FINALE

By Julian Beale

With
love and best wishes.
Julian
10 Jun '24

Chapter One

The human scream is an underrated form of expression. It can be the harbinger of hope or signal a descent into despair. It can advertise delight or disappointment, pain or fulfilment, surprise or suspense, horror or happiness. And in all these emotions, the scream offers a further benefit: it is multilingual.

The scream which shattered the warm, still evening air seemed to mix fear and pain with both surprise and outrage, but it was vaguely muted by the bulk of the imposing building from which it was drawn. In East Africa, the largest private houses are generally titled as 'compounds' and named for the owner or resident of the moment. The property which emitted the drawn-out scream was known as "Toto's Compound" and amongst the local population, the place provoked fear, envy and awe in equal measure.

Awe first: the building was some 150 metres long and about half that in depth. It wasn't tall, being just two stories high with a roof top balcony which covered the whole and beneath it were a series of interconnecting basement rooms. Toto's had been designed by an Ethiopian born architect in the mid 1960's and its construction was finally completed almost ten years later. The client who had commissioned the project was called Hasab al Barajidan. He had acquired enormous wealth and influence through ruthless trading in minerals, precious stones, construction equipment and some slavery as a highly profitable side-line.

Then Envy, which wasn't hard to understand. This was a country and a city which had descended into violent anarchy throughout the decade of the 1980's, with the great majority of its population just struggling to stay alive and often wondering if the effort was worthwhile.

Such pressure breeds Fear in anyone: fear of having nothing and nowhere to go. Even more fear if you do have something and you're surrounded by people who can and will take it from you. Most fear of all if you are suspected of having some dangerous knowledge. With that, you might well disappear inside the Compound and never emerge again. Which is why they called the man "Toto". In the local slang, that signified 'it's over, you're finished, you're dead and gone'.

A roughly finished concrete wall, some two metres high and topped with coils of razor wire, protected the entire length of the Compound. Beyond it lay the coastal road, now simply a track along which very occasional traffic would crawl, slowed to walking pace by the dust filled potholes and the trenches opened up by rocket attacks. In the month of June 2011, this was the highway bordering the Indian Ocean and running south from Mogadishu, Capital City of the lawless State of Somalia.

In the bowels of the basement, in a large rectangular room devoid of all-natural light, a group of about a dozen figures perspired under the fierce effect of powerful spotlights mounted on wheeled stands which were ranged around a full-sized billiard table. The walls of the room were bright white painted plaster on concrete blocks, the floor was covered by large white tiles, each a metre square. The only other furniture in the entire room was an old-fashioned wooden dining chair, with elaborately carved arms, cane seat and back. The chair stood in one corner and was occupied by a spare, grizzled man of advanced years. He sat slouched by habit, bent by arthritis and full bearded by custom.

A much younger figure detached itself from the group around the table and with lithe and fluent step, went to stand in front of the chair. Another male, this one, but far younger, barely out of teenage years, full charged with energy, passion and anger. The old man in the chair hooked one scrawny leg over the arm of his chair and started to scratch at his crotch, a dismissive gesture of authority as he looked up into the immature face bending over him. He spoke.

'Be very careful. I warn you that you are testing my patience. This is something which must be done. You know that. It is our practice and our right. It has been so down all the generations and is accepted by our tribe and our family, including your own mother and father. Who are you to question my decision? You do not argue with Toto! Now … stand aside and say no more'.

The young man looking down on him hopped from foot to foot as he mixed fear with fury, finally unable to contain himself as he burst out in response.

'But she is my sister - my only sibling! I am here to guide and protect her .... and she's only a young girl - still a child.!'

With a roar of exasperation, the old man sprang from his chair.

'If she's old enough to bleed then she's old enough to butcher,' he bawled as he swept his grandson aside and signalled to those around the billiard table. The gesture was unmistakeable as they moved towards their victim, an old crone at their head wielding her knives and others rushing forward to pinion the pathetic body of the girl on her back on the table, her legs spread apart, her wrists and ankles held firm by strong arms.

A still sharper scream, mixing horror, pain and indignation drove the patriarch back to his chair and then there was a sudden silence as a grimy rag was thrust down the throat of the victim. The only sounds remaining were a little whimpering, the clicking of knives and the hoarse grunting of the old woman as she wrestled with needle and camel gut.

Then the lights failed, and the roof of the basement started to collapse on them. When all the dust had settled, there were only two survivors and the empire of Toto had gone forever. Another militia, led by another Warlord had seen the wealth, coveted the possessions, aspired to the authority and

hatched a plan. Evidently, it was good enough for purpose and the residents of the shacks and tents and abandoned vehicles in the area surrounding the Compound would have to start to accustom themselves to a new voice of command and a new regime.

Chapter Two

I'm in my favourite place at my chosen time of day: dawn on the beach outside Century City, Millennium, on the west coast of the Continent of Africa.

I was christened Oliver - Oliver Aveling - but most people call me Olty. It's my birthday today, New Year's Day, the 1st January. This morning, we move into 2036 and I'm forty-five years old. It's now about 6.30 am, not yet fully light but getting there fast. My father, Oscar, rang about an hour ago from home in a much colder and completely dark Herefordshire in England to give me some unhappy news which I have been steeling myself to expect. It sounds as if my mother will not be with us for much longer and when I have composed myself in this habitual walk along the sand, I'll go back to my apartment and speak to my siblings - my brother Edward who is a land agent in the UK and my lawyer sister Christina, who lives in London, is very down to earth in character and has a much greater medical understanding than either Dad or me of the circumstances and the prognosis. My father sounded close to meltdown on the phone - distraught of course but also exhausted: that would be the effect of driving at least twice a day over the last three months from our house to the Hospice outside Leominster, a journey of twenty minutes minimum in each direction.

Just one of my many shortcomings is that I have a wandering mind which gets too easily and quickly distracted. Even as I walked and pondered on the distress of my mother's imminent demise, I couldn't stop my thoughts heading off at a tangent towards the Southeast and Hippo Province in which, word had just reached me, a resurgence of game poaching was active. I would need to get a further report on this later in the day. And then, before I had walked more than another few metres, my conscience assailed me again with concern about Oksana, the woman with whom I have been living for the last five years and whom I have been thinking is the love of my life... and yet, and yet.

If all of this is not enough, I glance over my shoulder and see the smoke cloud still billowing - it seems for miles up into the clear, early day sky of Millennium. I know its source is twenty-five kilometres north, right in the heart of Century City and I know it's being generated by the still burning hulk of the ship which was hit by an enormous explosion in the early hours of today. Why, how and with what implications are questions to which I hope I'll get some answers when I meet Police Inspector General Maurice Odinga later this morning.

I've now reached the fallen palm tree which rests as a half-buried log on the beach and is my turning point for home and breakfast. But as I start to swing round, I catch a glimpse of a figure way further down the beach - my eyesight remains pretty good, and this must have been at least half a kilometre distant. I say 'figure' but this one isn't human: it's a dog and I believe it's Absalom. I don't shout or whistle and I don't flap my arms about. I just stand where I am, watching as he works up his best speed and comes flying down the beach towards me.

He's an imposing, powerful dog, Absalom: about five years old with a heavy build and a thick, lustrous coat which makes him appear even bigger. He's a German Shepherd and when he knows you, he has a lovely nature. When he doesn't, he's not to be argued with.

I'm very lucky to live out here at Rainbow Beach. I walk straight out onto the seashore from my two storey, duplex apartment which sports four en-suite bedrooms and two balconies from which to gaze at the ever-moving ocean and the frequently spectacular sunsets. Less than two kilometres north of my building, there's a small mall with a pharmacy, a convenience store and a reasonable Italian restaurant: also, an ATM and a liquor store. From the front entrance to my apartment, it's barely a thirty-minute drive into my office in the City but I admit it would take a bit longer if my job didn't rate a government car and driver.

Rainbow is a popular beach. It's convenient for day trippers, for joggers and walkers looking for early or evening exercise, for car cocooned lovers looking for a decent background view to enhance their romantic activities. And there's more. There are three separate campsites / caravan parks along this stretch of our coast, and they are all pretty full at this time of year, especially with families coming out of the country to the seaside to holiday while they celebrate Christmas and New Year. That's the explanation for the remains of sandcastles which have survived the tides sweeping over their construction the previous day, especially if the young architects and builders have chosen a protected site for their creation - as in the lee of the fallen tree which is my turning point.

Absalom bounces round me and starts to worry at what's left of the considerably deep moat which must have been the fundamental for the castle which I'm now skirting. Suddenly, there's a cloud of sand whirling around me and through it, I see a small but familiar form springing up from the beach and I hear a surprisingly deep voice speaking in a foreign tongue as it welcomes and calms the dog: Troy is on the scene.

Troy is San: that's to say he's a Bushman from the deep Kalahari Desert of Namibia. He's short in stature, hardly more than a metre and a half, slight in build, wizened in facial features which have been burned by sun and blistered by driving desert winds. It's impossible to guess his age, it could be anywhere between 40 and 60 and I couldn't pronounce his San name even if I knew it. Troy is also the most completely competent human being I know, and his talents are extraordinary. Prime amongst these is his ability to disappear and yet be ever present. He and I never met formally. We weren't introduced. We just found each other, by accident. That was at least five years ago. It could even be six, but I do know for sure that it was at this time of year. High summer for us and marking my birthday, I had joined a party of likeminded animal safari enthusiasts - eight of us in all plus an entourage of drivers, cooks and bottle washers - all in high spirits as we journeyed southeast over rough roads and progressively more bush tracks towards the international boundary which marks the limit of our nation's territory. There's no natural or manmade barrier there to mark the spot but that was the whole purpose of our expedition. Word had come through from Millennium's Wildlife Department that elephants, long expected, were coming up from the south. They kept us waiting nearly a week in our camp, growing ever more impatient and nervous before they finally passed by us almost three kilometres away to the west: the matriarch leading their way, of course, about a dozen young but breeding females and amongst those, as many young, most between two and three years old but three much smaller and one so very small as to appear almost new-born.

It was a triumphant and touching moment which thrilled me as the cavalcade hove into view, making its majestic passage through the sparse bush and our party lingered until the light was fading away before we returned to our camp to start packing up in readiness for a dawn departure on our way back towards Century City.

Only then did I notice the diminutive figure busying itself around our firepit. This was, of course, Troy, making his entrance into my life for all that I didn't know at that point anything of his provenance, nationality or even his name. In the early morning, he simply attached himself to us and made himself useful so that by the time we had regained the City boundaries two days later, Troy had become a part of life. It took very much longer, of course, to establish anything of a working relationship.

Not that the practical difficulties, especially communication, seemed to matter very much at the time. Once he had arrived, he was simply there with me, involving himself in my life in a manner which was so subdued and subtle that I really didn't recognise that it was happening. But there were a couple of developments during that first year which made the whole process that much easier. The first of these involved living quarters for Troy. When he first arrived with me, he lived in the two bays allotted to me in the car park under my apartment building. This was adequate but not an ideal arrangement for either of us. In the second week of November - a Springtime month for us here in the Southern Hemisphere - I had a busy working schedule which included an overnight visit to Pretoria. I got home on the Friday evening to find Troy gone, apparently left without any message of why. Honestly, I didn't give his sudden disappearance much thought that evening. I was tired from travel and some fractious meetings which had preceded my journey home, so I helped myself to a large nightcap and went straight off to bed. But matters changed in the morning when I took a typically early call from Hugh Dundas. Even today, Hugh will ring at an ungodly hour: although the man has just turned ninety, he remains astonishingly energetic, and his brainpower seems undiminished. Back then, of course, he was mid-eighties and permanently humming as I have much cause to remember.

'Have you lost something', he demanded, never one to beat about the bush.

Just for once, I was ready for him. 'Well, I have lost someone', I replied and knew from the ensuing silence that I'd guessed right. It didn't take Hugh long to confirm.

'Troy turned up here around sunset last night', he announced. 'He slept in the old shack by my boat shed and he's been tidying it up since dawn. D'you mind if he stays?'

'That's more for you to say than me, Hugh. Troy's a free agent ... but anyway, how are you managing to communicate between the two of you?'

'No secret there, Olty. I'll explain, but better in person. Why don't you come by for a couple of drinks and a meal this evening?'

'What better, Hugh, thanks. I'll see you about seven.' There was a grunt of affirmation as I hung up.

It all became clear over an excellent dinner. Troy had moved to be with people who spoke his language. Some years earlier, Hugh engaged a couple who had travelled from Windhoek in Namibia to join the first wave of immigrants into the newly created country of Millennium. They were called Erasmus and Delilah. She had some nursing skills and experience so that her prime responsibility soon came to be the care of Janey Dundas, Hugh's wife who was wheelchair bound and demanding in character. Delilah's husband Erasmus, a skinny scarecrow of a man who was almost twice her height, had been born outside Walvis Bay and was in family background and by every inclination a man of the sea. So, at a stroke, Hugh had found a solution for two problems: first, caring companionship for Janey and then finding for himself a boatman with the right levels of expertise.

Chapter Three

I've almost finished my morning walk now, just about back at the entrance from the beach into the rear hallway of my apartment block.

To complete this account, I need to start by compressing thirty-five years of history into a summary which informs without confusing, providing detail without drama, facts without feelings.

With the dawn of this century, on New Year's Day 2000, this country and this seaside city were invaded by a polyglot assembly of about three thousand souls who arrived in three ships and one aeroplane to take over, partly by force and mostly by guile, a long-established sovereign State which had evolved over hundreds of years.

The *coup* was masterminded by a middle-aged Englishman named David Heaven and, in its execution, he was supported and encouraged by three close friends who had been undergraduates with him at Oxford University thirty years previously. These were a French born lady called Alexandra (Alexa) Labarre, a British Army professional turned security consultant, Conrad Aveling, often called 'Connie' and a rumbustious Priest named Rupert Broke Smith who went under the sobriquet of Pente. In addition, there was Kingston Offenbach, a lanky black American from the deep south, a little older than the others as he had spent a year at Oxford on post graduate studies, sponsored by his career employer, the CIA of Langley, Virginia, USA.

Then Hugh - Hugh Dundas, a man of business and finance, a colossus who had bestrode the commercial globe from his base in Hong Kong for ten years and more prior to its return to China. *Project Zero,* the act of brazen piracy which had enabled David Heaven to fulfil his dream, could simply not have happened without Dundas who brought to the monumental exercise his calm power of analysis, his immense personal wealth, his knowledge and his contacts. Yet for all these powerful attributes, Hugh could have been undermined by his own self-doubt, a persistent thorn in his armour of confidence which was nurtured by the nagging guilt he had continued to feel since the car accident for which he was responsible which had crippled his then fiancée Janey, shortly afterwards his wife, severely compromising her quality of life for over thirty-five years until her death in 2002, here in the beach house which he had built for her, tended to the last by the loyal and caring Delilah. Long before then, back in 1987, Hugh had met and fallen under the redeeming spell of Alexa - nee Alexandra Labarre, widow of Peter Bushell, to whom she was briefly married whilst living in Sydney. Hugh and Alexa were a sublime and devoted couple, much loved and loving for many years before their relationship was solemnized in 2008 and today, embarking on her eighty ninth year, Alexa is as spry as her husband, continuing despite the passage of time to combine feminine characteristics with grace and dignity.

During years now long gone, Alexa had her own powerful demons with which she had to battle and independently of this pressure, she exercised commitment and influence in the planning of *Zero.* Connie Aveling, Pente Broke Smith and King Offenbach, all three were hugely involved and played their different roles. Pente is, remarkably, still with us and living on his own - a large, shambling, rambling man - still fond of his beer and his noxious smelling cigars but now much reduced in stamina in his mid-nineties and growing tired of life. Not that he is troubled: Pente is a man of absolute Faith and, as he puts it, is looking forward to going home soon. Connie died many years ago as a result of a drama in London and Offenbach slipped away peacefully in a nursing home deep in the hills of West Virginia.

David Heaven, Hugh and Alexa Dundas, Conrad Aveling, Pente Broke Smith and Kingston Offenbach. Six individuals, spawn of a single generation, both united and divided in pursuit of an outlandish dream and probably surprised by the extent of its fulfilment. There were others, too, who played significant parts in the creation of this country: Sol and Martin Kirchoff, David Heaven's long time business partners, Fergus "Cogs" Carradine who was the expedition's military commander at the time of the invasion and who remained a mentor and good friend of mine until his premature death. Key members of his team including Rory Trollope and Simon Goring, the latter of special memory. Which leads me on to a little more history and to describe how I, myself, fit into this overall scene.

David Heaven was my maternal grandfather, but I didn't come to know this until fifteen years ago when documented proof of the lineage was handed over to me by Guy Labarre, a relative in her French family of Alexa Dundas. David had assembled for me a personal letter together with a mass of memorabilia before his sudden death of a heart attack in May 2013. He left this treasure trove of memories and explanations with Alexa, his close friend of a lifetime, perhaps because he was fearful of making an instant exit as his own father had done before him. Whatever, Alexa had come to be herself anxious about the responsibility of remaining guardian to this material, so she had passed the little suitcase in which David had stored his journal to her nephew Guy and he had in due course found the opportunity to pass it to me. I have kept a copy of most of it but gave the original to Jack Kirchoff, son of my grandfather's partner in the Mansion House business. Jack is also the historian amongst us and the author of the definitive account of our nation - *The Making of Millennium.*

Now comes the complicated bit of background: you need to know the outline but I'll try to keep it simple and concise.

I was born and brought up in the wilds of Herefordshire, one of England's prettiest and most rural counties. My father, Oscar, was a country solicitor, very active in his Practice and much involved in many local endeavours. Anna, my mother, delivered State education throughout the County and in addition to raising me and my two siblings, she served for many years as a dedicated Classroom Assistant until the dementia which is about to claim her started to take a real grip.

Oscar and my uncle Peter are twins, born out of wedlock in Cambodia to my late grandmother, Antoinette, who was then still a schoolgirl, and the boys were conceived by vicious, multiple rape. Antoinette, even then universally known as Tepee, was rescued and taken to live in Singapore. There, when her sons were four years old, she chanced to meet Conrad Aveling. They fell in love and married, Connie was happy to accept her sons as his own and they went on to have a third child - a daughter. Twins feature also on my mother's side and in a previous generation. Anna is the only child of Ouye, the daughter of a notorious rebel leader who flourished for a while in Angola, Southern Africa. Jonas Savimbi died in a firefight with Government forces in 2002, by which point he had a much depleted following. He had several wives and many children. It is said that his favourite amongst the former was a woman of Irish descent and a fiery disposition. She bore him twin daughters, Ouye who died for lack of proper attention whilst giving birth in remote bush country to Anna who was then nurtured and raised by Ouye's sister Aissata, generally called Aischa. The twins met David Heaven in 1970 when he fathered my mother, Anna. Subsequently, David was reintroduced to Aischa a few years later when she was established in Lisbon, and they started a relationship which would endure for a lifetime. They married in Millennium in 2000 and Aischa predeceased her husband, dying in May 2003. When still very young, Anna met Oscar by chance encounter when he was on a holiday break in Lisbon, and they bonded very happily. They married soon afterwards, and I am the first born of the union. I completed my education in England and then came out here to make my life. I have returned to London and Herefordshire on a regular basis during the past twenty – five years but Millennium and its capital, Century City rapidly became home to me and it's here that I expect to live out my remaining time. So, I guess this makes for a suitable opportunity to set down more about this country, my life and occupation here and my aspirations for the future.

Millennium is situated on the West Coast of the continent of Africa - about halfway down. We are a medium size country for Africa with a ground area of some quarter of a million square kilometres, nearly one thousand bordering the South Atlantic with a coastal strip which moves into a hilly spine and gives way to savannah land in the south and east. We have a tropical, humid climate.

Prior to my grandfather, David Heaven's invasion and takeover on New Year's Day 2000, this country had moved into independence from being a colony of France. The population then was only a little more than a million souls, concentrated in the capital and two other major centres. There were disparate tribes, many local dialects, very little agriculture, thus a dependence on imported food. The infrastructure was extremely weak, transportation and power supply poor and erratic, a shortage of foreign exchange and a reliance on financial aid from the developed world and multinational institutions.

Thirty-five years on, the change is dramatic and may be presented as justification for what was claimed at the time to be an act of 21st Century neo colonialism and piracy.

We are a wealthy country for our size. We husband carefully the reserves of high-quality crude oil which flows from the offshore field known as The Tamalou Trench and which is estimated to retain fifty years supply given a declining world demand. Our population has increased by more than tenfold, our life expectancy has gone out from fifty to seventy, our power is provided by wind, wave and sun: our water comes from springs and a dam in the highlands, much supplemented by desalination plants. We are now about thirty percent self-sufficient in food, mostly in vegetables and fruit but with also a contribution from locally raised meat. We export cut flowers to the USA and Europe. Our infrastructure is well established with an excellent main roads network and internal air services. There is no railway. Throughout the country, three languages are widely spoken - French, local African dialects and to an increasing extent, English. This last has really become a lingua franca over the years because, at the last count, we have welcomed immigrants from fifty-three countries around the world and almost all of them step onto our shore for the first time with a smattering of English, however slight.

I think that brief summary is enough for now about how this country was established but you need to know more about how it works today and how I fit into the picture. I'll cover that as I'm driven into my office in the city centre by

Jerome who has just appeared in one of the fleet of Government Mercedes, diesel powered in deference to all the oil we're still pumping.

I'm now shaved, showered and suitably suited. I tiptoe out of our bedroom, leaving Oksana asleep although I hear a squeak of farewell. Today is a National Holiday as in most countries in the world but I'm on parade for a few critical matters, starting with seeing the Chief of Police and here is Troy, with Absalom at his heels, to see me off. The road trip in would normally take thirty-five minutes but today it'll be barely half that.

I'm sitting back comfortably, relishing the sight of the high-rise city centre as we sweep along the undulating Autoroute.

I arrived in Century for the first time in late September 2014 when I was twenty-three and this road was a rough track hugging the coastline. Earlier that summer in the UK, I had completed my time at Bristol University, gaining a 2:1 degree in languages with a bit of politics and some time spent at Grenoble on secondment. Uncertain of my next move, I had joined a French friend who wanted to experience something of Africa and was attracted by the prospect of seeing this brand-new country. He stayed a few months whilst I'm still here. At that point, I knew next to nothing about the history, no idea of my relationship to the buccaneering man who had come storming in here at the turn of the century.

I was twenty-four before I became reasonably established, with a small apartment tucked away in an inland suburb and a permanent post in the fledgling Department of International Affairs. It wasn't much but I loved the lifestyle, the climate and the company I kept. There was variety, challenge and a permanent feeling of excitement both at work and play. Prospects seemed bright so when I went home for almost a month's leave based on my parents' house in Herefordshire, I was happy to see them, my siblings and a good few old mates from school and days at Uni, yet I found myself yearning for my return to Millennium. At the outset, I'd been happy to find just a job which paid me a living wage but now I was waking up to the realisation that I had found a career.

When I started in the Department, I was lucky to have a good deal of access to the top boss, an Armenian born man called Joe Kaba. Joe was an inspirational figure, a driving force with brain, presence and a clear strategy. His vision was that Millennium should command respect around the globe but particularly throughout the continent of Africa. In this, he was reflecting the aspirations of our Founding President, David Heaven, also of Hugh Dundas who followed David into that post for a further two years. During the time that both were in Office, I seemed, at Joe Kaba's behest, to spend most of my time on aeroplanes. I flew North, South and East, always with the diplomatic mission to establish and improve our relations with the Governments of any and all African States, both large and small, democratic and autocratic. Since Millennium was relatively wealthy thanks to our oil but was also the new kid on the continental block and as our existence was widely perceived as resulting from a neo colonial land grab, our visiting delegations were sometimes received with suspicion, occasionally derision and sometimes overt hostility. But no matter the challenges, Joe Kaba kept us at it and in small steps we made progress even though they could be two forward and one back. We were helped by stability at home which first David, then Hugh and in later years his successors managed to maintain.

Over time, Joe became a mentor to me and a loyal friend, so I came to spend a fair amount of leisure time at his house and with his family. It was from Joe that I came to understand how the terrorist twins had come very close to a success in 2001 which would have completely torpedoed our fledgling state, barely a year after Heaven and team steamed over the horizon and when I was still a schoolboy. It was about then, when Joe was recounting this history that he made the opportunity to introduce me to Fergus Carradine, the very professional soldier without whom the invasion might well have failed, and the twins might have triumphed. Fergus - or "Cogs" as we call him on account of his fearsome general knowledge became an instant close companion and I often turned to him for advice.

And as for other crises, with immense effort and skill, Hugh Dundas got Millennium through the world financial crash of 2008, an extraordinary achievement since we were then still struggling to find our feet and by good fortune, we were not too hard hit by the Covid virus in '21 with its devastating effect worldwide although we were very much more damaged by the later pandemic in 2026.

But I'm getting a bit ahead of myself. In November 2021, I went to London as the front man to prepare the way for Joe Kaba to spend time with the British Prime Minister, seeking support for a high-profile conference which we were to host in Century City the following January.

That autumn visit to the UK remains caught in my memory for a second reason also. It was then, for the first time, that I could see and appreciate the first signs of my mother Anna's dementia and I spent an agonising weekend in Herefordshire trying to find some comfort for my father as he poured out his distress to me.

And then Joe Kaba had a heart attack which meant that I had to do my best to cover for him before I returned to Millennium with a workload inevitably increased by his incapacity. They thought he would make a good recovery, but his angina grew worse over the next couple of years with another three attacks before the last which silenced him for ever in July 2025. I wept a lot of tears over Joe, and I miss him still.

Following Joe's unexpected death, part of me thought and much of me hoped that I would be promoted into his role, but our then President, the charismatic and effective Alberto Gonzalez, Cuban born who had arrived in the First Fleet, felt I was a bit young plus he thought that all the diplomatic hosting required by the job made it better suited to a married man. As it turned out, however, he gave the post to a woman, a soignee lady who had come to Millennium from Egypt. Perhaps Alberto was right and anyway, I soon got over my disappointment as he fast tracked me through several staging post appointments in our Civil Service before he relinquished the Presidency.

I was confirmed as Director of the Secretariat on 1st September 2032, so I have now been in the job for something over three years. The work is demanding but very fulfilling. It can also be confusing and that's mostly a result of how the governance of Millennium has evolved over time so I think it would be helpful if I explain just a little of how we operate in this country.

Millennium is a democracy and we do have a written Constitution, but it is unusual and that makes it harder to explain. The short and simple version is as follows. The country is divided into thirteen Provinces, four urban and nine rural. Their shapes and boundaries are determined mostly by topography but also with some influence of history and the preferences of the former Colonial French power. Each Province sends five Provincial Representatives (PR's) to our National Assembly, which is physically located here, in Century City. Technically, we're a Presidential Republic but we've cobbled together a lot of other people's ideas to produce a form of government which seems to work for us, particularly recognising that the majority of our population wasn't born here. So, there's a bit of the UK, a bit of North America, some Australasian and some more from Western Europe.

We hold National Elections every five years. Local, Provincial voting follows the same pattern and at this level, personalities get promoted and political groups are formed. Local Government is extremely important to us, and our Founders saw it as fundamental to encouraging commitment and contribution from all the hundreds of thousands of immigrants who have given up a previous life to make a new one in Millennium.

Every citizen aged eighteen and over gets a vote. Anyone entitled to vote may put forward their name to be elected to represent their Province in the National Assembly, but here the Founders introduced a novel requirement. Two out of the five Representatives from each Province must demonstrate that they hold a professional qualification and are of independent means. You must show that you have a medical qualification, that you're a lawyer, a Minister of Religion, a School Teacher, an agronomist ... whatever it may be. The list is long and varied but the objective is constant. The expectation is that candidates who meet these criteria would likely be successful in winning a seat in the Assembly and would be prepared to stay for a second term of five years. That means that forty percent of the Provincial Representatives from across the whole country are exerting a significant influence in the Assembly and on the Executive Panel which exists to advise and support the President.

There's a bit more to say about the Executive Panel which equates in business speak to a Board of Directors. There are nine PR's making up the Panel, plus the President in whose gift is the allocation of Portfolio responsibilities on the Panel. Members serve two consecutive terms. The Constitution forbids them to stay longer and their most important responsibility is to select, by simple majority vote, which of them is to ascend to the position of President, thus succeeding the current incumbent. This means that a new President must have served for a five year term on the Panel before assuming the top job.

We've almost arrived at my building, and I haven't said anything yet about the Secretariat which is simply our name for a Civil Service, an administrative body which exists to keep the wheels of government turning as smoothly as possible. It's my responsibility to run the outfit nationally with the help of nearly fifteen hundred people located here and in regional offices across the country. It's not just a job, it's a way of life and I wouldn't want to lose a minute of it.

Jerome slides the car to a smooth halt by the side entrance and I hop out to make a quiet entrance into the Reception area. Glancing behind me, I see parked an official car with a uniformed Police driver standing by it: evidently, the Chief is already here.

Chapter Four

Maurice Odinga gets to his feet as I approach him. He is a short man with a pretty round figure and a completely bald, cannonball head. Nevertheless, he exudes command and authority, smart in his tropical uniform with badges of rank, cap tucked under his arm and baton in hand.

We greet each other warmly and I lead him towards the wide staircase which will bring us up to the first floor where I have my corner office. This, the Secretariat HQ building is colonial in style, about a hundred years old and ideally located being fifty odd metres by underground passage from the Assembly.

Beatrice, my good friend and marvellous PA has already organised coffee and I pour a cup for Maurice as we settle ourselves in the window seats which look out over the Assembly lawn: the sun beats down from a Millennium blue sky on this New Year's morning.

'Thanks for seeing me today, Olty,' says Maurice crossing his short legs and looking apprehensive, 'I'm afraid I don't have much good news for you.'

'Go on,' I reply. 'Is this about the *Dawn?*'

He nods. 'Yes, of course. I was down there myself this morning and I had breakfast with Lenny Williamson, the Marine Engineer. Do you know him?'

'I've met him, yes, and I know his reputation. He sounds to be very well qualified.'

Maurice goes on. 'He's certainly that, I agree, and I'm confident that he'll give us an expert assessment and a detailed report on the damage and what it's going to take in time and money for repairs.'

'Assuming the vessel is not so badly damaged as to be beyond redemption?'

'That was the most interesting and unexpected thing which Lenny had to say to me, Olty. Good news and bad really, both together.'

My expression asks the question. I don't need to say anything, and Maurice continues.

'He thought the damage would be a lot worse than it is. He's found where explosives were detonated in the engine room - although that's been out of commission for over twenty years now - and then quite a number of hotspots throughout the ship, all in the public spaces, the auditorium, the main dining room and the large lounge. Locations in which there is a fair bit of fire damage, but no threat whatever to the fundamental structure of the *Dawn.*

'Was there any loss of life?'

Maurice shakes his head. 'Not directly, no. But one member of the security staff who was on the night shift went to investigate smoke coming from behind the dance floor and was caught in a secondary explosion. Pretty unpleasant burns but he'll survive OK.'

'So, What are your conclusions, Mo?'

'Olty, it's much too soon to be thinking of conclusions. Right now, I'm just surprised and being of enquiring and suspicious mind, I always harbour a concern when I'm surprised. But look. I've got my best team on this one, we'll keep going over whatever more we can find and I'll keep talking to Lenny. Give us a few days and then maybe I'll have something which I can present as a conclusion. Meanwhile, we'll shut the *Dawn* down, cancel or postpone any bookings for parties, receptions or conferences over the next month or so, plus make the vessel safe and have a review of security arrangements. Horses and stable doors etc' and he sat back with a wry smile, clasping his small, neat hands over his slightly bulging tummy.

I'm joining him in the smile and thinking it would be good to get a next date agreed before we part this morning when I see Beatrice approaching at a run, heels clicking on the parquet and her pretty face streaked with tears. Obviously, she has news, and I can guess what it is. Beatrice had got close to my mother during the few visits my parents made to Millennium during the past years.

In the end, I spent two weeks in England, a couple of days in London, the rest based at Gable Farm, my parents' house outside Leominster and our family home.

Mum was cremated in Hereford, and we followed that solemn but simple ceremony with a celebration of her life and a bit of a binge at Gable Farm afterwards. Nearly 300 people crammed themselves into our Parish Church for her Service and nearly all of them seemed to come on to the Wake.

That volume of humanity made a strong impression on me. She had lived there all her married life, raised her children, socialised and contributed to the local community, so it was to be expected that there would be a large turnout amongst friends and contacts living in the neighbourhood. But they came also from much further afield - from London and Bristol and adjoining counties, from Worcester and Gloucestershire. There was the warmth of enthusiastic comment too. Nearly everyone there seemed to want a few words to express sadness, appreciation, admiration, sympathy. Of course, my father was besieged by queues of people waiting patiently to give him a hug with a few words of comfort and not many fewer stood in lines and groups for the chance of a word with me or my siblings, Edward and Christina.

My mother was only sixty-six when she died and in reality, had left us at least a year previously as the dementia had taken a vicious hold. During the days that followed, I had many a long walk and talk with my Dad, Oscar, and it became clear to me that he would be particularly hard hit. They had been such constant companions, such very good friends and I was immediately fearful that he would retreat into a lonely shell to be distracted only by his many contacts and colleagues in the legal profession. I was confident that my brother and sister would be forever there for him: it's good that Edward lives less than an hour away with his growing family, but Christina is unmarried and currently unconnected in her busy London life. There is one other upon whom I can always count. My father's twin brother Pete is a polar opposite in character. Pete finds and sells exotic cars from which he makes a fine but unreliable living. He has no children, has had countless alliances but has never married, lives a slightly rackety life in the wilds of Dorset but is the most marvellous company when you can get hold of him. I spent an hour on the phone with him and implored him to contact me if ever he felt concerned about my Dad's equilibrium.

And then it was time for me to go. In every way, I had to get back to work.

Chapter Five

Having taken the day flight down from London, it's a real pleasure to find Jerome waiting at the gate for me and I'm grateful to Beatrice for organising this welcome. As we are driving around the Ringway, heading for the Autoroute home, Jerome tells me that he was into the Airport only yesterday, dropping Oksana for a trip down south to Capetown. I know this already as I spoke to her from Gable Farm just a couple of days back when she told me about this two day symposium. Oksana is a highly qualified microbiologist on a permanent contract to inform and advise our Department of Health, so she travels internationally on an irregular but frequent basis.

It's getting towards dusk when Jerome drops me. I can't see a sign of Troy but reckon he must be about halfway through his 3km walk up the beach to Hugh's, so I hump my bag into the lift and up to the apartment.

As soon as I punch in the entry code and walk through the front door, I know something is going on, something has changed. It's just somehow in the atmosphere.

I walk into our bedroom and there's an envelope lying there in the middle of the bed. A couple of kisses are scrawled on it but there's no message inside. I fetch a beer from the kitchen and sit, nursing the can, in front of the wall screen of the TV in our living room. Oksana's face lights up immediately but I pause it to study how good she's looking, very smart in a black business suit. She's wearing the pearls I gave her the Christmas before last. I drink my beer and listen to her message. I listen to it twice before I switch off, pour myself a large whisky, select a cigar from the box and then move out onto the balcony to sip and smoke while I reflect.

Oksana has left. She's left me and she's not coming back. She's resigned her job, is fulfilling her final commitment by attending this gig in Capetown and from there she will fly straight back to Belarus, home to Minsk and the husband she has never divorced. In her message of farewell to me, she is elegant, composed and fluent as always with just that tiny trace of accent which attracted me from the first. Right at the end, she lets slip her guard and dabs a tissue at her eyes, but she remains determined and constant. There's no room for compromise. I sit out on the balcony for a long time, conflicted in my thoughts. Part of me is tortured by the accuracy of Oksana's comments. We have been together for more than three years, sharing some very good times and inevitably, some not so good. She never actually met my mother but in the early days, they spoke on the phone on several occasions, so Oksana felt involved and was much distressed when we heard together the news of the diagnosis. She is herself a very family oriented person, close to her parents and her only sibling - an elder brother. She used to talk easily to me about Karol, her estranged husband who sounds to be highly regarded by her family. I'm sure they'll be thrilled to have her back and will be hoping that the marriage will be restored.

But this is dangerous ground. If I have another drink, I'll start getting all maudlin and feeling sorry for myself. I must not do that as this is all much more my fault than hers. She was forever telling me that I didn't leave enough time in life for myself - let alone for anyone else : perhaps she's right and maybe I'm learning the lesson too late.

Despite my better intentions, I did, of course, have another whisky - in fact I had several more so when I woke late this morning, I felt still tired from travel, made worse by over indulgence in the bottle. As I struggled to find focus in every sense, I recognised that I was in mourning for both my mother and my lover. But neither is coming back and it's time for a new chapter.

I had intended to drive myself to the office that day but when I stepped out of my building, Jerome was already there and waiting. A good thing too. I was in no condition to be driving that morning. Beatrice was waiting for me with her own brand of warm and caring welcome. I had with me a copy of my mother's Memorial Service and I was touched by how ecstatic Bea was that I had remembered. Then she told me that for my first day back, work would not be too onerous: no meetings planned, no 'must call at once' messages, and best of all, no crisis. But Bea was obviously pleased when I asked her if she would check with the President's entourage to see if I could have an appointment for some time later in the day.

'Sure' she said approvingly, 'and you're right to ask, Olty. It's only good manners to confirm you're back.' Bea is a stickler for manners, spelling and syntax. But I'm not complaining now, and I didn't then. We all of us need to follow a protocol.

The President's Office is in the Assembly complex, hardly five minutes' walk from the Secretariat and I'm probably a couple early for the twelve-noon appointment as I approach the rather forbidding, five metre high double doors in fine mahogany which guard the entrance to the Presidential suite.

There's a guard just inside the door and a male Private Secretary appears to give a welcome before guiding me into the inner sanctum. The President is standing as I walk in, and she directs me to a round table in the bay window. There are four upright, leather upholstered chairs on rollers and we sit down opposite each other. She has a coffee tray in front of her and she pours me a cup.

Laetitia Valbuena is the second Lady President of Millennium, and she took office last year in 2035, so she will be in charge until the end of '39 when I will be turning fifty which is a sobering thought. Our first female President was Helen Menendez, for whom I had worked directly after my then boss, Joe Kaba, was smitten by a heart attack in 2020. Mrs Menendez was herself unwell at that point and she died of kidney failure in '23 or '24. She was a splendid person, and I really felt her loss.

President Valbuena is a striking personality and a significant force. She's Spanish born, formerly a philosophy professor and a citizen of Seville. She came to Millennium in 2026 with her husband Hector who had been for a while a pro tennis player and good enough to be on the international circuit for a time. With them arrived two daughters, Carmen and Melissa. The girls were then about nine or ten, I suppose, but I didn't know until later that they had much older siblings - another daughter and a son - neither of whom left Spain as they were both victims of the pandemic which swept through Europe during the second half of 2025 and they died in hospital in Seville. The impact of this tragedy was sufficient to drive their parents to risk a brand-new start which is why, in their early fifties, they became citizens of Century City.

Laetitia Valbuena is a supremely elegant woman. She's tall, slim, marvellous bone structure, habitually wearing her jet-black hair scooped up into a chignon, immaculate, if heavy, make up and impeccable dress sense. She's as smart as ever today in a cream linen suit and her radiant smile is a welcome in itself.

Without preamble, she asks me : 'How did it go, Olty? What a very sombre time for you and very hard, I expect, for you to leave your father.

'You're right, Madam President,' I reply. 'It was a sad farewell indeed and all the worse for it being this time of year in England, but he's a resilient man. He has his work, his many interests and a wide circle of friends who will help to sustain him. He has my brother and sister who will be on hand and best of all, he has his recollections.'

'I do hope so. Hector and I were so sorry to hear the news from Beatrice and we have been thinking of you. I hope we may expect your father to pay you a visit here in due course of time. But now, 'she continues, shifting gears, 'You will have much catching up which you will want to get on with, so I won't detain you.' But by now, I have come to know her well enough to recognise when she has something on her mind, so I put down my coffee cup and sit back, waiting. As always, she goes straight to the point.

'There's something going on here, Olty, a quite subtle change in the pattern of Millennium life and I'm developing suspicions ... or perhaps concerns would be a better word for it.'

'Tell me more', I invite. Is this something which has cropped up while I've been away?'

'No, longer than that. It's been building slowly over the last few months - really since the start of the current academic year.'

I must have looked puzzled, and I was, because she hurries on.

'Carmen is nearly nineteen now and she started at Uni this year. She seems to have settled in well and is enjoying her course which is in history of art with a great emphasis on Chinese culture. She's got plenty of friends already, a fair bit of sport and lots of partying with too much drink - everything as it should be at that age and stage.'

'But there's a but - something troubling you?'

There's quite a long pause and I'm starting to wonder what to say next when the President rattles her coffee spoon in its saucer and I realise in a flash that she's nervous, unsure of how to express herself which is most unusual for her. I'm silently composing what I hope will be a calming comment when she places both hands on the table between us and rushes on, the normal steely look back in her eye.

'Actually, it's more to do with our younger daughter and her age group. Melissa's still at High School, she's fifteen and a half, more or less, pretty bright, completely happy: quite normal teenage up's, downs and hormones. They've just started back for the new term and suddenly - pretty much out of nowhere it seems, there's this passionate debate about how we should be lowering the voting age in this country, giving the right to all when they turn sixteen. It's a view apparently popular also amongst university students so I've learned most about it from Carmen who gets quite steamed up over the subject. It seems that the chief protagonist is a post graduate student aged about twenty-five or six doing a Master's in theology. He's called Luc de Houlette and he sounds to be a bit of a rabble rouser.'

I'm quite mystified and I say so. My instinctive reaction is that this is all juvenile stuff which really shouldn't take up a President's time. She agrees but then goes on to add.

'The latest thing, only yesterday Carmen tells her father that the Student Union want to hold a rally and press for a Referendum which could lead to an interim Election halfway through the current term.'

Suddenly, I'm feeling on safer ground, and I smile reassuringly as I speak out with confidence. 'Madam President, this is all absolute nonsense. It has to be. Our

Constitution is entirely clear. We have a General Election only and always every five years. But even then, the population isn't choosing between political parties and competing manifestos. People are simply concentrating on the individuals they want to see representing them in the National Assembly. But you know all that, Madam President, and you know a lot more besides. You've been through it all and you've earned your place at the top of our tree: you're well established and you're secure - as you've got every right to be'.

I can see this little speech having an effect even as I'm speaking. She's looking calmer again and is quite recovering her poise to the extent of reasserting her authority before we part.

'Thank you Olty. I appreciate your reassurance but even so, have a word with Maurice Odinga would you please. I did mention this man de Houlette to him and asked for him to be checked out. Just to be sure.'

'Of course, Madam President. I'll do that and report back.'

As things turned out, I was able to do just that much more quickly than I expected. I had hardly got back to my desk and the piles of paper and endless Mails which had been building up during my absence in the UK when Bea appeared to tell me that Mo was waiting in Reception, very anxious for a short conversation and full of apology for barging in unannounced. I waved all that aside when he walked in a few minutes later and we sat down to talk over a coffee.

Mo is looking and sounding less ebullient than his normal self, but he starts with a warm welcome and expresses his sympathy for my mother's death. More surprisingly, he goes on to say that he's sorry that Oksana has left to go back to Europe.

'I was fond of that lady', he says, 'and I admired her'.

'Me too', I smile wryly, 'but how did you know?'

'I get the daily reports from Customs and Immigration at Heaven International.'

He's referring to our airport here in Century and I smile in understanding. I should have worked that out for myself. I go on,

'What's news from here, Mo?'

'First off, the explosion on the *Dawn*. You remember just before you had to fly, I'd got Lenny Williamson involved?'

'I remember.'

'OK, so he's reported back after going over the whole ship in fine detail and he confirms: no structural damage, all quite minor stuff which won't take too much money or time to put right. And I've had the Insurer in while you were away - there's going to be no problem in accepting a claim in full.'

'So why? What's your explanation?'

'It's a hunch, really, but my best guess is that the incident wasn't an act of sabotage at all. I think it was more of a prank that went a little over the top. A sort of gesture which went a bit wrong.'

'You must have something more to back that up.'

'I do, yes, but nothing else concerning the *Dawn*. There's been a few other things during the past couple of weeks. A minor but noisy protest gathering on the University Campus - no more than thirty students demonstrating to reduce our voting age and then three separate incidents in different parts of the city, all involving impromptu raids on small convenience stores: in two of these, minor thieving with a bit of damage to premises and the loss of some stock - liquor - the third resulting in a head wound for the proprietor who had a good go at the villains.'

Maurice Odinga passes a hand wearily over his bald head as he sums up. 'None of this is too serious, Olty, but I just wanted to let you know and now I'll get out of your way. I've got a long nose from so many years Police work and right now, I smell some mischief brewing. Do you know anything about Papua New Guinea?'

'Not a thing, no.'

'An old chum of mine - an Aussie - spent years in the Police Service there and talked about the permanent trouble they had with young tearaways, the gang culture, always causing trouble and up to mischief. They called them the Rascals and they weren't just a nuisance. When organised, they would threaten and terrorise people. We have something of the same in West Africa but here they're called *"vouyoy"* - a French origin equivalent.'

As he gets up to leave, Mo adds, 'Amongst your youthful contacts, check out a guy called Luc - Luc de Houlette. I know next to nothing about him but from what I hear, I have him down as potential trouble.'

Chapter Six

After Mo had left, I got my head down to some serious work and spent the next three hours going through reports, particularly from the provinces, and a fair mass of random paperwork. Then I paused for a sandwich and another coffee at my desk after which I picked up the phone and asked Pascal to join me.

Pascal Brana was born in Budapest and came as a child to live in Millennium. Both his parents have now died and there was no sibling. I'm never quite sure of his sexuality and I don't intend to ask. We don't mix socially but we are good friends, and we work well together. As my second in command here at the Secretariat, he is completely invaluable. Pascal is a long streak of a man - skeletal thin, a bit stooped and prematurely balding for his thirty two years but his knowledge is encyclopaedic and his advice always calm and measured. I simply couldn't do without his support.

Pascal joins me from his office down the hall and we sit together on either side of my desk, for almost three hours. It's a session of review and renew, looking over what's been happening since my unforeseen departure and an update on latest developments throughout Millennium. I'm particularly interested to know how goes the refurbishment and expansion of the Secretariat Office in Leopard Province (they're all named for the wildlife of Africa) and then here at HQ, what progress is being made by our newly appointed head of IT, a lady who hails from

Hong Kong which she left to avoid the ever more authoritarian regime from China. As a first priority, I have charged her with making an assessment of all our systems which I believe are getting old and tired, with a view to providing for speed, ease of use and security.

At the conclusion of all this, I feel ready to grill Pascal on the topic which has been introduced by the President and has been troubling Odinga. I have the feeling that it's about to trouble me.

Pascal is prepared. He's obviously been expecting this turn in our conversation, but he still manages to surprise me.

'Mr Edmund Ladoux.'

'Yes. What about him?'

'I think you should speak to him at the earliest opportunity.'

'Subject?'

'The *Dawn*. The incidents all over the city during the last few weeks. The student dissent and their agenda. Most important, this young guy Houlette.'

I stare at Pascal as he sits twiddling his old propelling pencil in his long, slim fingers. It's a sort of talisman for him.

I ask him, 'What possible connection is there with Edmund Ladoux?'

'I don't know for sure that there is one, but I have met this Houlette who does have some charisma about him but not a great brain. He must be getting direction, leadership from somewhere or someone and Mr Ladoux may have information on the subject. I have much respect for his knowledge and contacts.'

I sigh as I look him in the eye.

'What's bugging everyone, Pascal? First the President, then the Police Chief and now you. Which means me as well. Why the sudden concern about a little student unrest and a single troublemaker with the gift of the gab?'

Pascal shrugs and sits forward in his chair.

'Probably, there's nothing to this, Olty, but I do still think we should check it out - make sure there isn't something which needs nipping in the bud. The President is settling very well into her term of Office but it's early days yet and she does have a big programme coming up, especially over this next year. I figure it's worth wearing belt and braces.'

I'm always amused by Pascal's language: highly colloquial expressions in English from way back but delivered with the soft accent of his mid European ancestry.

'I'll humour you, Pascal, and make some enquiries. Let's get together again on this one in a couple of days.' Pascal nods in satisfaction and gets up to leave me pondering. Later, I ask Bea to warn Jerome that I won't be ready for our return drive home until about 7pm. Before then, I have another call to make, and I leave the Secretariat on foot. It takes me about seven minutes of measured walking time until I emerge from a pedestrian alley into Cathedral Square and make my way round the imposing building and into the old Cloisters which have long been converted into small mews houses for members of our Clergy and the Cathedral Administrator. Plus, one other and I go straight to knock on his door. There's some delay before I hear shuffling footsteps inside, then a fiddling with the lock and drawing back the bolt. Finally, the door opens wide and there stands the stooped bulk of Pente Broke Smith. With his great bushy beard, he looks like the prophet Abraham and moves with a deliberate care which respects his ninety-two-year lifespan but the voice booms with undiminished strength as he welcomes me.

'Olty! What a very damn pleasant surprise! I thought you were still in the UK but how good to see you home again. Come in, come in and take the weight of your feet. Have a cup of tea perhaps .... Or maybe a dram or two?'

'I shouldn't be too long, Pente, but a beer would go down a treat.'

When we were seated in his small, snug "parlour" as he insists on calling his neat sitting room which seems further diminished by his large presence, he started our conversation by asking the questions I had been anticipating.

'How did it go? I was thinking so much about you all on the day: and praying for you too, of course. It comes to us all and nobody has to remind me that I'm in God's Waiting

Room myself and it can't be too much longer before he sticks his head round the door and crooks a finger in my direction. Not before time, either! But tell me about it all. Was Vanda able to make it there?'

'She was, yes, but only just. She has to spend most of her time in a wheelchair now and it's obvious that she tires easily.'

'Not surprising. She's almost as bloody old as I am. But she'd have had Imogen to push her around?'

'Imo was there, yes, and looking terrific. Obviously very happy with her new husband who's called Freddie someone: Carswell is the name, I think. He's does something in farm machinery, and they've bought a place in Yorkshire. Freddie's a widower with two teenage children. Imo has her little Edward by that desperate Dan from whom she is now finally and painfully divorced. She told me that she and Freddie are now trying for a joint production.'

'How very candid of her!'

'Wasn't it. But she's every inch her mother's daughter and just as forthright as Vanda.'

Pente's eyes mist as he passes a ham hand over his face. Vanda Deveridge had been the love of his life as they grew up together in the depths of Herefordshire but when still at Oxford University, he had jilted her in favour of the Almighty and had joined the Priesthood. But their lives had remained entwined down the long years, and he used to make an annual pilgrimage from Millennium to England to see Vanda, her daughter Hannah and granddaughter Imogen. These excursions had ceased about ten years ago when Pente had declared himself too ancient for air travel, but these two nonagenarians continued to embrace modern communications as they exchanged news and views across the world. I know also from my infrequent

Church attendance that Pente ensures the loving maintenance of the simple but striking memorial in the grounds of the Cathedral which guards the remains of Simon Goring who died there thirty-five years ago, still mourned by Hannah who had loved him so, although not remembered by their daughter Imogen who was too young to be affected by his tragic and dramatic passing.

Pente jerks his head up and I notice the hand on his glass is becoming shaky.

‘And your family at home, Olty. Forgive me as I should have asked before. How are things for them now after this tragedy of losing your mother?’

So, I go again through my little summary of the time I spent with my Dad and my siblings while he looks both grave but also calm. And then suddenly, he says,

‘But you didn’t just drop by on a whim, Olty, did you? What’s on your mind?

This old man is extraordinary for his prescience but I’m grateful for it and I give him an abbreviated account of my conversations with the President and with Pascal while

Pente moves around opening another couple of beers for us. He collapses back into his chair and peers at me from under his shaggy eyebrows.

'I can't tell you much, Olty, but I will pass some comment on young de Houlette who is a regular firebrand and something of a pain in the derriere - to borrow his own language. And therein lies the clue, if you like. Perhaps you don't know this but "Houlette" in French means a Shepherds Crook. It's none too subtle, just a bit of a pointer. The name is an invention, I'm pretty sure of that, a sort of nom de plume. And it certainly suits the operator because young Luc is all about gathering disciples about him, the more the merrier!'

'But what's his pitch, Pente? What's the point and purpose?'

'He's a Pied Piper. His call is to young people. Just teenagers - the fifteen to seventeen year olds who want fewer rules and more independence. And didn't we all want such liberty at that age. Even I remember feeling the urge for it, over seventy years and counting back into the mists of time. So, his appeal is to sweet sixteen of any gender, background, creed or colour and don't forget that for most in that age group, you want to be *in* the crowd, not stand out from it and I can tell you for myself that Luc has a talent for touching the heart strings of his young audience. I've heard him speak ... from a discreet distance and I was mighty impressed.'

'If you say so, Pente, and you of all people know how to spread a message ... but I still don't get it. What *is* the message and what's he trying to do with it?'

To my astonishment, Pente leans forward to make his arthritic fingers grapple with the lid of a sandalwood box which lies on the table between us. Finally, he extracts one of the short and evil smelling cigars for which he is notorious, and he rasps his old lighter to fire up.

'I'm on very short rations these days', he mutters as he blows out a cloud of smoke and then continues.

'The message, you ask. That's very simple. It's a call for support. To encourage these youngsters to put pressure on their parents, their schoolteachers, older siblings, community leaders. And what they're after is influence to change the law of this land to recognise the age of majority being reduced by two years. They want adult life to start at sixteen rather than the current eighteen. That would mean that from your sixteenth birthday, you can drink, smoke, buy legal drugs, drive a car, have sex as you choose. You would cease to be a child at that point.'

'So, this is the drum which de Houlette is banging?'

'That's it, Olty, that's it and all about it, except that there's more of course.'

'What - fact or speculation?'

Pente gives his trademark booming laugh. 'You know me well! It is speculation but pretty obvious. Little Luc may be the Piper but who's calling the tune? That's the question. Who ... and why? What's the full agenda?'

'Three questions then,' I remark, smiling at him and before he can respond, 'but you're not alone. Pascal also concludes that something more significant is afoot and he wants me to start by grilling Edmund?'

'Ladoux?'

I nod my head and he looks pensive. 'Maybe', he says after a pause, 'but for my money, I'd start with Kane Merrick.'

'Yup. A reasonable thought and I'll act on it. But for now, Pente, I'm not saying anything to the President. She's worried enough because their younger daughter is a developing disciple of Houlette but much more than that are the implications. For anything approaching this barmy idea to turn into reality, there would have to be a change made to our Constitution. That can happen only following a formal proposal to the Assembly by the President of the day which would need prior endorsement by the Panel. And frankly, I can't see that there would be any appetite for such a move. We have enough in the way of road accidents and sex exploitation in Millennium without changing the law to encourage more of both!'

'Oh, I do agree, no error, Olty but you know whoever is pulling the de Houlette strings must be intent on fermenting a national row which could lead to an exceptional Election, bringing forward the established timetable. That would itself introduce a regime change which, imagined that way, starts to look like a bloodless coup. Wouldn't you say?'

I started in my chair and put down my glass with a thump.

'I can't blame travel tiredness so I must be being bloody stupid or I'm going prematurely senile because, by God Pente, you have an alarmingly good point there and I'm already wasting time just lounging here and enjoying your beer when I should be out asking questions. And Edmund is the man to start with.'

'You might have a good opportunity sooner than you'd expect and on quite a casual basis too. When you get home, I fancy you'll find a message from Tina, welcoming you back and inviting you to one of her famous soirees. I've been invited and the word is that Edmund will be there amongst a few others. I'm much too old to drive after dusk these days so would you please divert some and give me a lift.'

Chapter Seven

The invitation - more of a summons really in her true style - turns out to be for the Friday evening and I decide to ask Jerome to drive us, but in my car as this is not official business. He arrives about seven and we start off in the wrong direction, going back into the city to collect Pente from the Cathedral Close. He complains at climbing up into the back of my old Grenadier but settles into silence as we move westwards in light traffic. It's nearly 40 km's to the little village in which Tina Fullerton has lived alone for the last thirty years since her beloved Bill dropped on the spot, felled by heart failure.

Bill Fullerton had been a contemporary of Hugh Dundas and by all accounts a larger-than-life character. As young men, the two had been very close friends through schooldays and the start of their working careers in the City of London. Hugh had provided the brains and the contacts for both of them, Bill the entertainment. The Fullertons had followed Hugh to Hong Kong and whilst there had introduced him to Alexa Bushell, nee Labarre. They had all arrived in Millennium on the first day of this Century, all vital components in their own way of the grand plan executed by my grandfather, David Heaven, to establish a new order in Africa.

Tina Goranko was a good deal, almost twelve years, younger than the Englishman she met in London towards the end of the nineteen swinging sixties. She had been born and raised in the plains country of North Dakota, USA, had proved to be an exceptionally bright student with a promising future in whatever profession she chose but she forsook all such opportunities when she married Bill Fullerton who, by his own admission, relied on character and charisma to make up for a lack of brilliance and application. He was nevertheless the constant friend upon whom Hugh Dundas relied for support, so they made a formidable team together.

This Friday in January evening in the year 2036, Tina must be only just shy of eighty years old yet she remains a striking looking lady with her long, languid figure, erect posture, flawless presentation and commanding presence: all that and with language to shock and sometimes to outrage. She greets us in the middle of her huge, oblong shaped reception room with its floor to ceiling windows looking out due East over gently undulating, seemingly endless plains country. Tina always says that the view reminds her of her native Dakota, although 'thank Christ, we don't get the god damn snow here'.

Already there are Ken and Veronica Sanchez - he runs our national airline. They are a pleasant couple, reliable company if not too exciting. Also, Jerry and Jules, an affable, entertaining pair of old queens who came to Century City from Boston, USA over ten years ago and who preside over the city's arts and culture elite. I'm interested to see that Mervyn Tredinnick is here and imagine that he is present to even up the numbers. Quite apart from that convenience, I know that Tina still can't resist flirting with entirely unsuitable men who are aeons younger than her age group. Mervyn would fall into that category, in addition to which he is tall, good looking and appears to be frighteningly fit: as well he should be as he is by profession a London Special Branch policeman who is here to check us out and get to know the place over the next few months before starting his real job for the next year or so. He is the personal protection officer to Humphrey Corton, son of the British Prime Minister, who will shortly turn nineteen and start a course at our university.

Pente has been hobnobbing with our hostess since we walked in but now he makes way for the Coberleys - Vincent and Marylin - who have just arrived and they cluster as a group by the remarkable structure which makes such a feature of this huge room. It's a circular wall, knee high for most people, built of locally quarried stone and capped with a cushion covered mahogany rail on which you can perch quite comfortably although not for long. The wall has a diameter of about two metres and within is an immense firepit, above which is suspended a copper chimney mouth which draws away the rising smoke to escape through the upper storey of the house and out into the Millennium sky. A log fire is always burning but it's muted at this, the height of our warm summer and lying, snuffling amongst the comfortably warm ashes is the celebrated Trumper, possibly the oldest and certainly the ugliest warthog you could expect to find throughout the whole of Africa. Trumper, named by Tina for a long gone US President, is as controversial a sight as his namesake and in like manner, he attracts immediate attention.

I'm anticipating that there will be twelve of us in this party but that only ten will sit down later to dinner at the table awaiting us at the northern end of this huge hall of a room. The explanation is that Hugh and Alexa Dundas will join us for a drink but will not stay for long. Both of them weary at the end of these long, hot days and prefer to return home before it gets too late. I chat briefly to Alexa, still strikingly elegant but a little hampered by her poor hearing in this vast space with its vaulted ceiling. I greet Earl Schneider, the Mister Media for our country as he owns the principal Television Channel and half a dozen publications, national and regional. I acknowledge James and Elizabeth Clark, both practising lawyers and socially very active and then I don't have to turn round to know that Kane Merrick has arrived with his booming laugh. This is useful because I should get the chance to have a word with him about this youth movement business. I move towards him and his diminutive wife, Elspeth, but I'm intercepted by Liz Clark with a stranger standing beside her.

'Olty', says Liz, 'I'd like you to meet Helen – Helen Priest who has only just arrived in Century. She's going to be staying with us for a while - well, for as long as it takes us to find her the sort of accommodation she would like for her stay in Millennium.'

Then, turning to her guest, she adds, 'Helen, let me introduce you to Olty: Oliver Aveling. He runs the Government Secretariat which makes him our senior Civil Servant ... and a most useful man to know!'

Addressing myself to the lady, I remark, 'How nice to meet you. I already know your name well: there have been many messages about you from both London and Geneva.'

She has a surprisingly deep voice and the very slightest of accents which I place as Middle Eastern - maybe Lebanese. She smiles, 'With my name, I bet you were expecting to meet a Minister!'

So that was the very insignificant start of it - a relationship which will last for less than a year but will dominate my lifetime. But at that time, of course, all I knew was that I was meeting for the first time a young woman in her mid-thirties, tall, slender, a long neck and shapely, graceful hands (I always notice those). She was dressed in a plain cream blouse, open at the collar and tucked loosely into black silk trousers above plain black pumps on her feet. She wore what looked like a Cartier watch with a square face, held on her left wrist by a heavy crocodile strap. She had no rings (I notice that too), just simple pearl studs in her ears and a gold crucifix, suspended from a thick, gold chain. Very little make up, a light blush on her lips. Her hair was a very deep russet in colour, lustrous and heavy as it hung to her shoulders. The eyes twinkled their piercing violet colour. The face was almost angelic in its composition, made more interesting by its slightly imperfect nose and the smile as she looked at me was impish, speaking of character and humour. She was very attractive indeed ... and she knew it.

There was no time for further conversation as Abel, Tina's major-domo, a huge, hulking man who Is Ghanaian born and has been a fixture in this house since the long-gone days when Bill Fullerton was still alive, sounded his foghorn of a voice to announce that dinner was served and we all moved towards the table, leaving Hugh and Alexa Dundas to make a quiet and dignified exit.

There's no ceremony in this house: Tina will install herself at the head of her massive table, choosing whom she wishes to sit on either side of her which did not include me on this occasion and leaving all other guests to sit where they will. Liz Clark shepherded Helen away and I sat between Kane and Elspeth Merrick. They are both good company, but I find it hard to relax entirely in his presence.

Kane is not especially tall, but he is a great bull of a man who will impose himself forcefully on all those surrounding him. He was born and brought up in rural Zimbabwe, the scion of a wealthy ranching family who owned a considerable tract of land outside Gueru stretching south towards Bulawayo. Kane lost both his parents and his birthright to the marauding bands of Robert Mugabe at some point during the late nineties, after which he abandoned his land, scooped up Elspeth and their two boys and came to establish himself with a new life here in Millennium. A new life, but constant in his profession and over the last twenty-five years, he has built up a ranching empire which sprawls across our central highlands region. The headquarters of the operation and their main house are located outside the burgeoning town of Highworth, but Kane and Elspeth have another house here in Century City as their sons now run the business and Kane needs to be in town as he is the Panel Member responsible for Agriculture which is a key finance earner for Millennium. There are three grandchildren, a girl and two boys, all of whom live in town with their grandparents during schooldays, returning to Highworth at weekends and for holidays.

Kane Merrick is never reluctant to express an opinion and he engages me forcefully on the subject of Luc de Houlette as soon as I mention the name over our starter of crab salad.

'The guy's a French pansy' he expostulates, 'out to stir up a bit of trouble and make a name for himself. I hope you'll crack down hard on him, Olty'.

'Not my province, Kane, whatever I may think. If he's breaking the law or inciting others to do so, then it's a matter for the Commissioner' I reply, hearing myself sounding Civil servile and a bit pompous.

From my other side, Elspeth chips in to comment 'trouble is, Olty, if he's inciting anyone, it's children, adults in body more or less but in law still minors and too young to answer for charges like this.'

It's a fair point. Elspeth Merrick looks timid but she's well qualified for this debate, being an educationalist and a respected lecturer at the University. She continues 'I do worry about our young people being led astray and this is a matter too close to home. Our own granddaughter Amy, just fifteen, is one falling under his spell and with a passion which is hard to dispute.'

'Could you elaborate on that?'

'Certainly, I can', says Elspeth, 'but probably it'll take longer than we have now ... and I wouldn't want to spoil Kane's beef which I know Tina is going to produce as her piece de resistance. But shorthand for now, Olty, what this is all about is youth, bursting with energy and exploding hormones, being persuaded that, collectively, they are being undervalued in Millennium's still quite new and developing world. These young things and a growing number of later teens/early twenties are being groomed towards a conviction that they should be getting a greater say and at a younger age in how their country is governed. "We can't contribute without commitment": that's the cry of the moment.

Elspeth is right about the timing: even now, waiting staff are collecting our crab plates, glasses are being refilled and the first plates of what I know will be the most delectable meat are being born from the kitchen. I am, however, startled to see that my driver has become one of the waiters. But it turns out that Jerome doesn't have meat for me: but he does have a message and he bends to whisper in my ear.

'It's the Police. Commissioner Odinga has phoned to ask you to join him urgently. He's in the middle of town and it seems he has a problem with these young protesters.

'Is that all? Where is he exactly and what sort of help?'

'He's at the War Memorial in Cathedral Close. Seems there's quite a gathering there. Says he won't have a problem in containing things and dispersing the crowd, but he would like for you to have a look. I'll have the car ready outside.'

I sigh as I push back my chair and Kane at my side mutters that he'll be in touch after the weekend so we can regroup to continue the discussion. I walk up to the head of the table to make my apologies to Tina and see that she has Pente sitting in pride of place next to her. Instantly I recognise that with this action taking place in the city location most dear to his heart, he should be with us. Over the hubbub of general conversation, I explain the summons and he turns briefly to his hostess before creaking to his feet to follow me out of the room and the house.

Chapter Eight

Jerome puts his foot down and it takes us a bare twenty minutes to get into the city centre. We swoop past the Secretariat building on the one-way system and as we round the corner and onto the cobble setts of the Close, I catch my breath in astonishment. This is a big crowd which is milling all over the large, chained off area which protects the entrance to the Cathedral building and in the middle of which stands our Memorial. It doesn't celebrate the War dead, of course, because the country which preceded Millennium was not involved in either of the two world conflicts of the last century, but it is a large, ornate and ever running fountain which marks the establishment of Century City in the year 2000. This is a centrepiece and has particular meaning for Pente, whose life over the last thirty five years has been so interrelated to this grand and historic building: it's his church. In every sense.

I had made Pente ride in the front with Jerome and as we come to a violent halt, he opens his door and slips out with surprising ease, but he staggers as he straightens up and looks around him. I'm out of the car myself by then and immediately I see Mo Odinga trotting towards me. He comes up, looking concerned but calm and still managing to exude authority.

'Thanks for coming so quick, Olty. I wanted you to see this before my guys break it up. I expect you're surprised by the numbers: I know I was when I got here about an hour ago and they haven't stopped coming since.'

They certainly seem organised. Twenty metres to my right, there's a sort of raised platform and it's got a lectern at the front of it with a microphone. There's plenty of background noise so I can hardly hear the stuttering voice of the slightly built guy standing there and I'm guessing this is my first sight of Luc de Houlette who's bellowing away but can't really make himself heard.

But suddenly he is elbowed away and his place in front of the mike taken by a great bearded thug of a man and we can hear him clearly enough. To paraphrase the message which is being shouted at the crowd with much gesticulation and spittle flying, Millennium rules and standard of living are being dictated by a handful of the old, elite and wealthy to exploit the masses and deny the voice of the young and emerging generation. But this stream of invective is being spouted by a man who looks like he must be in his thirties and the very image of a down and out to boot: greasy jeans and leather jerkin, bare but heavily tattooed arms, matted hair to his shoulders. Just listening gives me the chance to look around at the substantial crowd which is made up mostly of really young teenagers - both sexes, varied sizes, of course, a fair mixture of ethnicity but that's what you would expect in this city. A second, random glance reveals something more. Circulating quietly amongst this mob of young people are one or two motley figures - two men and one girl I spot - and all three are obviously of the same sort of age and just as scruffy as the speaker, who is continuing with his rant. I concentrate on the girl for a few seconds and see that she is handing out sweets to the young listeners. Except they're not sweets, I'm sure. They'll be twists containing probably coke but maybe some other party drug and is this a reward for turning up here this evening or an inducement to return on a future occasion. Probably a bit of both. My thoughts are interrupted by Maurice Odinga who asks, 'Seen enough?'

I just nod and Mo is already moving. He shoulders his way forward and climbs up the few stairs onto the platform. There's room enough for him to push de Houlette out of his way and I see this prophet figure jump down to the ground and move to disappear into the crowd. Then I see Odinga step forward and place one ham hand over the microphone. He's shorter than the speaker and has to look up at him but I'm close enough to hear their exchange.

'I'm the Commissioner of Police and I judge that this unlawful gathering is creating a disturbance. You will cease speaking and depart immediately or you will be arrested and charged with causing an affray.'

… 'and I'm a citizen who's entitled to air my views and concerns for society. So you can step down in your smart uniform and fuck off!!'

There's a clearly audible smack as Mo hits the guy hard across the face, twists one arm behind his back and pushes him off the platform where he sprawls on the ground. I notice that members of the Police team have materialised. and are grouped around their boss in support. But no one steps forward to challenge and Odinga pulls the mike to his lips and announces, 'This gathering is now concluded and all of you in the crowd are to disperse immediately. Go home and you will hear no more about this. But anyone remaining here in Cathedral Close in five minutes time will be arrested with your name taken and published on all media tomorrow morning. There will be no further warning.'

He stood, motionless, on the platform, watching as the crowd started to break up immediately. This seems a good point for me, also, to leave and I look around for Jerome. But first, I see to Pente and walk with him to his front door. I am fearful. For the first time in my experience, his ebullience has deserted him.

There is little more to say about that strange Friday evening and not much more about the weekend which followed it. Jerome drove me home and it was not late. I remember I made myself something to eat and then drank most of a bottle of a heavy burgundy, while leaning on the rail of my bedroom balcony, watching the restless ocean as it thundered onto the beach. A large part of me was filled with a foreboding to which I couldn't give cause or shape. Other than that, I brooded on Oksana with a mixture of guilt, longing and sadness. I was also stirred by the memory of Helen Priest, with whom I had exchanged barely a word but there had been enough to excite my interest and I was intrigued because I knew that I had to introduce her around and help her to plan the progress of her work assignment here in Millennium.

Chapter Nine

The next day - Saturday morning - I phoned Mo Odinga at home. He sounded bouncy enough, but I could sense the worry behind a calm exterior. I posed just one question.

'That guy who hijacked the event, Mo, and was sounding off until you shut him down. He's a grown adult, for Christ's sake. So, what was all that about and who is he?

'He's *vouyoy,* Olty, remember I told you? He's trouble, all the worse as he was doing as he's told.'

'And what about the random few I saw in the crowd dishing out what I'm guessing were drugs of some sort?'

'Yup. *vouyoy* also, no question. They'll all be part of one gang or group. We're working over the weekend to try and put some names to faces but you can be sure, Olty, that front man was being paid for his performance and it's not going to stop there. We need to find who's behind all this before it gets out of hand. Let's get together again next week and have a review.'

We hung up then and I brooded for a while before ringing Pente. But I couldn't get a reply, so I punched in another number and immediately heard a well-known voice.

'Dundas Residence'

'How are you today, Delilah? May I speak to Mr Dundas please ... or is he taking a nap?'

'Oh hello, Mr Oliver', she always calls me that and I must say that it always boosts my morale! And then,

'No, no. Mr and Mrs Dundas are both here. They're sitting in the shade on the terrace having a glass of punch while we all wait for my Erasmus to bring home some fish which I can prepare for lunch. Do you want to come over, Mr Oliver?'

'Not today, thank you Delilah: but I would like a word with Mr D if there's time before your lunch.'

She didn't respond - didn't need to as Hugh came on the line.

'Quite a testing evening, I gather, and Tina's party buggered up for good measure!'

'Yes, all of that and more. What have you heard, Hugh, and what do you make of it?

'You'll do better to hear from Alexa, Olty. She has a finger closer to the pulse. I'll hand you over.'

The calm, clear voice came over the line. There was never hesitation in this remarkable, vintage lady: never a single syllable wasted.

'Good morning, Olty. I'm glad you rang. I've been wanting to talk to you. Earlier, I took a call from the President, the third time she's been in touch in as many days ... and all on the same subject. She's getting increasingly concerned about their daughter Melissa and the malign influence which is so affecting the child.

'Melissa's the younger daughter?'

'Yes, that's right. She's a pretty, lively thing, fast moving from being a tomboy to a young sophisticate, but still very much a juvenile.'

'But they grow up very quickly these days, no?'

'Girls have always done that, Olty, but even so: at eighteen, you have experience, at fifteen, you're still fumbling. Believe me because I've been there, even so long ago!'

'And it's obvious that the President is worried?'

'She's desperate. Laetitia's a good friend of mine and she has been speaking very candidly. She's very conscious that in character, Melissa's vulnerable to the wrong sort of approach and influence.'

'So how do we handle this, Alexa. What would you have me do about it?'

'Olty, you're a very diplomatic character. Heavens, you used to be a professional diplomat before ascending to the dizzy heights of managing the Secretariat! Look, you know how things work and you know how to get the best from people. Hugh and I have talked this over - of course we have - and we've discussed it with Pente too. We think he's right. This isn't about that little toad de Houlette and his half-baked campaign. There's something and someone more sinister behind it and we need to flush them out. We need to understand the additional and main agenda. And then work out how best to confront it. Please could you do your best, then come over to us one evening later this week so we can compare notes.'

That's where we left it and I went on to spend a lonely Saturday evening, lost in not very productive thought. Sunday was better. I considerably extended my morning beach walk, working out my moves for the following day and a new week. Around noon, I walked up the road to the small Mall and bought a takeaway curry from the Indian restaurant where I've come to know the owners - an enterprising and entertaining couple who originate from Mumbai.

When I got home, had eaten and drank a good deal more of that Burgundy, my thought was to ring the Merricks and make a plan to meet again. I particularly wanted to hear more of what Elspeth has to say but then I changed tack. Trouble is that she wouldn't meet me on her own. Elspeth is extremely old fashioned, and she would consider such a proposition improper but as soon as you get Kane involved, you're likely to get bulldozed.

I acknowledge the guy's influence and admire his accomplishment, but he is inclined to overwhelm.

So instead, as dusk was falling that Sunday evening, I rang Edmund Ladoux and fixed to have lunch with him the following day. Edmund is my firmest friend and I trust him with more secrets than I should.

Chapter Ten

We met at noon in the Grill Bar of the Century Hotel in the heart of the city. This is one of our oldest buildings, now a small but luxuriously comfortable hotel with prices to match and the Grill is as close as we get to a Club. It's a good spot for fine, old fashioned dining in discreet surroundings.

That Monday, we spent an hour, two gins & tonic and most of a three-course lunch just catching up with news. We had not been together since I had been back to England following my mother's death and Edmund wanted to hear all about that trip and how my family was coping. Then there was Oksana, to whom he had been close and she was a subject on which he grilled me closely - and not for the first time either as he had long been constructively critical about what he saw as the casual way in which I had been conducting my side of the relationship. Not that he is well qualified to sit in judgement.

Edmund is a committed and active homosexual but there is no partner in his life, nor does he seek one. For most of the time, he is a confirmed, ageing bachelor, an aesthete who is most content in his own company. He lives by himself in a modest apartment, located somewhere in the depths of Pentonville which is not the most glorious of the Century City suburbs.

Just occasionally, Edmund will embark on an affair with some random stranger, sometimes more than one simultaneously, for a day, a night, even a week of torrid sex. Apart from this Jekyll and Hyde predilection, he is the most reserved and cultured man, with his carefully chosen words, considered opinions and urbane appearance. He is passionate about his opera and something of an authority on Renaissance art. Professionally, Edmund is a lawyer and preeminent in his field. He sits on our Panel and is the National Minister responsible for our legal system and our Constitution. President Valbuena is the third in succession under whom he has served which makes this the twelfth year in which he has held the post. He's an important guy and I'm glad to be sitting with him now, with a pot of coffee between us and a brandy a piece after our large lunch. I need his assessment of what I still see as an incident rather than a crisis. I need his advice and that will be the more valuable because we are close friends and I trust him completely. He's very tall, not much short of two metres, painfully thin with a bald egg head which appears uncomfortably balanced on the end of his long neck with its protruding Adam's apple. He has sallow, olive coloured skin and very slender fingers which he uses delicately to reinforce his debating points.

Edmund is a Somali by birth and moves with the calm and grace which seems to come naturally to people of East African descent. He is about my age - mid forties - but doesn't know precisely where or when he was born. He survived a childhood in the horrors of war-torn Mogadishu, escaping in his early teens to Thailand and thence Hong Kong, just in time to stow away on the *Orphan's Dawn* before she sailed on her maiden and only journey, arriving here on the first day of this century.

I ask 'You'll have heard about the demo on Friday evening, Edmund, and what Mo Odinga had to do to break it up. But what about this strange, meandering priest, Luc de Houlette, what d'you make of him and this talk of trying to drive down the voting age?'

'I think the bit of bombing damage on the ship, the *Dawn*, is just as significant - perhaps more so.'

I'm caught out by Edmund's reply.

'Why d'you say that? I thought you were barely conscious of the *Dawn* episode, and I know you and I haven't had a chance to discuss it before today.'

'Olty, you may be - indeed you are - my prime source of information: but you're not the only one. Anyway, as I see things, the demo was making a statement, whereas the bombing was to send a message. So, I conclude that whatever this thing is about, it's ramping up and we must expect it to get worse ... and quickly!'

'There's sparse evidence, little to go on, I agree, but what's your best guess as at today, Edmund. What should we, what should Mo and his guys be looking for: and what, if anything, should I be saying to the President?'

'Best guess, Olty? With nothing much to guide us, my gut tells me that someone is in an early but developing stage of mounting a takeover - another coup but this one being an internal revolution.'

I'm thunderstruck by this postulation and I feel my hand trembling as I carefully put down my cup.

'How on earth, Edmund, do you reach that conclusion?'

'Well, look, there's no process of logical, developing thought that leads me there: it's a gut reaction, that's all, with nothing I can prove. But that is what you asked me for.' He leant forward, placing his slender hands on his bony knees as he fixed me with that penetrating stare which I have come to know so well. He goes on,

'First, some person or people attack the ship to make a scene, to attract attention, to set out their credentials if you like. All they are trying to do is to evidence their capability and to leave a calling card. They choose the New Year because that's another anniversary of when Millennium came into existence, and they expect us to notice that part of the message. And then this voting age business. For me, that's just using our young people as rentacrowd. They're easily influenced at that age.

I nod in agreement but add, 'That's a reasonable assumption, Edmund, but I still don't get where you're heading with this theory. It does seem outlandish to me. After all, we have got things well organised in this country, haven't we? Of course there've been ups and downs over the years but look at Millennium here and now - as we're sitting here today. We've still got good income from our offshore oil,' I find myself ticking off the plus points on my fingers as I confront his gaze, 'We've got stability, equality of opportunity, space, security, full employment, excellent education and health care *and* a decent climate. I mean, what else d'you want?!'

'Olty,' he says, 'It's not about what I want, it's what some other bugger doesn't have but fancies to the point at which he/she/they is tempted to make a grab for it.'

I shake my head at him. I always have time for Edmund's thoughts but on this matter, I really do think that his vivid imagination is running away with him. I want to move the conversation on but I don't want to offend him so I sigh and say, 'I can't see such a threat, myself, but I'll put it to Mo Odinga and see if he has unearthed anything further yet'. Then another thought occurs to me, so I add. 'If there's anything to your theory, Edmund, there must be somebody behind all this. It can't be all down to a crowd of schoolchildren, a troublesome priest of doubtful qualification and a mob of rowdies.'

He nods in agreement and says. 'That's right: but the name of Merrick does come to mind.'

'You're not accusing Kane, surely?'

'I'm not accusing anyone, Olty, but Kane isn't the whole family.

'You're thinking of their sons?'

'Only one of them. The elder, Maximilian, doesn't register too strongly on the reality scale. Mad Max, they call him and it's not hard to see why. You may know different, but I don't think Max has ever contributed much to the family business. Since his teen years, he's been too preoccupied with cars, horses and women. He's a good-looking devil and charming with it but if he has any other talents, he keeps them well hidden. He's a brilliant horseman and an outstanding polo player but you can't be playing elitist sports for a lifetime and Max must be mid-forties by now. And God only knows how that Imelda has stuck by him over all the years since they married. Max is a serial adulterer and is said to couple with the last body in the bus queue if he's got five minutes spare.'

I was quite surprised by the bitterness in Edmund's voice. Max Merrick certainly has a reputation, and none too savoury at that, but equally he is known for his humour and generosity. He is a bon viveur with style and some attitude.

'I'm ashamed to say that I can't remember, Edmund, so please remind me: do Max and Imelda have children?'

'No, they don't … and presumably won't now. But then there is the younger Merrick son, Leroy, who ticks all the right boxes. He's bright, articulate, very dedicated to safeguarding the ranching empire which Kane has built up over the years and improving it too. It's Leroy who launched the beef export trade which is now contributing a lot to our national income and there's Merrick Trucking which distributes fresh fruit and veg country wide: that also was Leroy's brainchild.'

I'm thinking even as Edmund speaks that all this is true but also that Leroy is obsessive about his business and further burnishes his reputation with a sensible level of commitment to good works. I know he sits on the Boards of several leading Charities and is a Governor of Schools both in Century City and in the provinces. This is all admirable stuff, but the fact remains that he is also, in character, a worthy but colourless bore. I say nothing and my friend continues.

'It's Leroy and Rhoda who have provided the next generation: the twin boys whose age is just still in single figures and their first born, Lucinda, who's a fair bit older and now boarding with her grandparents and at school here in the city.'

I remember now my truncated conversation with Kane and Elspeth the other night at Tina Fullerton's, hearing their concern that the girl might be falling under the influence of Luc de Houlette.

'So even though his own daughter may be at risk, you reckon that Leroy Merrick may be behind all this trouble with a larger and more dangerous agenda?'

'Honestly, Olty, I don't know - of course I don't. All this is just by way of casual lunchtime conversation and I'm not laying blame at anyone's door. I can point to Leroy having the power base, the contacts and the brains but I'm not at all sure he's got the character for making a move.'

He paused for a while and then added 'Why don't you talk to Hugh about it. It would be a matter dear to his heart and he does remain remarkably clear thinking.'

'I know and you're right. I should do that, and I will. But for right now, I'd better get back to my desk and try to concentrate after that excellent lunch!'

It's my turn today so I pay the bill, then we rise simultaneously and make our way towards the door from our window table. On the way, we pass by Liz Clark who is engrossed in conversation with the striking Ms Priest - obviously covering for her some key aspects of Century social life. Liz introduces her to Edmund who bows over her hand in a courtly style. Helen turns briefly to me and says, with her enigmatic smile, 'I've received a summons from your Beatrice that I'm to be in your office tomorrow morning at ten sharp!'

'I'll look forward to it', I reply as we move on and leave them to finish their lunch.

Chapter Eleven

She was certainly very punctual. On the dot of ten the following morning, Beatrice showed her into my office, and we immediately moved together over to my table and chairs in the window with its fine view and a tray of coffee laid out on the low table.

She stood taller than I remembered from our first, very brief, meeting at Tina's: 1.75 at least or about 5'9" in what is now very old money. Her very slim but shapely frame was dressed for business. A plain black trouser suit over a cream linen blouse. A minimum of make up, no rings nor other jewellery, just an up to the minute CC hanging around her neck from an expensive looking gold chain.

I find myself speaking first and needing to start with an apology.

'I haven't done my homework: I do have the briefing paper but it came through just the day I left for the UK on personal business and I've not long been back. Sorry!'

'It's understood. Beatrice filled me in and you're OK with that, I hope. What a tragedy to lose your mother so suddenly.'

'Not so sudden really. We'd been losing her to her dementia over quite a time.' I'm touched that Bea should have taken the initiative to explain and surprised that I don't mind a stranger knowing.

'Were you close?'

‘Yes, we were, but only as close as we could be with her there and me here over the last thirty odd years.’

‘I know what you mean. My Mum has been gone a long, long time now …. But I still hear her speaking to me from time to time.’

I sit up straighter and pick up the dossier from the table in front of us.

‘Tell me more about yourself and how we can help you. I gather you expect to be with us for six months or so?’

‘That’s the plan but it could be a little longer depending on how things go: and how long you can put up with me!’ She smiles over the rim of her coffee cup.

I return the smile but don’t reply and Helen goes on.

‘Usually with these assignments, I spend a week or so working on a time plan, writing it up with objectives and to do by dates, discussing it to gain agreement from my host and my boss back at base…’

‘That’s New York?’ I interrupt her with my question.

‘That’s Geneva.’

‘I thought you’re with the UN.

‘I am, yes. But UNHCR: Refugees’.

She has a soft, low voice with clear enunciation and a timbre which suggests an American mid-west background. I have the sense that she neither wastes nor minces words.

‘Of course,’, I remark, ‘we don’t have a classic refugee challenge here in Millennium: in principle, we welcome all from everywhere.’ I feel that I’m sounding pompous and self-righteous, but Helen seems undeterred as she continues.

‘Quite. But that’s the purpose of my mission, Mr Aveling. Once I have gained some understanding of your circumstances in this country, I’d like to discuss with you and your colleagues the prospects of Millennium receiving a regular and perhaps an increasing number per annum of dispossessed and desperate people from hotspots around the globe.’

Immediately, I’m on the defensive and hear myself mouthing well-worn platitudes which I have used often enough before.

‘Well, we already do our bit, Ms Priest, and have been doing over the last decade. We do take in immigrants from DRC for example, escapees from repression there, some from Zimbabwe, less frequently others from the Balkans and from the Middle East, people who may have skipped through several different sovereign states before finding their way to our borders.’

‘And some of them you send back?’

'It happens, yes, but only after exhaustive investigation into background and circumstances. We don't condemn anyone to persecution.'

There's that whimsical smile again as she crosses her legs to lean forward for her coffee cup.

'We're going too fast here. I need to get myself better organised before I start grilling you! But let's anyway skip the formalities: I'm Helen'.

'Good idea! I'm Oliver … but most people call me Olty'.

'Maybe so, but then again, I'm not most people and I think Oliver's a fine name.'

There's a long pause while I'm deciding what to make of this. Then I say,

'Tell me more about your background, Helen, and tell me how I can help you get started with your assignment here.'

OK. Well here's the short version. I'm forty-three, single, never married, no kids, no attachments, no parents now, no siblings, no relatives. Born and raised in Mogadishu, Somalia. Always hungry, always threatened, always in danger of one sort or another. Escaped when I was about fifteen. On a pirate boat to Yemen. Knocked about, molested, just survived the journey. Aden almost worse than Moga. Destitute, starving, sleeping on a rubbish tip. But then I got seriously lucky. I was taken in by an American couple who took me from Aden to Muscat, Oman where he had a posting for three years during which I became part of the family, received some education, came to understand a bit of how the world works. Still stateless, of course, no passport, no nationality, no fixed abode. But my couple of saviours, bless them, wouldn't let me go. I was adopted and taken home to Washington with them. By then I'd found that I had a brain and started to use it. I did a law degree and a Master's in marketing and business Administration at Harvard. By then, I reckoned I was overqualified, and it was time to go to work. I found a job with the UN and an apartment I could afford, both in New York and both on the same day. I stayed there for three years before I had the chance to transfer into UNHCR in Geneva. Being pretty much a refugee myself, it seemed the place to head for and I've never regretted the move. It's home now and I doubt I'll develop an urge to live anywhere else.'

'Not even here in Millennium?' I'm smiling, trying to make a joke of it but she comes straight back at me.

'Particularly not in Century City - not anywhere in Millennium. You're a pampered lot and you've had it too easy for way too long.' There's no levity in her response.

'But you've only just arrived here: isn't it a bit soon to form such a certain opinion?'

Now there is just a slight and rueful grin as she says,

'Yup. I guess you have a point there, Oliver. I should have a look around before I confirm my thoughts. Just don't go expecting a change of heart.'

Suddenly, I have a bright idea and as at that very moment, Beatrice appears with a refill pot of coffee, so I ask her,

'Bea. When does Mervyn leave on his round trip?'

There's no hesitation: Bea's knowledge is encyclopaedic. 'He leaves on Friday, Olty, and reckons to be about a week or ten days on his travels. He wants to spend at least a couple of days in Rheina Blanca, checking on arrangements at the diving club. I've fixed for him to take Jerome and your car. I hope that's OK?'

'Of course. I can look after myself for a few days. What this means, Helen, is that you can have a guided tour round our country: see what you make of us and what we have to offer.'

'Sounds good to me. And it will be good for the Clarks, give them a break and perhaps Liz will have nailed down an apartment for me by the time we're back. But one thing: who's this Mervyn?'

'You might have met him at Tina's dinner party : a tall guy. He's a policeman out here from the UK for a year or so. He does personal protection and he'll be looking out for young Humphrey Corton who's a VIP and only eighteen but will be doing a stint at our University.'

Helen just shrugs. 'But isn't eighteen rather young for Uni? That's more high school age. Who is he anyway? It's surely tough to be landed with a name like that.'

Before I can reply, Beatrice breaks in to comment. 'Humphrey's the son of the British Prime Minister, Helen, and him coming here for a spell is important because it shows that the UK is taking us seriously and developing confidence in Millennium. The Head of the Government's family is entitled to protection, even if there is minimal risk.'

'Well, whatever,' Helen says, 'Thanks for the help, Bea, and the arrangements. I'm sure Mervyn will be good company.' She stands and pivots elegantly, scooping up her handbag as she makes towards my door. I have time to think that something has upset her: she doesn't like being 'arranged', she likes to be singular and independent?

I have very many other things to do and life is busy. I get immersed over the following days, then suddenly I realise that they've been gone for almost a week. At the same moment, I'm conscious that I'm looking forward to her return.

But now arrives a seminal event, taking place on a day I'll never forget.

I'm at my desk in the Secretariat, just finishing up a routine meeting by video link with two of the Regional Offices. It's nearly midday on Tuesday, 29th January 2036 when my personal, private screen lights up with a short, meaningful message which reads. 'It's nearly time: come now if you want to say farewell. UC.'

'UC' is Ulick - Ulick Connor, our hulking great Irishman from County Cork, strongman rugby international in time past, now coach, also a fine friend and an excellent doctor. I knew immediately where I would find him, and I left my office at the gallop.

Chapter Twelve

It took me just a few minutes to run round from the Secretariat building into the Cathedral Cloisters and I found Ulick standing outside the door of Pente's small house. He was signalling me to slow down as I came up to him.

'There's no rush, Olty' he said in his surprisingly soft Irish brogue, 'Bejasus but he's a tough old bugger in spite of the recurring malaria, all the whisky and those bloody cigars! I'm amazed he's kept going this long'.

'Bloody lucky you were here, Ulick. Who found you?'

'You'll not believe it, but he called me himself! Asked would I come round and check him out as he reckons his time has come. Well, he's right there, but not quite. You'll find him in the garden, Olty. He's still conscious and muttering to himself but damned if I can make out a word of it.'

I passed by him and entered the little house, pausing in the familiar, cluttered room which Pente insisted on calling his parlour, dominated by the huge television screen which occupied all of one wall, noting that his ancient desk top computer was alight and awaiting instruction, glancing at the narrow staircase up which he would squeeze his portly frame to the single, en suite bedroom above. I went quietly on into the small courtyard garden which was almost entirely enclosed by the prolific vine which blotted out most of the sky whilst giving shade from our burning sunshine. The small birdbath with gurgling fountain - Pente's most prized possession from his spiritual home, the

Monastery of the Order of Saints, near the village of Slaley, in Northumberland, England - was chattering to itself in one corner.

He was sitting in his scruffy old wicker chair with his back to me. The whole scene was so familiar: it seemed that I had been there a thousand times before and would be coming again. Except that I knew in that instant that I wouldn't. I knew this was the last time.

I moved gently around him and stooped down so I could see his face, but he was holding it so low that he was almost on his knees. His hands were fluttering, and his arms were jerking spasmodically. I looked round to ask Ulick what was happening to Pente, the wild thought running through my brain was that I was witnessing some sort of death throe. Then some sanity returned because I caught the sound of speech but so very faint that I had to slip to my knees and press my ear almost to his mouth before I could catch the words. This was no 'muttering' as Ulick had reported. It was the Song of Simeon. Pente was reciting over and over the opening verse of the Nunc Dimittis: *Lord, now lettest thou thy servant depart in peace.* I had no doubt that the Almighty would grant him this wish, so I stood and walked out to join the Doctor. A short time later, Ulick went back into the house and returned to confirm that Pente Broke Smith had died.

The following week passed for me in a whirl and a daze. The whirl came from all that had to be done, the daze because I couldn't believe that he was gone.

Rupert Broke Smith - known for almost all his adult life as 'Pente' - was not far into his ninety-third year when he died. Born in November 1943 to elderly parents eking out a precarious existence in extremely rural Herefordshire, his rather lonely childhood was brightened by his friendship with a local farmer's daughter called Vanda. Their relationship blossomed, developed, was consummated. They might well have married and lived happily ever after but Rupert was a bright young man and won a place at Oxford University. In the long vacation of his second year, he journeyed to the Indian subcontinent and spent some weeks in the high country of the Hindu Kush. He returned with a vision and a calling which led him into the priesthood and a monastic life with the Order of Saints. When he had completed his induction and training, he undertook the first of many missions of behalf of his Order which saw him living in different countries throughout Africa over the next thirty odd years. Despite this itinerant existence in generally harsh surroundings, he maintained the four close friendships which were forged during university days, leading to them being known as 'The Oxford Five'. Yet more important to him, he never relinquished his love and regard for Vanda, the girl he left behind when he became a priest.

Pente lived here in Century City for the last thirty-five years of his life: he was the mainspring of the Cathedral, having been the prime mover behind the renovation of the building. He gave valued advice to a succession of our Presidents, and he was a source of spiritual comfort to a countless number of visitors to his house here in the Cloisters. So, he was well known, highly regarded and much loved in the towns, villages and communities which make up this young country. The news of his passing spread very quickly and soon, television and radio stations, daily newspapers and weekly news sheets, above all social & personal media were alive with tributes, reminiscences and commentary. Since it was generally known that Pente had been a celibate bachelor priest, living on his own, a fair amount of correspondence in whatever form came into the Secretariat and despite the best, caring efforts of Beatrice and her colleagues, much of this landed on my desk to keep me fully occupied along with a normal intake of work to be completed. In addition, I was an Executor of his Will, along with James Clark who was also his lawyer. We were both surprised by the extent and variety of his worldly goods and by the complexity of the arrangements that he specified for their dispersal. This was all set out in an old fashioned, handwritten file which I found prominently displayed on his desk shortly after his death. It was no sort of a shock for me to appreciate that he must have sensed the imminence of his demise in time to leave in good order the trappings of his existence in this world. I expect he was content in the knowledge that he was reaching the end of his road and looking forward to the start of the next.

There were a very few - three to be exact - who warranted a personal account of Pente's passing. I had driven out to see Tina Fullerton first and found her feeding titbits to Trumper in his firepit.

'Ah, Jesus Christ', she said, 'I fuckin' knew this was coming. I could see it in his eyes the other night when you were all here. He was such a terrific guy, Olty. I did love him so .... and so did my Bill! But d'ya know, I'm glad for him: I reckon he'd had enough and deserves his rest.' Unchecked tears were rolling down her cheeks and ruining her make up as I left and drove on to the spreading house and grounds on the beach which were the home of Hugh and Alexa Dundas. Hugh had been the financier and grand planner who had supported my grandfather David Heaven in his vision of Project Zero which had brought them storming in to found the country at the turn of this century. He had always regarded Pente as his Priest and the loss would hit him hard, especially in the frailty of his own considerable age. But more important still was his wife, Alexa. Born Alexandra Labarre with Anglo French parentage and then married for a while to the Australian Peter Bushell before living with and finally marrying Hugh, it's Alexa who shares more background with Pente than any of the rest of us because they were undergraduates together at Oxford University so many years ago and with David, formed the nucleus of the 'Oxford Five.' She is now the only one still alive.

I'm not surprised that Alexa takes the news phlegmatically: she has suffered much distress and trauma during her own long life of just on ninety years last month and she has a calm serenity about her which is a constant source of wonder.

'I'm relieved for him, Olty, and just glad that Vanda went before him as she wouldn't have been strong enough to come out here to see him off. I imagine you're planning something special for his funeral?'

Her question had put me in mind of something that had been troubling and puzzling me, namely that I had been unable to find a single word of instruction or guidance in all of Pente's papers about a farewell Service. I didn't say anything about this to Alexa as we had a quiet cup of tea together, but I left the Dundas house to drive back into town, returning to the Cloisters to find Moses waiting for me in Pente's house. He had a slim file under his arm which explained it all.

Chapter Thirteen

Moses Chirungu comes from Malawi and is our Bishop. He is short, rotund, black and bald so that he and Mo Odinga could be taken for twins. But not when they are dressed for work. Mo's dress uniform is smart enough, particularly impressive when complete with badges of office, gold epaulettes and his ivory tipped swagger stick. But he can't compete with Chirungu in full regalia, formal vestments, Bishop's cope and mitre, the thick chain around his neck carrying the heavy gold cross, nestling against his chest: not that he's wearing any of this as he stands to greet me in Pente's parlour. In his jeans and an open necked shirt, he hands the file to me, saying,

'He left it with me about a month ago, Olty, but I didn't open it until this morning. Pente always said that he didn't want too much fuss but equally, he loved a grand occasion and a big statement.' He taps the file as he adds, 'this qualifies as I think you'll agree.'

I certainly did and now, a week on, there's a group of us in the Cathedral, running through a bit of a rehearsal before the big day tomorrow. Bea is standing between Moses and me. She's making notes of things still to do but has found time also to tell me that she has heard from Mervyn and Helen that all has gone well and they're on their way back, hoping to be here for tomorrow. What with all the palaver over Pente, I'm ashamed to say that I have not been giving much thought to their expedition around the country but I'm glad to hear this news.

Then Jack Kirchoff dashes past: he's a very good friend and right now is by way of being the master of ceremonies here. Jack's grandfather, Martin, was the business partner of David Heaven from whom I'm descended, so Jack and I are much the same age and have a lot of history together. He's the family historian and archivist but here and now in this Cathedral, he is being as creative as only Jack can be.

He's had giant screens erected throughout this cavernous building and they are electronically linked together and driven with an audio input from a single command point which is way up beyond the High Altar. We're just having a demo from Jack and his team of geeks and wizards. It's magical, I must say. Assembled mostly from photographs - many ancient and grainy in black & white - and interwoven with some very sparse script, the rolling presentation tells the long story of a pretty remarkable life. Jack has arranged it all so that we move from Oxford to a Seminary somewhere in England (we're not told exactly where), to South Africa during the Apartheid era, then to Tanzania, on to Mauritius, back to Tanzania, to London, then the Order of Saints in Northumberland and finally here to Millennium, to Century City and to the National Monument at Acacia Grove.

Many of these photos were taken by Pente himself: I recognise some of them from his personal books and records but taken as a single account, as Jack has contrived it, this is not just a celebration of one man's life, it's living history. As I watch, I'm suddenly struck by the realisation that we won't be seeing the old bugger again, not hearing the booming laugh nor smelling his noxious cigar smoke. I will surely miss him, and the thought brings a tear to my eye which is further encouraged by booming music. The Cathedral's mighty organ, being played by a slip of a girl hardly out of university, is thundering out Elgar's Nimrod and I can see that in their stalls, the male voice Choir of the Order of Saints, which has travelled out specially for this occasion, has risen to their feet in recognition. And this is still just the rehearsal.

I feel a hand pressed into mine, giving it a squeeze of comfort. To my complete surprise, I find that Helen Priest is standing by me. She says,

'I thought you looked overcome.'

'Just very touched, really but yes, a little overcome by memories. Thank you .... and welcome back. I do hope it went well?'

'There'll be time enough to tell you everything later. Just concentrate on this for now.'

I did as I was told, and the following day was a triumph: a suitable and worthy celebration of a great life of accomplishment and devotion. At the end of it, when I was back home on my balcony overlooking the restless sea, I felt content that Pente Broke Smith could, and now would, rest in peace. But, of course, the business of life had to go on.

Chapter Fourteen

In the middle of the following week, I hosted a meeting at the Secretariat with Mervyn Tredinnick and Helen Priest. Beatrice was in attendance, and she organised an audio/visual recording, with a copy to go to each of us. This was nothing to do with security or protocol, it was just to provide a reminder of facts and opinions exchanged in conversation. I thought that Mervyn, in particular, might find it useful.

They had visited just about every point of interest within the borders of Millennium: our two regional centres which are large towns bordering on cities, all seven of my Secretariat outposts, very many medium sized settlements, a mass of villages and miles of varied country in between, including that remote spot in the extreme south where I had seen the elephant troop march over the border and met Troy for the first time.

They both had much to say about Rheina Blanca, but for different reasons. They had spent two full days there and had been accommodated for three nights in the Yacht Club, in which they had been well entertained. Mervyn had insisted on inspecting every detail of the Water Sport Centre where Humphrey Corton was expected to want to spend relaxation time away from his university studies here in Century. The Centre in RB serves also as the base for the Diving Club and its many activities. This being the young man's passion, I could see why Mervyn needed to check out all the facilities and the safety regime there but in addition, he took it on himself to approve the intended accommodation and catering arrangements.

'In this job', he remarked in his attractive, sing-song accent, 'you need to see and understand things in advance. It's no good waiting 'till the train's rolling like to find you've got a carriage disconnected.'

For her part, Helen had an understandably different agenda and it turned out that her focus had sharpened as soon as she perceived that Rheina Blanca has developed over the past several years to become our prime centre for the Muslim community. Our country has a completely open policy of absolute tolerance towards every colour and creed. But that doesn't stop people of like mind, background and custom wanting to co-exist in close proximity. I couldn't say (and nor could anyone else) quite why RB had attracted over time such a high proportion of the Muslim faith but that's the way of it. In sharp contrast, the township of Tamalourene, nearly a thousand kilometres due East, is home to the descendants of the native African people who had been dispossessed by my grandfather when he came storming into this country thirty-five years ago. This is as far from the ocean as you can get in Millennium and the local topography reflects it. The surrounding country is dry, harsh and sparse. It's savannah, encouraging the establishment of plains game which now abounds and with their growth in numbers has come their natural predators. Lion is to be found here now and some cheetah, sustaining themselves with ease from the large herds of impala, kudu and zebra which roam across the broad landscape. Towering above Tama is the Palace, the vast and ornate structure which had been commissioned by the President of a bygone era to celebrate his origin somewhere in the poverty stricken back streets of Tamalourene town. He had died a bloody death in David Heaven's invasion and his son, Jago, had retreated into an isolated exile. The ostentatious Palace was never completed but the immense shell survived to play a brief but notorious role in the first crisis to hit Millennium back in 2001. About ten years later, the vacant property was acquired by an American owned international development corporation, and it now flourishes as a mega luxurious hotel and country club, a magnet to attract the extremely wealthy and self-important from around the globe. I gathered that Helen and Mervyn had spent one night there but found it too opulent for their taste although he had admired the golf course, and both had enjoyed seeing the rich and rare in their personal planes passing through the private airport.

We finished up our debrief with both thanking me for the loan of Jerome and my car. The former had been a superlative guide and comforter, as well as a great pilot: the Grenadier had carried them in style and safety over some testing terrain. I knew just what they meant in both cases, and it was very rewarding to hear them express appreciation. Helen got up to go then, but Mervyn asked to stay on as he had news for me. I called out to Bea, asking her to set up a date for Helen and I to continue discussion over a lunch. I could sense that she had more, much more which she wanted to say to me.

I turned to Mervyn.

'My news is a bit of a worry, I'm afraid,' was his opening comment. He seemed rather diffident, so I didn't respond immediately, thinking it better to give him time to get into his stride. Finally, Mervyn continued.

'I've heard from my people in London. Just yesterday I took the call which was placed to the British Embassy here on the secure link. It didn't make me happy.'

The Welsh accent is strong in his voice as he goes on.

'London - specifically MI6 - has been picking up gossip about a plan to kidnap for ransom young Corder whilst he is here in Millennium. It seems that gossip has firmed up to become intel which must be taken seriously and can't be ignored, particularly not so close to Humphrey's planned arrival here which is now just a few months away. Strictly speaking, I'm out of order in telling you this as my first point of contact is Police Commissioner Odinga but I figure he would want to tell you anyway and right now is not an opportunity to be missed. I hope you agree, Olty.'

'I do. D'you want me to get Mo over here now?'

He shakes his head. 'Not yet. Better, I think, for me to tell you in private first a little more of the background. The Commissioner will have operational responsibility on the ground from the minute young Corder arrives in September but let's keep this between ourselves for the time being.'

'Very well, I'll let you call the shots, Mervyn, just give me all you can - in guaranteed confidence.'

'OK and thanks for that. Now to start, Olty, these sorts of threats to our Premier Family are more commonplace than you might imagine. They've been happening for years and through succeeding generations. They're reason enough for those of us in the Protection Squad to exist. I'm paid to be at the sharp end but there's more than a hundred of us in the back office in London, bright and experienced brains who are forever enquiring, analysing, sifting through data and rumour which comes to us from many different sources, including our colleagues in the Foreign Office and the Security Service. When you get down to it, the motivation of the suspected bad guys is always about money or political influence, sometimes both. And that applies equally if you're talking about victims who are wealthy or well known in any walk of life. Ransom is big business and has been since the dawn of time, just about.'

I interrupted him to remark, 'Something tells me you're about to say that there's a difference in this case.'

He points a finger at me. 'A good guess! Yes, there is something different and it makes the threat just a bit more credible than the norm. The word is that the possible perpetrators are not ordinary criminals with their sights on cash or possessions but that would be unlikely anyway. No, there was always going to be a political (he drags the word out to be embellished by his Welsh lilt) motive here but what's different is the source.'

'What are you saying here, Mervyn?'

'Well, see, there are any number of disaffected groups around the world, aren't there? Groups in China, Russia, the Balkans: but especially through the Middle East and perhaps the Horn of Africa. But what we're picking up here comes from the Indian sub-Continent and that *is* unusual, plus the rumour and talk has been corroborated by several different sources - too many to be ignored.'

'But I don't understand. What do we have here which would be the inducement. We have no political influence outside Africa, not even so much here, come to that.'

'Maybe so, Olty, but ask yourself what you *do* have here in Millennium: you have space and stability, commodities which are much prized but in short supply around the globe.'

As Mervyn speaks, I hear Edmund Ladoux's words coming back to haunt me, but I made no mention of this and concentrated my attention as Tredinnick continued.

'Whatever else, there's to be no announcement, no debate and no change to the plans. My boss at base is very clear about this. He's told me that the Prime Minister and his wife have been fully briefed and have made their decision. They want Humphrey's visit and university course to proceed as they have always been determined that their children should benefit from the learning curve of as normal an upbringing as can be managed. They have expressed complete confidence in the Personal Protection

Force. They have agreed, however, to one additional arrangement.'

Without speaking, I raised my eyes in a question mark.

'I'm to have support and back up. A second officer will travel out here with Humphrey and remain throughout his stay here. Again, in the privacy of this conversation, I can tell you that I do know the guy who has been selected and I think he's a good choice.'

'Can you tell me more?'

'I can, yes. Most of the guys and girls on our team are recruited from the Police, the majority from the London Metropolitan Force. But this Officer has a different background. His name is Royce Harrison, a native of the Caribbean. Born and raised on the island of St Kitts, he completed his education in the UK, joined the Royal Navy as a boy, was put through University at the expense of the Service, transferred and commissioned into the Royal Marines and was later picked to serve in the SBS - the Special Boat Service.

Royce is in his early thirties, quite a cerebral character, very cool, calm and unhurried except in emergencies, but he brings a real bonus. I'm a landlubber, myself but he's very waterborne. The sea is his element, and his speciality is under water and in particular, deep diving. So, ... very helpful and suitable!'

'Yes, I can see the advantage in that. But while we're talking, Mervyn, tell me what you think of this unrest amongst our young people: and this character Luc de Houlette, not to mention the *vouyoy* issue, which I bet Mo Odinga has raised with you?'

'As to the first, I guess you're thinking that Humphrey might get caught up with them?'

'It's crossed my mind, yes.'

'Well, look, I'm confident you can relax a bit on that one. For starters, he's a bit older than the age group who were out the other night and I'm certain sure he wouldn't be influenced by the Houlette fellow who's a right drippy character. Humphrey Corton prefers his men to be manly.'

'How can you be so sure?'

'Because I know him. I've been on the team assigned to Humphrey for quite some time - since just after he turned sixteen so his last two years at boarding school. At that age, most of us – and he's no exception – tend to nail our colours to the mast. You need to be older with more life experience before you learn how to hide your feelings and shield your personality.'

'What about the rest of it?'

'The *vouyoy*, d'you mean'.

'Yes, I do. All that.'

He pursed his lips and shook his head.

'Frankly, that worries me more - much more since I've been talking to my chief. Apparently, we have a mob of them in London now. Have had for a few years and they've spread around the country, in all the major cities and some rural locations too.'

'You're not telling me they come in from Asia?'

Mervyn chuckled as he shook his head. 'Lordy, no. All our lowlife villains are home grown but they did pinch the name and now it's gone viral. The root of the problem lies in drugs, as is so often the case, and particularly in how they are marketed and distributed. The drug trade is the bane of our existence in this century and the smart thinkers say it'll get worse before it gets better. They're so cheap, you see and so accessible yet still making enormous profits for the fat and ruthless cats at the top of the food chain. I'm afraid I get a bit passionate on the subject: bit of personal history you see.'

'Do you talk about that?' I phrased this as a question, and he responded immediately.

'Oh, I don't mind. The pain is behind, like. Well mostly anyway and you just must keep going.' Then a pause before he spoke again.

'I lost my nephew about three years back, the oldest of the three boys born to my sister and her Owen. They live in a modest little house on a grimy street outside Caerphilly, in one of the Valley villages which were built originally to house mineworkers. All that is long gone, of course, so our

Owen never had to follow Grandad down the Pits - no more did I come to that. Owen works clean, doing shifts at a big Builders Merchant in Newport, South Wales but he and Anwen live a quiet, frugal sort of a life and they seem content enough with their lot. Of course, they have only the two sons now and they're still hurting. Their firstborn - another Mervyn by the way - he was the pick of the litter, you might say. Very bright, studious but no bookworm, a good sportsman, an entertaining character and a fair musician with his guitar. The apple of his parents' eye and it all looked so promising. Then disaster and tragedy. It only took three months or thereabouts. He fell in with the wrong crowd at school, recruited by a 'county lines' gang, started running errands for them and distributing, almost all cocaine. He liked the money it made him, became addicted himself, started skimming a bit of the cash he was collecting, next thing Owen and Anwen hear is that he's dead, found with his neck broken in a rubbish skip left outside their local supermarket. That was a week after Mervyn's fourteenth birthday.'

'So, this was murder', I said, 'Savage and horrifying. Was anyone convicted?'

'Well, the case has never been closed and I have a lot of time and respect for my colleagues in the South Wales Force. They won't give up on it and they won't stop trying. But they won't succeed either. No, they won't.'

Tredinnick gave a deep, distracted sigh before running a hand through his hair as he continues, 'but the bottom line lesson to be learned from this sad, bad tale, Olty, is that society in whatever country throughout the world needs to recognise what goes on under our very noses, to learn and to take action before disaster strikes, not simply to wring our hands while we offer tea and sympathy to both victims and perpetrators alike.

'That's a generality,' I said, 'get specific.'

'Well look,' he banged down his coffee cup and fixed me with a fierce stare, the lilt of his Welsh accent strengthening as he spoke, 'these *vouyou* are everywhere on the planet. These gangs call themselves by different names in different places but wherever, their advantage lies in their anonymity. They're not an organisation. They don't have membership, don't have a command structure or leaders. They don't have bonds of relationship or codes of conduct as in a *mafia*. They're just casuals, an itinerant workforce of individuals who come and go as the fancy takes them, crossing boundaries, changing locations, taking occasional advantage of opportunities as they find them: sometimes, they're a rentamob at a demo such as you've just had here, other times they're enforcers ... or drug mules ... or in sale and distribution, most likely of coke. Or it could be pushing people smuggling - refugees.'

I didn't want a global lecture, my interest starts and stops with Millennium, so I responded sharply, shaking my head.

'Mervyn, you know what you're talking about, I've no doubt, but none of it applies here. We don't have a drugs trade in this country and our refugee immigrants are planned, not smuggled'.

'You're misleading yourself, Olty, if you're taking comfort in such an assurance, really you are. You've seen the *vouyou* at work with your own eyes and I can promise you that I've seen the drug trade circulating in Century City. As for the refugee situation, listen to Helen as soon as you have a chance. That girl has a lot to tell you.'

Mervyn left me at that, and I sat brooding for a while, depressed and uneasy in my mind. Here I am, I thought to myself, the senior Government official and Administrator in this still fledgling country and I'm pretty damned unhappy to have to admit that there is obviously a lot happening in Millennium of which I should be aware and yet have been blissfully unconscious. It follows that I'm not on top of the job and I had better shape up urgently, while I still have the opportunity to do so.

I'm thinking that the best place to start must be with Maurice Odinga when Bea taps at the door. I'm not surprised at her mission.

'I have Helen Priest on the line, Olty. She wants to make an appointment to come in and see you. She says for a couple of hours as there's a lot of ground to cover, but looking at the schedule, we're all booked out already over the next three days. What d'you want me to say?'

'Say you'll call her back with some options.'

In the end, we had to settle on a lunch date for the end of that week, on the Friday, 1230 at the Club: it wasn't ideal because I didn't want to be interrupted, either by hovering waiters or chance encounters but even more, I didn't want to wait through the weekend before having this conversation. Being honest with myself also, I just wanted to spend some more time with her.

I walked in there a little early and was content that Luigi, the Maître d' who hails from Padua, showed me to my favourite table which has a pleasant view overlooking the waterfront but more importantly, is partially obscured behind a pillar, thus affording some privacy.

Chapter Fifteen

Helen Priest arrives bang on time, and I rise to greet her with a handshake. I had expected to see her in her business suit ensemble but today, she has chosen to look much more relaxed: she wears figure hugging jeans in a deep blue which is close to black and a loose fitting, floral print blouse, gathered at the waist. No jewellery, just a neat, square faced watch which speaks of Cartier and around her neck, the ever-present *sese.* The Communications Centre, CC or *sese* for short, is just about de rigueur these days for the wealthy, the fashionable, the movers and shakers. It represents all the advances in micro technology over the last fifteen years or so. Entirely voice activated by the owner, it can be worn on the wrist or as a pendant, acting as a phone or a tablet in a former era so providing for constant communication and information flow. I'm guessing, but I think Helen's model is from the same manufacturer as my own which is produced somewhere in a complex of factories outside Pyongyang, Republic of Korea. Since the final dictator from the megalomaniac dynasty fell to obesity and heart disease about ten years ago, the formerly separate Republics of North and South on the Korean Peninsula have bonded together with unexpected speed and success to form a powerhouse of high technology manufacturing, driven by a population now approaching 75 million people producing an output which gives China some real opposition. Seoul is the Capital and political centre of the combined nations while the commercial and economic heart beats in Pyongyang.

Helen and I agree that we benefit from the output of this country which not so long back was in every sense divided, with the autocracy of the North a constant threat to world stability.

Luigi arrives with the menu, but I know it off by heart and ask for my normal of a clear soup followed by the pasta dish of the day. Helen doesn't hesitate in following suit. She declines alcohol and wine, requesting just still water while I order plain tonic with a chunk of lemon. We get down to business immediately and Helen launches in.

'I enjoyed very much the introductory tour around your borders, and I must say that I was well impressed by your regional outpost offices: nice, helpful and well-informed people at every stop.'

I incline my head in acknowledgement. 'I'm glad to hear it …. but thank you for saying so.'

'It's just Rheina Blanca which I'd like to talk about, Mr Aveling. It's there that I think you have a problem.'

'Really? I'm surprised at that.' I put the spoon back in my soup as I look into her eyes. I am indeed surprised and I'm disappointed. We've put a lot of investment and effort into the development of RB: I think it's a settlement to be proud of, but I don't want to be drawn into debate just yet, so I simply say,

'There's no call for formalities. Call me "Olty": most people do.'

'I know it but I think it's a pity to abbreviate a decent name, so I'd rather call you "Oliver", unless that offends?'

'Certainly not.' I smile and wave a reassuring hand although I'm puzzled and a little affected. The only other person in my life who has insisted on keeping to my Christened name in full is my father. But this isn't a matter of moment and I continue.

'I'm intrigued. What, exactly, is the problem you see in RB?'

'It's a people thing. More than a quarter of a million of them. All pretty much from the same place, and they won't mix. So, they're not integrating, and that's likely to lead to trouble, if not in this generation, then the next.'

'What about the city?'

'Oh, nothing wrong with that. RB's a fine town, well laid out, expanding sensibly, decent and varied facilities. It's not the physical aspects, it's the inhabitants.'

'But you can't make people choose their neighbours, not decide who they mix with. There aren't any ghettoes in RB: there aren't no-go areas, surely?'

'Not as such, no. But look below the surface, Oliver, and you see currents.'

By this time, we're into the pasta and I reach out for a bread roll from the basket which sits between us. I'm playing for time whilst thinking.

I ask her, 'How long were you there for? A couple of days, wasn't it?'

'Two and a half. But in this job, you learn to spot the signs early on, plus I must say that I was much helped by Selina. She's a bright girl, Oliver, very knowledgeable and an excellent communicator: we hit it off immediately and I spent just about all my time there with her.'

I nod in agreement, but I don't need persuading about the talents of Selina Kebir. I promoted her to take over the Secretariat Regional Office in Rheina Blanca two years ago on the death of her predecessor after a long illness which had expunged his efforts in the job. Selina is a South African of Indian extraction and Beatrice, my right hand here, is her twin sister.

'Tell me more, please Helen, about your job and your brief for this mission. What are your priorities on this visit?'

'They never change, really. I seem to be forever travelling, always short stay visits, always on the lookout to see what's working well, what's bad, what could be improved and how. Each time, I finish by going home to Geneva, back to my office in the UNHCR complex and reporting in to my boss there.'

'Who is?'

'Right now, it's a man. A guy called Lee van Troung, a US citizen of Vietnamese extraction, whose grandfather is still alive and living in San Francisco with memories that date back to the Vietnam war in which he fought for Ho Chi

Minh. Lee is more American than Asian, very capable, done extremely well to get to be Operations Director at forty-one years old.'

I ask her, 'Who's the Director General of the Agency now? Is it still that Cambodian whose name I can't pronounce?'

'No longer', she says, shaking her head. 'He retired last year and now we have in charge a Greek called Prosper Aguilas. People speak highly of him but I haven't met him myself: not yet and perhaps not ever. We're such a huge outfit now, nearly 20,000 staff all told - most spread around the globe in just about every country but even so, there are thousands at HQ in Switzerland.'

'Do you enjoy the work?' Helen has a soft timbre to her voice with just the slightest trace of an accent which I can't quite place. I am keen to keep her talking, even by resorting to a banal question.

There's a slight pause before she responds. 'I guess I'd say that it's absorbing and mostly fulfilling but there are times when you feel overwhelmed by the sadness and distress which you can't help but witness.'

'They say, don't they, that the poor are always with us. Does the same go for refugees, d'you think?'

'Well, yes, of course Oliver.'

There's another silence and I can feel that she's working up to a speech. She finishes her pasta and pushes her plate aside as she continues.

'When I started work for the Agency - and that was nearly nine years back - I was employed as just a helper, an assistant to a regional supervisor who answered to the then Ops Director. My immediate boss was a woman, a lady in her mid-fifties who was born in Honduras. She's retired now and lives in France, but we keep in touch and I still have time for her and much respect for her views. This Juanita took me under her wing from almost day one: I was a very small cog in her wheel, but she somehow found the time for me. She would say that was because I was myself a refugee, which was true enough, but there was more to it. We were sort of fellow travellers, we found conversation flowed easily between us and she soon got me to tell her everything about my own life experience, so I shared with her a much expanded version of the potted history I've already given you.'

By now, we have both finished eating and coffee has been brought to us. I press her into having a glass of Armagnac to go with it and this encourages her to start talking again.

'Juanita has a gift for reducing the most complex problem into a digestible analysis. I was about 25 or 26 when I started work in her team and the whole size and scope of the UNHCR both dazzled and confused me. It was Juanita rather than colleagues who sorted it out for me. She gave me the history: how the Agency was first established after the Second World War in 1950: how, by 2020, the Organisation was doing its best to cater for some twenty million refugees and spending nearly nine billion US Dollars a year doing so, the whole of this sum being generated from donations worldwide but chiefly from the US and European Union Governments. Since then, of course, all the statistics have been growing further. Today, it's more like thirty-one million displaced people and a budget of a bit more than twelve billion US: per year!'

It's hard to know how to react and I hear myself saying, rather lamely,

'Those are certainly impressive figures, frightening even. What does the future hold and how do you plan for it?'

'That's the big question and honestly, no one has an answer to it. But here's the thing, Oliver. Throughout the history of this planet, there have never not been refugees. It comes down to the basic human condition. The never-ending conflict between the haves and the have not's. It's that which produces the dilemma and poses the question - fight or flight. Down all the ages there have been individuals, groups, families and tribes growing into multitudes who've decided that they will give up an unequal struggle and simply move out, move on, move away. They may not know what they're going to but whether they were with Moses two thousand years ago or whether they were confronted by the latest African genocide only last year, you're talking about people who just want out.'

She presents all this very fluently and there's passion in her voice with its beguiling inflection, but I'm feeling the need to move the conversation on and closer to home - my home. She's about to continue her theme, I can sense that, so I lean forward with my elbows on the table and cradle my coffee cup as I look her in the eyes to say,

‘I get it, Helen, the challenge is huge and the pressure on you and your colleagues must be constant. The numbers are stratospheric and with the world as it is, they must keep growing exponentially. Politicians are never going to find a short term fix - still less a permanent solution. But ... and forgive me for a blunt question .... where does Millennium come into this? We already take in our fair share of migrants - misfits, political refugees and victims of conflict amongst them. We’re pleased to do so and will be happy to continue but our sheer capacity to help will always have its limits.’

‘That’s the very point, Oliver. This new country of yours is a beacon of hope and one of the very few that is willing and able to offer refuge and the prospect of stability for displaced people. But the problem is integration, ... in a word.’

‘I’m not sure I can understand what you’re getting at. This whole country is built on mixing people from different cultures and backgrounds: different colours, creeds, languages etc. What’s that if not integration?’

‘It *is* just that! It’s integration but here’s the distinction. Everywhere I went on our grand tour, I met people who had all made their own choice - first to come to this country, then to decide where to live, work and establish themselves in Millennium. Of course, not everybody has arrived from someplace overseas, you have your indigenous population, some of whom can trace their roots back through generations. But you know Oliver, it's only in Rheina Blanca that you find pretty much the whole population is made up of those who arrived under pressure, refugees who decided on flight not fight and came here in desperation to escape from something wretched or life threatening or both. And having made it this far, they haven't moved on: they won't and don't mix. In effect, they're simply recreating the manner of living from which they ran to escape'.

I can feel myself getting irritated: this sounds to me like the start of an attack on our achievement. It's an assault on success.

'Oh, come on, Helen. That's unfair and it's not even accurate. There *are* migrants into RB who move on out, I could introduce you to a few here in Century and elsewhere. I grant you the majority stay put there but they are no longer threatened by whatever drove them from their original homes and livelihood. They used to be persecuted: here they're welcomed and they're safe.'

'It's nearly three o'clock,' she says abruptly.

'What's that got to do with anything?'

'Nothing, Oliver, except that you've started to sound pressured, and I don't want to make it worse by outstaying my welcome. You've already been kind in giving me lunch today.'

I wave a hand at her. 'Honestly, no difficulty in that and don't stop now. I've got another half an hour or so. Go on, please do!'

Shaking her head and giving me her pretty, winning smile, Helen continues.

'There's too much to cover it all today but let me just leave you for now with a couple of thoughts but please stop me if you think I've got any of the background facts wrong.'

I nod at her, smiling back in agreement.

'OK. Well here goes!'

She spoke for the next few minutes with great fluency. She didn't hesitate, she didn't repeat herself, she allowed herself only one or two brief pauses in the monologue, but these anyway served to add emphasis. She had no notes with her, but I did see her glance from time to time at the *sese* hanging around her neck, enabling her to check on pre-recorded facts and figures as she spoke.

'Rheina Blanca', Helen begins,' is the third largest settlement in Millennium but RB is a Province as well as a City. The total population is just over a quarter of a million, of which nearly two hundred and twenty thousand live within the City boundary. This total breaks into two almost equal parts. You have in RB a hundred thousand citizens who are Rohingyan refugees and about the same number who were born as Uyghurs. The Rohingya started arriving here in 2016 and '17. All were fleeing from the ethnic cleansing campaign instigated and vigorously pursued by the Government of Myanmar and most had escaped first to Bangladesh before transiting on to Millennium. The Uyghur originate predominantly from Xinjiang Province in Northwest China and were victims of cultural genocide. But the Uyghur people are to be found also in Central Asia and quite a proportion of those in RB emigrated from Uzbekistan and Kyrgyzstan.

Now both of these two groups started to arrive here between fifteen and twenty years ago so we are seeing now the results of some generation change although less so amongst the Uyghur because so many of the first women to settle in Millennium had been sterilised whilst still in China on orders from Beijing. In terms of religious belief, both the Uyghur and Rohingya are, in the majority, Sunni Muslim but quite a proportion of the latter follow Sufism.'

I interrupt her flow, 'What's the significance of that?'

'It means that this group, a few hundred or maybe a thousand max practice a particularly rigorous self-discipline in their Faith. You might call them obsessive.'

I feel myself start to fidget. I shouldn't but can't help myself. I have things waiting back in the office and I do want to get away promptly this afternoon. It's Friday and I have a round of golf set up for this evening before the light goes. So, I say simply,

'OK, Helen, I think I get it. You've got a whole bunch of people who won't or can't mix quite as we might like them to. But isn't that just life and humanity for you? As a society, we can provide and organise, but we can't make people what they aren't and apparently don't want to be. Isn't that right?'

'Maybe, Oliver. There is a fair bit more to tell you but it's not for now: you're a busy man with a big job, I know. How about I write you up a summary to include my ideas and perhaps we can meet up again soon to discuss things further. Thank you for lunch anyway.'

She was rising as she spoke, and we walked out together before going our separate ways. Helen had given me much to think over but in the immediate aftermath of that conversation, I found that I couldn't concentrate on the content of it: I was just conscious of how impressed I was by the depth and speed of her analysis and, face it, by how attracted to her I was becoming. So, I put the core detail to one side in my mind while I chased through some admin work and got to the Clubhouse on time. Edmund Ladoux drove in right behind me, and we stood around together, chatting, until our opponents arrived. Pete and Chuck are both Americans and both here on three-year assignments from their US employers. One is in Oil and the other Water, but they seem to mix well enough together.

Banana Beach is named for its shape and the colour of the sand. Along its full length of nearly two kilometres, the ground rises quite sharply before levelling to make an idyllic setting for a Links course. With a couple of short holes, you can get round in a bit over two hours which is a useful bonus in our climate in which dusk comes in so quickly.

That evening, I was hitting it long and straight enough but my putting was rubbish, so the Yanks ran out winners. Edmund had been reliable as always and was gracious in defeat. We had a beer together and they left Edmund and I to have a supper - steak and a salad while we shared a bottle of the house Rioja. I told him something of my talk with Helen over lunch and he listened intently before commenting.'

'She sounds like an astute lady, Olty.'

'She's all of that. And now I'm left wondering what's coming next, especially this summary she talks about.'

'I'm sure you'll handle it OK, whatever. But there's a complication, isn't there.'

It was a statement, not a question, to which I nevertheless played dumb, toying with my wineglass as I replied.

'What d'you mean?'

'Well, you fancy the woman, don't you.'

Edmund is always direct, sometimes painfully so, and it's because he has no interest himself in the opposite sex that he tends to home in on straight relationships.

I temporise, saying simply that I certainly do find Helen attractive but that we are simply working together. He gives a wintry smile which tells me he thinks I am being a pious poser. Then, again typical of the man, he goes off on a completely different tack.

'Tell me, Olty, if you're allowed to, when does our youthful VIP reach our shores?'

'No secret there, Edmund. It'll be sometime in September. I don't have a precise date yet, but it'll be early in the month.'

'What do you know about his family? On a personal level, I mean. Have you met or corresponded with his parents?'

'I haven't, no,' I replied, 'but of course the President has had quite a bit of contact. And for my own interest, I've done some research.'

'Oh really,' said Edmund, 'please tell me more.'

'Well,' I continued with mug of coffee in hand, 'Humphrey's great grandfather was a Dutch Jew called Maximilian Cootzee living with his wife, Esme, in Amsterdam when they were swept up in a purge by the German controlled Police in early 1942 and transported to the Concentration Camp at Sobibor in Poland. Esme died there but Max was one of the few escapees following a prisoner uprising in October 1943. Against the odds, he made it back to Holland and was hidden by friends in The Hague until the end of the War. In 1946, he arrived in England and settled to a new life in Peterborough, finding work as an archivist at the Cathedral and progressing to become a Visitor Guide to the building.

In 1950, after a prolonged courtship, Max married a war widow named Beth Hargreaves who had lost her first husband in a bomber over Cologne. She had a son Robert, always called Bobby. Max adopted him as his own and at the same time changed the family name to Corton, reflecting his gratitude to the country and the community of Orton, a village suburb of Peterborough and in which he and Beth put down roots.

By 1971, Bobby is married to a local girl, Sandra Evans, and they are living in Coventry where Bobby is well established, working in the Trade Union movement. They have three children, two daughters and a son, Edward, born in 1981. In 2006, whilst on a skiing holiday, Edward meets and subsequently marries a Swiss girl called Annelise Swinnberg. Edward is now embarked on a political career and fights, unsuccessfully, two By Elections on behalf of the Labour Party. He and Annelise live in Norwich and they have three offspring - Simon, born in 2009, Portia (known as Tia), born 2011 and afterthought Humphrey (2018).

The political landscape in the UK is fundamentally changed. Labour won a substantial majority in 2024 but mishandled the second and more serious Covid Pandemic which swept through Europe in 2025 and '26. The resulting dissent and economic crisis lead to the formation of the Revive Party, a coalition between the Conservatives and the short-lived Reform Group. Edward changes horses from Labour and his career takes off. He is elected to Parliament as the Revive MP for Hartlepool and progresses through a series of Opposition Ministerial appointments. He becomes Party Leader in 2030 and Prime Minister when Revive wins a snap election in 2033.

And now, in 2036, his son Simon is also in Politics as a SPAD, Tia is a Doctor in general practice and young Humphrey has just left school to spend a few months with us before going up to Cambridge.'

Edmund looked at me and smiled. 'A very comprehensive history, Olty: thank you'.

We chatted for a few minutes more as we finished our coffee and the wine, before leaving the Clubhouse and going our separate ways.

The Monday morning brought its own imperatives. The President let Bea know that she wanted the scheduled Panel Meeting brought forward to this week and to include a review of Luc de Houlette and the *vouyou*. All this added a good deal of unexpected work so that we reached another Friday before I realised that I hadn't heard from Helen. I consulted Bea before I left the office for the weekend.

'I haven't heard either,' she said, 'but leave it with me and I'll have a ring round. She's got a base now in Number 23 so I can check there, and I'll speak to Liz Clark. Also, Olty, I have my sister Selina coming up from RB to stay the weekend. I might get a clue from her. I'll ring you at home later.'

Number 23 is quite a plush address for us. It's a tower block, very centrally placed and offering about a hundred apartments. For a long-term visitor, it's a good alternative to one of our hotels, plus it has 24/7 Porterage: style too and prestige. The name is not a postal address. Apparently, our building here is the twenty-third such development constructed by the Brazilian outfit which owns it. Jerome drove us past the grand entrance, and I wondered if Helen was in there now, hopefully at work on the document she had promised me. Back home, I poured myself a drink to take onto the balcony while I considered what I could be doing with myself over the weekend. I'd hardly started before the phone in my watch bleeped at me. It was Bea.

'Selina and Arthur are just leaving RB now, so they'll be hours yet. But she has called to tell me that Helen's staying out of the city with Tina and they want us all to join them there tomorrow for lunch. 1230 prompt.'

I was pretty stunned by this news and had too many whisky's as I sat on the balcony, smoking a cigar and pondering over its meaning. Finally, I got to bed but remained restless all night, disturbed by strange noises outside which were probably imagined, by endless speculation as to why Helen had sought some sort of refuge with Tina and no doubt by my self-inflicted indigestion.

Chapter Sixteen

It was exactly 12.30 when I drew up in front of Tina's house - too early to be polite, really, but this was not a normal social occasion. I could see that Bea's electric Peugeot was already there, together with a large, double cab 4x4 which must have brought the Baines from Rheina Blanca the night before. Abel was on hand to greet me and to guide me through the well-known entrance and into Tina's enormous reception room.

They were all gathered in a group by the firepit in which I could hear Trumper snuffling as he stirred up a small cloud of ash. Tina, enveloped in a brightly coloured kaftan, was perched on the balustrade with Helen Priest next to her. The other three were standing, glass in hand. Arthur Baine is a Yorkshireman. He came here with his parents from a village somewhere outside Maltby when he was only six years old: that must be thirty years ago and counting but he has never lost his accent. Arthur is a big man, and he moves with the ponderous, slightly shambling gait of a true countryman. He met and married Selina having moved down to RB to take advantage of a promotion opportunity: Arthur is a policeman. He is Number Two in the hierarchy of the Police Department in Rheina Blanca and he's also Head of Detectives there which leads him into quite regular contact on national matters with the Commissioner, Mo Odinga. His wife and Beatrice are twin sisters and physically, they are as alike as two peas in a pod. Selina, just like Bea, is a bundle of creative energy and enormously competent.

Abel appears at my elbow and on the tray he's carrying is a tall glass full of his special recipe of Bloody Mary: I take it gratefully, noting that the girls are drinking the same while Arthur is nursing a beer in his giant fist. This is also the cue to sit for lunch which is laid out at the other end of this huge room and on a round table which will give an easier chance of group discussion: Tina or Abel or both think of everything.

I have a chance to look at Helen before we all sit down. She seems subdued and she looks exhausted with a drawn expression and dark lines under her eyes. It's warm weather, of course, being late January and warmer still in this great room with Trumper's fire smouldering, yet Helen is wearing a sweater over her plaid shirt and jeans. She is a very good-looking woman but today, this morning, she seems to have aged in the few days since we last saw each other.

Lunch is cold - fish, meats and salad to which we help ourselves from a small side table. Tina arranges the seating plan. I notice that Helen is picking at the small selection she has chosen. We start to eat, and Tina sets the scene.

'Today's Saturday: Helen has been here with me since Tuesday evening (she pronounces it *Toosday* with a good Dakota USA twang) and she can stay just as long as she wants but I figured it would be right to get all you guys together so you can talk through what's troubling her. A fuckin' strange lotta business but maybe I'm getting too old to follow it.'

With that introduction, Tina sits back in her chair and reaches for her glass and her packet of Camel cigarettes. In a directly contrasting move, it's Selina Baine who sits forward, pulling her chair closer to the table on which she places her hands and starts to speak, her brow furrowed in concentration: it's a pose which is very familiar to me.

'I'll set the scene, Olty, and Helen can come in as and when she pleases.'

I nod in her direction as she continues. 'The key point in all of this is that Helen's boss has been in RB. He spent two days in the city about a fortnight ago. Helen knew nothing of this in advance, she wasn't expecting him to visit Millennium, nor were we, we none of us saw him and now he's been and gone. So, it was a mystery visit for which there's no explanation.'

I push aside my plate without finishing my food. To say that this is a shock, and a surprise would be an understatement. I look at Helen.

'This would be the guy with the Vietnamese background. Lee someone?'

She nods. 'That's right. Lee van Troung. I spoke to him just the night before I left with Mervyn for our tour together. Lee was definitely in his office at UNHCR Headquarters in Geneva. I'm quite certain about that. We spoke for just a few minutes. We didn't need more. It was just a routine check in call.'

'And he didn't say anything about a trip out here?'

Helen shakes her head. 'Not a word, no.'

'So, could this be a case of mistaken identity? How can you be sure that he's turned up, unannounced in RB? Who saw him and anyway, who else is there who would recognise him?

Arthur Baine intervenes. 'I ran a check on the CCTV, Olty. The cameras at the airport. Just routine, of course, but they pick him up clearly enough - coming in and then going back out again a day later. Here,' Arthur adds, reaching for a plastic file which he's put on the floor beside him, 'I've made a couple of photos from the TV footage'.

We passed the photographs around amongst us. Two different angles, both a bit grainy, but clear images of a fairly slightly built guy, medium height, sports jacket over open necked shirt and jeans: Asian looking with a pencil line moustache. Could be anyone.

Bea takes over at this point, saying 'I spoke yesterday to my friend in Security and Border Control at Heaven International. He confirmed the days and flights which Mr van Troung took. This was during the week before last. There's a direct flight from Zurich to Century on Wednesdays and he arrived on the 5th March but he had to return via London on the Thursday. No shortage of internal flights between Century and RB of course.'

She hesitates for a moment before adding, 'and Border Control confirmed his identity. He was travelling on a US Passport.' I know why Bea is reluctant to mention this proof that this man really was van Troung since without it we would be dependent just on Helen's claim.

The next question is obvious, and I put it to Helen.

'This Lee is a big wheel, isn't he: Operations Director, I think you told me, an important post. So, have you any idea, any best guess as to what brought him here in such a rush and without notice to any of us - particularly you?'

'Not a single clue, Oliver, no I haven't. And I've thought of little else since Bea broke the news to me.'

'Bea, you heard from Selina?'

'That's right, Olty.'

I shake my head. I'm becoming exasperated by this puzzle, and I turn to Selina.

'There must have been something else going on, surely? Otherwise, why did you suddenly start looking for a man you didn't know, had never met or seen and weren't expecting to be there anyway?'

There's quite a long pause before Selina replies, the silence amongst our little group broken by Helen shifting in her seat and the rasp of Tina's lighter. I catch Selina looking nervously at Arthur before speaking.

'There *was* something, yes. We were extremely busy during February and I thought things would slacken off a bit as we turned into March, but on Monday 3rd, (I have time to be amused while she is speaking that Selina is the mirror image of her sister - absolutely precise on dates and facts) there was a Meeting of the RB City Council. It was quite routine, happens every month and there wasn't a huge Agenda which, again, is not unusual during the summer months. What *was* unusual was the big turnout of both Uyghur and Rohingya origin citizens. They're all represented on the Council as you know, Olty, but there was a fair turnout that evening of those just listening and spectating. There would have been at least fifty whereas normally we'd get maybe a dozen.' She glances again at her husband who nods in agreement. 'As the Chairman is winding up the Meeting at about 9.30, he invites final questions from the floor. There is only one and it comes as more of an announcement but wrapped up as a question. You know what I mean?'

It's my turn to nod in understanding - all too well - and she continues.

'It's a funny, wispy sort of little man who stands up and asks if Council Members are aware of the movement for change which is spreading through Century City and is expected to roll out across all of Millennium. The prime aim, says this fellow, is to bring down the voting age to better reflect our national population and he expects this to be a popular message amongst the large Muslim communities of Rheina Blanca. To finish off, the guy says there will be more information to come soon, and that The Council should expect an important visitor from overseas to arrive very soon. As he's sitting down, the Chairman thanked him for his contribution and asked his identification for the record.

‘I am a priest’, he says, ‘and my name is Luc de Houlette.’

This news alarms me, although I try not to show it. Finally, I look at Arthur to ask him, ‘Was he with anyone or did he seem to be on his own?’

Arthur runs a hand over his almost bald pate. I take the gesture to indicate that he feels awkward, somewhat diffident but his answer comes quickly enough.

‘It’s a bit of both, really. I was only there on the off chance. I didn’t know who I was looking for, but I’d had a call from Commissioner Odinga, asking me to be on the watch for this character. He told me about the bit of crowd trouble that you had up here in Century last month, guessing that the guy might chance his arm in RB …’

I break in on him. ‘Did he tell Hervey?’ Hervey Mueller is German born and came to Millennium from the Hamburg Police Service. He’s Arthur’s superior, Chief of Police in Rheina Blanca, but he’s a sick man, having treatment for stomach cancer so I’m not surprised to hear Arthur continue by saying, ‘No, and he told me to leave Hervey out of it, given his current circumstances, but I was to report to him directly on this one.’

‘OK, Arthur: please carry on.’

‘Well, I was standing at the back of the Hall, so I could see well enough. As soon as the audience started to disperse, this chap climbed up out of his seat and made straight for the exit doors. At that point, he was alone right enough but as soon as he’s through the doors and into the foyer, he was joined by three or four others, and they left the building in a group.'

'What then, Arthur? Did you lose them then?'

'I did not!' He sounded aggrieved at the very suggestion as he hunched over the table, his great ham hands clasped together as he fixed his gaze on me and continued.

'Almost immediately, a big black pick up pulled up and they all got in - two in the front seat with the little priest fellow squashed up next to the driver and another two who hopped up into the load bay behind. As the vehicle took off in a hurry, I noted the make and number as I was getting on my phone to Rodriguez who was in support with another guy from my team, travelling in an unmarked car.'

I interrupt him again. 'Just a minute, Arthur. The three - no, you said four - who took de Houlette away: were they locals? Did you recognise any of them?

He shook his head. 'I didn't know them, but I know the type well enough. They were what the Commissioner calls *vouyou*.'

'OK, so what next?'

'Well, I kept the line open to Rodriguez as he tailed them to a house in the Quartermain district. He and his partner sat there for almost two hours, parked up discreetly but so they could watch the house. There was no noise or disturbance of any kind but eventually, another vehicle slows and stops outside the house. This one is a small saloon, colour white and my guys note the details before the priest emerges, seems to say a quiet and civil farewell to the people inside, then gets into the saloon which drives off immediately. My team follow it clear across the city to another nondescript house in a quiet street, this time in the suburb of Malaika. He's obviously expected there and spends a further couple of hours inside before the same car takes him to a hotel in the City Centre. It's one of the Countrywide chain of motels. We maintained surveillance all through that night, but de Houlette didn't come out and he had no visitors.'

'And he left in the morning?'

'No, he didn't. He stayed on there for two nights.'

'And you kept watching him all that time?'

'Yes, we did. Round the clock which is what Commissioner Odinga ordered. De Houlette kept the same room and didn't stray out of it. Never had a visitor, didn't return to either of those two houses in Malaika and Quartermain. I kept the Commissioner informed, ringing him twice a day. We discreetly followed the priest when he went out for a bit of exercise, walking in Central Park. On the Tuesday, he went to Mass before going on into the Park, where he stopped for a while just next to the central fountain and there gathered around him quite a congregation of young people - twenty or more teenagers whom he seemed to be haranguing. He was speaking softly, and we couldn't get close enough to hear what he was saying to them but when I reported this to the Commissioner, he told me to relax as he'd heard it all before. We spotted a few of the *vouyou* there on the fringes but it all passed off quite peacefully. Otherwise, nothing. The next and the last we saw of him was when he left the Countrywide on the Wednesday afternoon and took a cab to the airport. We followed and watched him hang around for an hour or so, presumably waiting for an incoming flight, and sure enough, the early evening plane from Century landed and de Houlette met the man we now know to be Mr van Troung in the Arrivals Concourse.'

'So, this means that Luc de Houlette went down to RB for the main, if not the only purpose, of welcoming Lee van Troung and setting things up for him. I wonder why they didn't arrange to meet in Century and travel together. I imagine the priest flew down there?'

'No', says Bea, 'he didn't.'

That leaves only one alternative unless he drove himself which I instinctively doubt. Millennium does not have a Railway. In the Colonial days of the last century, there was a single track running from the then active bauxite mine in the extreme north of the country down to a deep-water seaport south of Rheina Blanca. Following the invasion in 2000, the newly formed Government Administration evaluated on three separate occasions during the next ten years the prospects for creating a national rail network but, as Hugh Dundas once explained to me in detail, it was never going to be a viable project, being prohibitively expensive and without the guarantee of sufficient human or goods traffic to justify the cost. So, our investment went instead into building a network of modern, multilane highways to connect major towns and centres. Up and down these today roll a fleet of highly specified coaches, all two decks, most hydrogen powered, many hauling trailers for passenger luggage/light goods transportation, all with two drivers and marked with the distinctive livery of Millennium Roadways, an outfit which was one of the first and most successful of Kane Merrick's enterprises.

National service schedules are frequent, and this is a cheap way to travel. One glance at Bea confirms that this was the means of travel for de Houlette.

Arthur pursed his lips as he snapped shut the notebook to which he had been referring occasionally.

'Not much to add, Olty. The same big black pick up appeared to collect the Asian and it took off immediately. The priest stayed put on the pavement and presently he wandered off to the Coach Station where they pick up passengers for RB Central and those travelling long distance. He joined the queue waiting for the Coach to Century and that's where we left him. I let Rodriguez go then and drove myself home but via that house in Malaika. The pickup was parked outside.'

It's time now to draw the strands together but I pause as Moses appears with tea things on a large tray which he deposits on the side table. I give everyone the chance to help themselves before I start in with a summary.

'Let's see what we've got so far .... and please break in if I'm missing something.

First off, we have this senior colleague of Helen's - her immediate superior in fact, Mr Lee van Troung, who makes a flying visit here, passing through Century City to spend a bare twenty-four hours in Rheina Blanca. We don't know who he came to speak to, and we don't know why. But I think we can be sure that he went to that house in Malaika and wherever he spent the night, it's a safe bet that he paid a call in Quartermain also. Is everyone agreed on that?'

I look around the group: there's no dissent so I continue.

'Then there's Luc de Houlette ...'

At this point, Helen does interrupt as she rises from her chair, removes the *sese* from around her neck and holding it in one hand, she makes for the door out onto Tina's terrace.

'Excuse me for a few minutes please. I'm going to make a call which I hope will be helpful in giving us more background on that.'

I nod in agreement, thinking it likely that she wants to speak to the lady who was her mentor back when she joined UNHCR in Geneva: Juanita is the name, I think? I continue talking to the remainder of the group.

'Is there significance in the places which he visited that evening after the Council meeting. I don't mean the houses; I'm thinking more of the places - the suburbs.'

Arthur, Selina and Bea looked at each other. It's Selina who answers for them.

'Well, yes, Olty, there might be. Malaika is a pretty congested suburb. Plenty of small houses, mostly terraced, back yards rather than gardens, the streets narrow and on top of each other. It's always been popular with Rohingya immigrants, and they're crammed in there now, often with two or even three families in one small dwelling. Quartermain is much more spacious. The houses are bigger, more modern and each with a bit of space both front and back. The whole area feels like it has more room to breathe ... and it even has its own park, complete with a playground of sorts. Quartermain is southeast of the city and borders open bush land. Not surprising that it attracts the people who've come here not so much from China as from the 'Stans: Uzbek and Kazak.'

'So, what do you think that means?'

This time, it's Arthur who replies. 'I don't think the congregation of people with different backgrounds and ethnicity means anything, Olty. The puzzle for me is why a man of status and influence should choose to jet in from Europe, going to some pains to keep his visit secret, spend just a few hours here and all of them, as far as we can see, with these two diverse groups of people. Why would you do this? There must be some special agenda. But what? That's the question. I might be able to find clues to answer it, but only by returning to those two houses and sitting down with the occupants. I can't do that without revealing an interest and perhaps ringing some alarm bells. It's your call now, Olty. Do I do this or don't I?'

'You don't,' I say, 'at least not for now. I really appreciate the offer, Arthur, and you've done very well indeed so far - all three of you have because you've put your finger on a problem which we didn't know we had. But now, I think the two priorities are first, let's see what information Helen is getting right now,' I gesture outside as I'm speaking, and we can all see her, deep in conversation as she strolls up and down Tina's terrace, 'and secondly, I want to hear Mo Odinga's take on the whole, murky situation. So, I'd like to ask you please to stay on an extra night up here with Bea and then all go to have a talk with the Commissioner on Monday morning. Take him through everything you've told me and let's get his view on where we go from here, including what do we do about Luc de Houlette who we must expect to be up to further mischief in and around Century City? Does that plan work for you all?'

'Sure.' Beatrice responded immediately. 'It'll be a pleasure to have Selina and Arthur with me for a bit longer and I'll set up a visit to the Commissioner's office for first thing Monday. I'll keep you advised, Olty, and see you at the Secretariat later in the day?' I nod in agreement, and she stands as she continues, 'for now, I think we should get out of Tina's way and leave you to get a debrief from Helen when she's through with this call.'

Arthur picks up his papers and the three of them make a quiet exit, murmuring their thanks to Tina as they leave. Helen I can see still speaking, and as we are left alone, the next surprise comes from Tina who lights another cigarette and points it as me as she announces, 'speaking of staying, Olty, you should reckon on being here with us overnight. I dunno what Helen's getting from this marathon phone conversation but apart from all that, the gal's got another bombshell to drop on you and it's going to take some talking through.'

Before I can reply, the terrace door opens to admit Helen who slumps into her chair as Tina calls for Abel and drinks. I check the time and I'm surprised to find that it's gone 5pm already. I can see that it's a clear, calm evening outside: it feels rather too warm here inside this cavernous room which seems strangely silent. Tina is sitting motionless except for her outstretched hand as she accepts the glass which Abel is proffering. I sense that Helen is stirring and turn so I can look straight at her. I'm shocked by what I see.

She is weeping gently and silently, the tears making tracks through her elegant make up down her face, but she makes no move to check or clear them. Her expression is blank but there is a faint tremor in her lips which speaks of distress, and I feel the need to break the spell. I lean forward to put a hand on her knee as I ask.

'You were talking to Juanita?'

She nods and that very movement completely changes her demeanour. She snatches up her table napkin from the floor by her chair, runs it roughly over her face, sits up straight, crosses her legs, clears her throat and starts speaking in those clipped tones and spare sentences which

I recall instantly from our lunchtime conversation as marking her style,

'It's more disappointment than disaster but 'Nita had a lot to tell me about Lee v T and all of it confirms that he certainly did make that short visit here although it doesn't add much to our understanding of why.'

Tina puts down her glass to chip in with 'Run the whole goddam call past us, Helen. You were speaking with Juanita, right? And did you record it?'

'Juanita, yes, often called 'Nita by her friends and yes, I've got it all but won't need the full nine yards to give you a meaningful summary.'

'Then just shoot, girl: you have a captive and interested audience.'

Helen doesn't hesitate. 'Lee van Troung has been the UNHCR Operations Director for three years now. I wasn't myself surprised at his appointment - a bright guy, excellent linguist, solid background experience and with clear leadership qualities: maybe a bit young for the post but all the better for that. He replaced 'Nita when she retired but he didn't take over from her. That's to say there wasn't a handover period as you would normally expect - a few months of working together, being introduced around, maybe some time out travelling which would be usual for such an international outfit as ours. But none of that could happen because Juanita was forced to retire sooner than she planned. She had a diagnosis of breast cancer confirmed and she wanted to start the recommended treatment without any delay. A good decision too as it seems to have been entirely successful and she hasn't had a recurrence.'

Speaking to Tina and me, Helen appears to be relaxing. She reaches for her drink and steals a smoke from Tina's pack, lighting up and blowing a trail as she continues.

'Juanita has just told me that she was having some doubts about Lee but only just before she left Geneva in a state of preoccupation with her own health and at a point when it would have been too difficult to back out of his appointment.'

I interrupt to ask, 'What were the concerns?'

'That's the right question, Oliver. The "concerns" were never formalised, nothing was put on paper and certainly Lee was never challenged, not asked to explain himself. What we're talking about here were just rumours, scuttlebutt, tittle tattle but it was at a time when the whole UN Organisation was taking broadsides to its reputation. You may both remember that in 2002, a limited number of our people were being accused of improper behaviour in both Sierra Leone and in Haiti. In the first, the charge was that UN Personnel were profitably involved in running South American sourced drugs, all cocaine, through Freetown and on into mainland Europe for general distribution, especially throughout France and Benelux. It was a completely different matter in Haiti. That was all about sexual exploitation with UN Officers either having or selling sex with locals in the harbour suburb of Port au Prince.'

I break in again, puzzled. 'But surely, Helen, from all I remember and read about those cases, UNHCR was never involved. Weren't the charges laid against members of the UN Peacekeeping Force?'

She nods, 'That's right, but that was over thirty years ago when LvT was just a young man in his early twenties. He was then one of many young staffers, doing a first job, recruited straight out of full-time education, most of them motivated by nothing more than wanting to see a bit of the world, experience the rougher side of life, help people born less fortunate than themselves. Not Lee, however. 'Nita reckons he was always out for himself, determined to amass huge wealth and to indulge his fantasies while he did so. He was always a compulsive paedophile but in the Haiti episode, the attraction for him wasn't the girls: it was the small boys ... and the younger the better.'

'So why didn't Juanita do something back then? She must have had her suspicions.'

'Don't forget that she was forging her own career and she could only listen to rumours. Plus, Lee didn't get taken on full time by UNHCR until 2009 or '10.

He was recruited as a Field Officer and spent all of the next fifteen years attached to various different Missions globally.'

'But mostly in Africa, I bet.'

'Yes, that's correct. But he didn't come within her orbit until 2025 when he arrived in Geneva and started to climb our corporate ladder. He was immediately recognised as a highflyer and he was obviously of critical support to Juanita as she was on the verge of winning the top job, Ops Director, the post from which she retired with her health problems.'

'And all the while, he was feathering his own nest and setting himself up for promotion?'

'Right again. I guess that must be how it was.'

I look Helen in the eye as I ask, 'How does that make her feel now? What did she say to you?'

Helen shrugs and the tears are back, brimming as she replies, 'Juanita is sad. She's horrified. She's not surprised.'

Tina now stirs in her seat between us. She slurps at her drink and lights up again as she interjects.

'Tragic, but not a helluva lot of fuckin' help! We still have no clue as to what the little shit's planning. Why was he here, for Christ's sake?'

'He's more than a little shit, Tina', Helen leans forward in her chair, her head in her hands as she speaks. During that long phone conversation, 'Nita told me more about what he has accomplished in his career. It's a lot: a lot for UNHCR and a lot for refugees worldwide. As we know, most of his field work was in Africa and I guess, from my own experience, that he had many small triumphs. That's the way it goes in this line. Building blocks, you might say, small steps which collectively make for progress. Except for one episode in LvT's case and that was Yemen back in the early twenties - '21 or '22. I read up on that and no question, Lee pretty much single handed faced down the Saudi's to get some relief for destitute and desperate locals. That took commitment ... and courage.'

Tins said, 'I'm surely glad to hear that. But it doesn't help us now, does it? Not unless you're saying that we're reading this all wrong? That his interest in Millennium is to save rather than to savage?'

Helen sighs deeply as she sits up straight and pushes back her hair with both hands.

'I'm not saying that Tina, no. I wish I could, but I can't. Juanita was quite certain in her conclusion. There's something here in this country which is holding out a promise which he just can't resist or refuse. That's the character of the guy. Rock solid for the most part until he arrives at a tipping point at which he can't help himself. He gets overtaken by temptation which leads directly to compulsion. There's one last thing of which she is quite certain. He won't be on his own in this grand plan, whatever it is. He'll have help: it will be some person or people already here and that won't be Luc de Houlette.'

Helen finishes talking and it seems to act like a cue for Tina. She rises to her feet, and I find myself admiring her for her poise and elegance which are remarkable for a woman of her age. She's a class act except, perhaps, for the language.

Tina says, 'I'm going to leave you guys to talk now. I'm getting too fuckin' old for late evenings with too much booze but you've got some more to get through. Abel will bring you something to eat and you help yourselves to the drinks trolley. And Olty, there's a room made up for you. I'll see you both for breakfast. Make sure you don't let Trumper out: he's inclined to wander.'

There was silence between us as Tina left the room and it continued in her absence. Helen and I stare at each other as if uncertain who should make the first move. At last, she speaks.

'I have more to tell you, Oliver, stuff I've already shared with Tina during the last few days, but with no one else, not even 'Nita over the phone.'

I just nod at her, wondering of course what's coming next. After a pause, Helen starts speaking again.

'I believe I know the person whom Lee van Troung came here to visit. He's a man and he's a kingpin, a vital link between LvT and all the others. He's a man well known to you. He's Edmund Ladoux.'

Chapter Seventeen

I can do more than to sit and stare at her without comment. I'm truly struck dumb by the accusation but also, in a way, relieved. There is no possibility, it seems to me, that this sensitive man with his prodigious learning and aesthetic taste can be involved in the sort of activities we are trying to investigate.

'Not Edmund,' I say firmly. 'He is above reproach and suspicion. He is also my good friend.'

'and he's my brother,' says Helen and she stops the world for me. I nurse my empty glass as I concentrate on finding words while she continues to hold my gaze.

'Helen. This is nonsense.'

'Oliver. I can assure you it isn't!'

'Look, I'm just talking about Edmund, the man, the character. He may be a lot of things but he isn't scheming, not dishonest ... and most definitely not evil. But anyway, Helen, you met him with me at lunch that day but you didn't greet him then as your brother: you didn't acknowledge him, you didn't give any sign of recognising him. If not then, how come now?'

Helen said nothing in reply: she just sat there, arms folded across her chest, a bemused and increasingly angry expression on her face. As we looked at each other, the silence stretched between us, abrading the atmosphere, creating a separation which spoke of fixed positions, dispute, aggression. I had been in too many tortuous negotiations on myriad different subjects over the years not to recognise the signs. But even as I was searching in my mind for a way back into constructive conversation, it was Helen who made a sensible suggestion.

'Let's not start fighting, you and I,' she said, adding with a wry smile, 'we've enough against us already.' And then,

'How about we take advantage of Tina's hospitality and ask Abel to bring us something to eat out on the terrace?' I nodded in relieved agreement, picked up my glass and followed her outside.

With his sixth sense of occasion, Abel had anticipated our move and had already set up a table, laid with plates, cutlery and glasses. It seemed to be a matter of minutes before he appeared with a tray - an omelette, a simple salad, fresh bread, a platter of cheese and a bottle of white wine, just opened and chilled in a bucket of ice.

As a diplomat by profession, I am certainly well practised - and I like to think quite proficient - in the art of casual conversation and small talk which I can manage with ease in any of three different languages but on that occasion, it was clear to me as we sat opposite each other to eat our supper in the peaceful setting of Tina's garden that Helen's concentration was wandering. Looking back, I think she was preparing herself for another gritty exchange on the matters of immediate concern.

But I forged ahead anyway, recounting more about the progress we were making, and the setbacks, in establishing our wildlife protectorate in the extreme south of Millennium. She nodded understanding and acknowledgement but gave no indication that she could share in this passion of mine so I moved on to thank her again for seeking me out with comforting support when the Cathedral preparations for Pente's funeral were in full swing and that gave me the opening to describe more of the big priest's character, background and accomplishments. After that, I was just embarking on the subject of our Founder and my grandfather, David Heaven, when quite suddenly, she pushed aside her cheese plate, lit a cigarette and plucked the wine bottle from its chiller to refill both our glasses. She took a sip before sitting back in her chair and fingering the ever-present *sese* round her neck as she looked me in the eye and spoke very directly.

'Oliver, I expect that your friend Edmund has told you that he was born in Mogadishu and that he came here from Somalia?' It was a question, but she didn't wait for my answer. She went on.

'That isn't true - or not the first part anyway. Our family originates from Bangladesh - specifically from Cox's Bazar which is in the extreme south east of this over populated country. Cox's Bazar is about a hundred and fifty kilometres south of Chittagong and is best known for being the tourist capital of Bangladesh, with its wide, sandy beach which is one of the longest in the world.

I was born at home, that's to say the family hovel on the beach, a shack fashioned from scrap packing cases and some old car panels to provide a roof. I don't remember any of this in detail, but I do know that my father scratched a bare living out of growing melons on a patch of land nearby which he sold to tourists as they strolled on the beach. I think I'm about forty now which makes my birth some time just before the turn of this century. I can just remember the inside of our rough shelter and I can still hear the waves rolling onto the beach, also the screams of my younger siblings - both girls I think - who came after me but didn't survive for long.

My small world revolved around my big brother Asif who, for some reason which I can't remember, I called Sala. He really acted as my parents as much as a sibling. As soon as I could walk, I would trail around after him except on those rare and happy occasions when he would pick me up and carry me along the beach on his shoulders. As a family, we were so grindingly poor that a day on which we had anything at all to eat was a cause for celebration, but Sala was my saviour and a worker of miracles. He would scavenge on the beach for articles dropped or lost by visitors and tourists. In my memories made dim by my age then and the passage of time since, Sala was endlessly resourceful in what he found and how he turned it into cash - US dollars for choice - and then into food or maybe sometimes a trinket which I could play with as a toy. It wasn't too bad a life and, of course, it was the only existence I knew.

All that changed when I was, I suppose, about four or five. One day, a stranger appeared at our shack, a man who was very short and fat: he seemed to roll rather than to walk. As far as I could tell at the time, he spoke a different language but that didn't seem to stop him communicating in some way with my mother and father. I could tell that Sala was worried by this visit because he took himself off for a long walk down the beach and he refused to take me with him. By the time he got back, it was too late for him to argue with our parents who had, in effect, sold us all to this strange man.

It took me months and the entire long journey to our new home to understand what had happened and by then I knew I had to keep well clear of Toto and do as I was told if I wanted to avoid a beating. We were not the only family in Cox's Bazar to become slaves of Toto or others like him: it happened so quickly and so easily. He flew in, spent a few days assessing the alternatives amongst the many hundreds, even thousands, of those just surviving in sordid squalor on that endlessly long beach and then he moved in with his offer which seemed too good to turn down. He would pay for safe and comfortable transport to his home in another country. There, he would provide lodging, food and payment for each of my parents who would enter employment as members of his personal staff. In time, my brother as well would be enrolled and later, perhaps me also. Toto didn't give my father a chance to change his mind so by that very evening, we had squashed our few belongings into a couple of carrier bags and were at the port, climbing aboard a smelly old fishing boat which rolled through the waves, heading west. The ancient engine fell silent on many occasions, one of which meant that we spent some days in the southernmost tip of Sri Lanka getting repairs done. As soon as possible, we went on across the Indian Ocean and moored eventually in the port of Mogadishu. So that's how we came to be Somalians, not whatever else Edmund may have told you.'

'How long had the journey taken?' I asked her.

'A couple of months, at least, maybe longer. I was probably four or maybe five years old when we arrived, and I have to admit that I quickly became used to my new life in the secure compound outside that teeming and dangerous city. There were other children of my age and although we couldn't speak the same language, we could play together. Both my parents seemed to be permanently at work and so was Sala. I missed his company especially, but I knew enough to appreciate the benefits of this new life and they were that I was getting enough to eat and that I had my own place in which to lie down and sleep safely.'

Helen ceased her monologue at this point for long enough to pour us both some more wine and to light another cigarette. I registered that she was smoking quite a lot and that surprised me. There's no law against it but so very few people do these days unless you are of a certain age and lifelong habit, like Tina, but then I noticed that Helen was also picking incessantly at her graceful fingers, and I reckoned that this journey for her so far back down memory lane must be having an effect. It was time for me to make a contribution, so I asked her,

'What sort of work were your parents and brother doing?'

There was quite a pause before she answered.

'That's a good question, Oliver, a very good question and I'm surprised I haven't thought more about it over the years: but I have had preoccupations as you will hear and I suppose that at that young age and being adequately fed and housed for the first time in my life, I didn't question anything much. I know that my mother spent almost all the time with the other women there. They acted together as a sort of housekeeping cohort - doing the laundry, sweeping out the rooms, in charge of the crèche, while Sala was kept busy with all the other young guys, washing and painting walls, cleaning out latrines, standing guard at the gates. But I remember best my father's job. He became one of three food tasters. One of them had to sample Toto's meals before he would start eating it: he had a paranoia about being poisoned.'

'And what was he like - Toto himself I mean?'

'Physically, he was short and fat with a huge paunch. He seemed to roll around the place. Most of the time he was good humoured and quite kind: he used to dole out sucky sweets to us young children, but he had a terrible temper when someone upset him. A very large man called Abdul, although I don't think that was his proper name, was Toto's guardian - always at his side - and he used to dish out punishment when Toto directed. I remember that one time, I saw Abdul tie a boy of Sala's age to the post in the middle of the compound and whip him into a bloody mess.'

I realised then that Helen was in some sort of daydream as she was describing all this to me: she was talking as if she was still a small girl of six years old. I wondered if there would be worse to come. I was soon to find out.

We finished our wine and sat looking at each other. It remained a very warm night, completely calm and still, peaceful under the night sky with the unseen bushland stretching away to the East and the silence broken only occasionally by the song of a night bird. I was conscious that if I was to hear more of this girl's background story, it had to come now. I called out softly to Abel and he materialised magically out of the gloom. I asked him for some more coffee and some of Tina's excellent Armagnac: before long, he returned with a pot, a bottle and brandy balloons.

We moved then from our upright chairs with the table between us to the L shaped wicker sofa with cushions seating which Tina has on her terrace. We sat decorously at right angles to each other, and Abel placed his tray on the low coffee table before us.

'Will you be needing anything further, Mr Aveling, or may I withdraw?' he asks graciously. I shake my head and smile my thanks. Abel departs, Helen pours coffee and I wrestle with the cork and bottle. When we are settled, I with a cigar and Helen another cigarette, she continues in her quiet, low voice, sometimes reinforcing a point with a mild movement of her right hand.

'For quite a long time, that's to say several years, I was experiencing more contentment than I had known previously in my short existence. Life was mostly an endless game with my playfellows, I had security, some comfort and enough to eat of a reasonable diet. All was therefore well enough as I grew taller and stronger. But I was also and inevitably maturing and that was to lead to my undoing.'

I interrupted her to ask, 'Before you move on with your story, can you tell me a little more about your surroundings, about the compound as you call it and especially about the man who now owned your family - this Toto.'

'It was called a compound because it enclosed a tribe. There were over a hundred of us in there and we were all Toto's people. He had several wives himself and any number of children but there was no distinction. Any and every human and animal living inside the wall which surrounded us was just one of his possessions. We existed to do exactly what we were told, at his whim and pleasure. We were an African kraal, and he was our chief with an absolute power over us all. The place was enormous: Sala told me that the compound wall stretched for over a kilometre, although that didn't mean much to me at the time. He said that it was three metres high and kept in immaculate condition, being permanently washed and painted by his army of slaves. There was no shortage of labour, and we were never lacking for materials. Toto was an immensely powerful man in the community of Mogadishu, with a finger in every pie and "commissions" or bribes being paid to him by every organisation in that lawless regime, including all the International Charities and even the US State Department during those years of the nineteen nineties which is when I was growing up there as just one of his subjects.'

Helen shifted in her seat, leaning forward with her arms on her knees, cradling the brandy balloon in both hands, gazing at the ground in front of her. I couldn't see her face clearly, but I guessed she was still in a dreamlike state, lost in the memories of nearly forty years ago. She continued, speaking calmly in her soft voice which barely carried to me even though we were sitting less than a metre apart. The night around us was very still, broken only by the odd snuffle from Trumper as he stirred ash in his firepit. She said,

'The days and months and years passed. I've told you already that I was content enough, carefree in play and with the comfort of my brother Sala to watch out for me when I needed guidance or help. But I was growing up, maturing, reaching the point of puberty.'

She leant back then, took a couple of sips at her Armagnac and looked me in the eyes as she went on.

'About half the world's population is female and we all have to go through the same thing, but age and stage is not the same for all of us. I was probably about thirteen years old when I noticed how much my breasts were growing and when I had my first period. My mother helped me a bit and I wasn't embarrassed to talk to Sala about it, but I was conscious of the more and different interest which some of the boys and men in the compound started to take in me. Abdul had to beat one or two of them off me and I heard him say that I wasn't to be touched - that Toto himself had plans for me. I remember feeling excited by that, privileged to be singled out: but I was living, for a short while, in a fool's paradise. Nothing changed for quite a long time - probably a year or more. I began to relax again, gaining more confidence in myself and my surroundings, casually certain of my future in the compound.'

Helen startled me then. Quite suddenly, she jumped to her feet and moved away from me, out onto the well-watered, lush grass which Tina keeps mown and manicured in the style of an English lawn: I have even played rough croquet on it on several occasions. She walked for maybe twelve metres or so, moving out of the patio lighting until I was beginning to lose her in the gloom. Then I saw her turn on her heel, moving with deliberation and a measured tread back towards me. As she re-entered the light, there was a determined look on her face as if she had just reached a decision. Abruptly, she spoke out with a harder edge to her voice.

'Oliver, how much do you know about FGM?'

I was unprepared for what sounded like a challenge, and I immediately sprang to the assumption that I was in for a grilling on another aspect of Millennium's perceived inadequacies, so sheltering in the habit of a professional lifetime, I played for time and said,

'Female Genital Mutilation? Well, I don't know a lot but I'm happy to hear the reports that the custom is dying out across Africa and that it's now very seldom practised here in this country.'

She came to sit down again and picked up her Armagnac and the half smoked cigarette which was still smouldering in the ashtray on the coffee table. She again fixed me with an unwavering gaze and shook her head as she spoke.

'Oliver, you're misinformed, I'm afraid. FGM is still prevalent throughout this continent and it's happening here in Millennium - probably as we speak. But I'm sorry. I'm not about to read you some UNHCR Riot Act. I raise the subject because it's part of my personal story. FGM is what happened to me all those years ago in Mogadishu and the effects are still with me - both physically and mentally. I can live with it, but I'll never get over it.'

I said something banal, trying to encourage her to tell me more whilst simultaneously regretting my casual assumption. But Helen didn't seem to notice my discomfort: she was keen to set out the history.

'I'll spare you the gory detail, Oliver, at least for now, but you should know about the background and how I came to be a target for attention'. She was back to speaking quite softly now but the night was so still that I could hear every word without difficulty. I took a pull on my cigar as she resumed.

'The practice of female circumcision has been going on for hundreds of years - perhaps thousands. It's estimated that over 200 million women alive today have been subjected to

FGM. The victims are mostly African, but they'll be found also in the Middle East and Asia, particularly in Indonesia. Age and the detail of the procedure vary but it's not at all clear what the purpose is wherever in the world we're talking. In some countries of Africa, they take girls when they are still babies for the treatment and in others, very much including Somalia, they wait for puberty before inflicting this barbarity.

As best anyone can understand it, the whole practice is rooted in gender inequality and seems to represent a crude attempt to control a girl's sexuality with ideas and notions about modesty, purity and beauty. Actually, I think this is mostly what singled me out and I can't talk about it without being entirely candid.'

In the gloom but with a little light spilling out from the house onto the terrace, I could make out that expression of determination which had attracted me at our first meeting.

I said simply, 'Please keep speaking,' and she did.

'I was one of about a dozen girls of about the same age in the compound at that time. We mixed and played together, were starting to get used to the chores and little jobs which we had to do, having our laughs and tears in a group. But I was conscious of feeling different, a bit apart from the others and, I'm ashamed to say, superior to them. After all, I was the only one getting special protection from Abdul *and* I had my brother, Sala, to assure me that I was worth looking after. Besides that, I was the tallest and slimmest girl in our group, I had the finest features. Like the others, I had zero education, but I was naturally quite savvy, had learned to communicate in the local language which for all of us was a sort of Mogadishu pidgin.

The point of all this, Oliver, is that I was pretty happy to be not just a possession of Toto - like everybody else in the compound - but something of a *prize* possession. I imagined that gave me status and benefit. I couldn't see that there would be a downside: more fool me!'

Sitting there listening to her, I was just thinking to myself that it was all very well for Helen to be analysing herself and her circumstances many years after the event, speaking now as a mature, highly educated, life experienced woman but articulating feelings that she had had as a simple child, but she anticipated me as she went on to say.

'I expect you're thinking that I am now being wise, but very many years after the event. Aren't you?'

'Something like that,' I smiled at her.

'Well, you're right, of course. That's just what I'm doing and have done hundreds of times before. But at the same time, I must recognise that I had my warnings and I simply ignored them because they weren't what I wanted to hear, although in my defence, there wasn't too much I could have done to help myself. I was only a child: I was a possession, and I had no chance of escape. I remember that I did say to Sala that I was scared but you know, even he thought that I was acting spoilt and privileged. I did try speaking to my parents. My mother took the line that she and I both were women in a man's world, better to accept it and make the best of things. My father was so consumed in his duties and commitment to Toto that he became progressively more remote and dismissive. There was someone else, a woman called Michaela, probably then in her mid-twenties but still good looking although permanently worn down by the bevy of children she had produced. She took me to one side and told me that she had once been his favourite, always at his beck and call, never to be touched by another man, so sacrosanct that she had been cut at about my age. That's what would happen to me, she said.

'I asked what exactly she meant by that, but she wouldn't tell me, just saying that I would find out soon enough. She was certainly right about that.'

I realised then that Helen was close to tears and thinking, hoping to spare her some pain of recollection, I broke in to ask her a question.

'What about your friends, the other girls in your group? Were none of them being singled out?'

She rose to her feet again and moved out of the pool of light on the terrace. She carried her Armagnac with her and raised the glass to her lips as she gazed up at the moon, splendidly bright that night.

'A fair question, Oliver, and the answer is that we were all in the same boat, all in for the same treatment. As I have told you, we were not all Somali born, most from the Indian sub-continent, one or two from west or central African countries. But we were all female and we were all slaves, in effect.

So yes. Some went before me. It always happened after Friday prayers. They took a group of three together one time. Two returned in agony, the third never came back, so she must have died under the knife. We never heard.

And then one week, without warning, it was my turn. But before, just the day before in fact, I had another chance conversation with Michaela. She was washing clothes by the pump in the main courtyard, and I stopped to talk to her as I was passing by. She told me that she never saw Toto these days. He never spoke to her, never acknowledged her. As she put it, 'my day is done. I used to be a favourite for a short while, but now I'm a nobody in his eyes'.

Then she went on to say that none of the six children who surrounded her had been fathered by Toto. She explained, although I'm not sure that I really understood at the time, that Toto was incapable. I remember that she said, 'he's all powerful but he's impotent'.

Helen came to sit down again beside me. She reached for the bottle to top up her glass and lit another cigarette. It was clear to me that we were reaching a denouement. I said nothing. She continued.

'So, there's the explanation and the irony, Oliver. No doubt Michaela wasn't the first and I wasn't to be the last, but it seems that Toto's favourites were neither used nor abused.

They were his vassals. They suffered in his ownership; they were ostracised by their peer group and they were ultimately rejected by him. Not that rejection was my fate - I wish it had been.'

I made to interrupt her, but she put up a hand.

'Not yet, Oliver, let me tell you the next bit first. It's hard to describe and I warn you that it makes for difficult listening … but you need to know.

The day after I talked to Michaela was another Friday. My mother made sure that I was placed next to her for Prayers and when this was over, she tucked her arm in mine and steered me as we walked together. We didn't speak. I was already trembling in fear and anticipation but of exactly what, I didn't yet know.

We went into the main entrance of the large, low building which sat in the centre of the Compound. They called it "The Centre". I had never been in there before. Normally, we were not allowed. We entered through the double doors which stood open and expectant. My mother walked us across the empty hall. It was eerie with no noise or people. I can remember the smell of it, even now. The walls of the place had recently been whitewashed and the concrete floor swept. It was pristine clean with not a stick of furniture. It should have been welcoming. It wasn't.

In one corner of the hall, opposite the main entrance, there was a staircase going down. My mother guided me across to it and we descended together. The stairs doubled back in a second flight which arrived into a large, rectangular basement room. Here there were already people, about ten or so and all women as I could tell from their white robes which everybody wore for Prayers. In the centre of the room was a wooden table, covered with a sheet and around the table were two or three stands of arc lights, illuminated to make the whole place incredibly bright and hot.

There was no delay.

I felt my mother squeeze me arm briefly and then she was swept away. In her place, several pairs of wiry, strong arms gripped me. I struggled, of course, but all it got me was a couple of slaps round my head before I had the clothes torn off me and was lifted and thrown onto that table, cracking my head on it as I fell. I was dizzy from the blows and the bang, as well as the shock of it all but then the same or similar hands were hauling my arms above my head, pinning me to the tabletop while others were at my ankles, spreading my legs wide apart. I was in a star shell position, naked, defenceless and powerless. I was young and naïve, Oliver. I didn't know then much about my body or how it worked. But I knew enough to be grossly offended by the indignity of it all.

I struggled, whimpered and screamed. I could see nothing but the blank, white ceiling which seemed to be so far above my head. But I could hear the strident, shouted objections from Sala and the coarse, emphatic rejection from Toto, mingled with breathless instructions from the old crone who sounded to be in charge of the gaggle of women restraining me. My head was again banged down in the tabletop: there was to be no escape. I felt the questing, searching, probing fingers making invasion into my most intimate privacy.

Then came the pain. It was excruciating, excoriating, excluding all my senses so that I couldn't see or smell or hear. I was submerged beneath this great wave of agonised suffering, so intense that it stopped me breathing.

I thought that the explosion, when it came, was part of the pain and that it would carry me away into peaceful death. I cared for nothing except for the sharp knives to cease and the insistent pricking and pulling to fade away.

Suddenly, my consciousness returned enough for me to recognise that the hands at my wrists and ankles, the weight of the bodies holding my own in place on that table, all these had miraculously disappeared. I was free to move, even though in intense pain and half covered in blood. The room was in deep gloom, the overhead lights dimmed, and the arc lights extinguished. There was a still silence all around me, also a choking dust cloud which dulled the faint noise of some moaning and groaning.

I forced myself to sit up and was rewarded by hitting my head on something cold and unyielding. I could make it out to be a long, thick metal spar but bent so that its ends rested on either side of the table. I wriggled out from beneath it, gritting my teeth against the pain from between my legs. Then I was able to sit, resting my feet on the very edge of the table with my knees pressed together as I held myself and felt my blood dripping out onto the floor. The dust was beginning to settle, and I could see a little more clearly.

The place was a charnel house. The explosion had brought down most of the roof of that basement room and I could look up to see the top of the stairs down which I had walked with my mother and into the hall we had crossed together. All around me lay the dead and the about to die. Body parts were strewn over the floor and on the bodies of other victims. Amazingly, my own robe was lying by me on the table, thrown down I suppose after it had been torn off me. I pulled it over my head and down as far as my waist. I felt illogically better to have covered the nakedness of my breasts. Looking around me, I was struck by a wave of sick revulsion, made worse when I saw an arm lying by itself, severed from the body but with its hand still whole and attached. It was from this that I recognised my mother and that was the last I saw of her. I called out for Sala, hoping that he would appear to rescue me as he had so often done before. But he was nowhere to be seen or heard and my only other clear memory is seeing the top half of Toto seated in a huge chair with arms, placed not far from my table and presumably to allow him a good view of proceedings: his legs and lower body had disappeared, replaced by a pool of gore which was dripping down onto the floor.

I was shaking now from the pain and the shock of whatever it was that had just happened. I couldn’t move. I was petrified. Then, behind Toto’s chair, I saw the figure of the man I later came to call Sinbad, although I never did get to know his real name.

He was tall. He was moving swiftly, flitting through the dust and the gloom in that nightmare scene. He was dressed in western style clothes - jeans, T shirt, I couldn't see his feet but he was carrying a gun in one hand, just a pistol and in the other, a long club. He was wearing a baseball cap.

I was transfixed, just sitting there, still hurting badly but quite unable to make myself move. This guy is working his way round the room, seeming to be checking on whether the people lying there are alive or dead. If he's in any doubt, he lashes out with this club and once he used his firearm. I wondered what he was going to do when he got to me and, d'you know, I found I didn't much care. Anything to take away the pain.

Quite suddenly, he was at my side and bending down to peer into my face. Then he didn't hesitate. I heard his club drop to the floor and felt myself grabbed under his arm. We went flying up that double flight of steps into the expanse of the hall and then, without pause out into the blazing sunshine. Immediately in front was a pick-up truck, engine running, two or three men in the back, one of them manning a machine gun which rested on the roof of the cab. I was thrown into the back, landing on sacking in the cargo area. I was still bleeding, of course, still in agony. The truck began to move immediately, and we went squealing out of the compound, bouncing onto the rough dirt road. I was thrown backwards and bashed my head against the steel wheel arch. I lost consciousness.

When I came to again, I could feel that I was still bleeding, my head was splitting and the pain between my legs was intense. The sun felt very hot and there was noisy shouting all around me. I felt very sick as well, partly all the pain, partly the shock and confusion but also due to the motion of waves. I was on a boat, and we were heading through some rough water.

I was relieved to find that I was still in the robe which I had pulled on in the basement. It was filthy dirty and soaked in my blood but it covered me and I was able to find the hood to pull over my head. This gave me protection from the sun, the salt spray and from seeing more of my surroundings. I didn't sleep but I did drift off again into a form of oblivion.

I don't know how long I lasted in that state. I wanted the relative peace to stay but of course it didn't. Suddenly, the hood of the robe was ripped away and I found myself looking up into an ugly, wispy bearded monkey face, pressed close enough for me to gag on the foul body odour. I heard a chortle of satisfaction as hands reached for me, grasping at my breasts as I was pushed flat on my back, the rough decking digging painfully into my spine. Then worse, a knee pushing its way between my legs. I screamed with the agony of it and the horror of this man's crotch coming into view. Honestly, Oliver, I wanted to expire - just then and there. I'd had enough of life.

But then, all change again. The mean, monkey face vanished and the knee disappeared. Another body blotted out the sun and I looked up to recognise the lanky figure of Sinbad who had snatched me from the basement. Now he had an arm around the neck of my assailant, and I turned my head slightly to see him walk no more than two metres to the side of the boat. Standing there, he used both hands to swing monkey face up above his head and I heard a despairing plea as the man was thrown over the side. The boat did not slow or change course.

I suppose I was becoming inured to shock on this day of crazy tumult, and I just lay where I was until Sinbad came padding back and swept me up in his arms. I was conscious of being carried off the deck out of the blazing sunshine and down some narrow steps. Then we were in a small, narrow room, the walls lined with bunk beds and pervaded by a powerful smell of grime and sweat.

Sinbad put me down on one of the low bunks. He stood looking at me for a minute or so before walking away, balancing against the sharp movements of the vessel. He ducked low and vanished through the small door at the front of the cabin, vanishing into what I was later to discover was a sort of kitchen which they called the galley. I curled myself into a ball to ease the cramps and waited. When Sinbad returned, he was carrying a tin mug in one hand and a long, curved pipe in the other. He bent down and encouraged me to drink from the mug. The liquid was very hot, almost scalding but I recognised the smell of green tea and could feel an immediate sustenance as I took a few tentative sips. He held the mug steady in both hands with the pipe in his mouth at which he sucked vigorously. Then he put the mug down on the floor beside the bunk, placed the stem of the pipe in my mouth and ordered me - there was no mistaking the command in his voice - to suck on it. At first, I gagged but then grew calmer as the effect started to take hold. I knew what this was: it was hashish, strong and pure. My father and brother used to smoke the pipe, proclaiming the soothing benefits which the drug introduced. He took the pipe from me and laid it on the floor. Then he stretched me out and removed the robe from me. I was completely naked to his gaze and his touch, but I was too far gone in pain and misery to protest or to care.

Sinbad was gentle but also firm. There was to be no disobeying his instructions. He started by grabbing bedding from the bunk opposite. There was a sheet and a blanket of sorts. Both looked dirty and smelt but without any delay, he prised my legs apart and pressed the bedding up to and against my vagina, putting on pressure to hold it there and soak up my blood. He kept one hand thereto apply the pressure whilst with the other, he picked up the pipe again. I grabbed it eagerly, happy to seek the relief which it brought. In a little while, he relaxed the pressure, removed the bedding and started to examine me.'

Helen broke off at this point and fixed me again with her penetrating stare.

'Now for the gruesome bit, Oliver.'

She started walking up and down again as she continued but in the absolute still of that night, her voice carried clearly to me.

‘The barbarity of female circumcision is absolute but the detail of how it’s practised varies according to local convictions and habits. These are influenced by ethnicity, geography and the age of the subject. In my case, I was about fifteen and well into puberty which made me average material for the east coast of Africa whereas in Asian and west African countries, they start cutting girls almost from birth. Anyway, for most girls of my age and stage in Somalia, they concentrate on the clitoris - incising and removing the hood and glans. No benefits to health have ever been claimed, much less proven, to result from this sordid process but the true purpose was and remains a matter of custom and habit, perpetuated in the name of honour and to ensure that girls are not subjected to social exclusion. There’s quite a lot of saying “what was good for your grandmother and your mother *must* be good for you”.

She went on without pause.

‘That’s as far as they got with me, but it seems that more was intended. As Sinbad was feeling and prying and poking around, he said he could see the signs of my flesh being punctured which would mean that they were going to go on to the process of infibulation. This involves sewing together the lips of the vulva, leaving just a small drain hole for the passing of urine and menstrual fluid. For sexual intercourse, the vagina can be opened …. and still more for childbirth.’

This was a revelation which horrified me, and I had to interrupt her, bursting out to say, ‘but that’s putting a sort of zip into your sexuality!’

Helen nodded. 'It's a desperate, senseless torture of a business and those whom it doesn't kill are mostly left maimed, as much mentally as physically. In my case, of course, the intent to sew me up could also have been explained by Toto's infatuation to keep me inviolate. I'm pretty sure it was the treatment he had meted out to Michaela.'

'But how did Sinbad know about such things? Tell me more about him.'

She was sitting down again now, and I topped up our glasses while she lit another cigarette, blowing a stream of smoke into the quiet night. She spoke.

'Well, Sinbad became immediately the centre of my shocked world: a protector and a father figure, if you like although I guess there was a strong element of Stockholm Syndrome to it. I had seen my mother blown apart and I had to assume that my father and my much-loved brother, Sala, that they were both gone also. I had no one left except this stranger doing his best to help my ravaged body. But all that's obvious.

I can't tell you all that much about Sinbad but what there is goes like this. He was born in Kandahar, Afghanistan. Grew up in poverty. Left home and went travelling when in his late 'teens. Returned home once, when he was about twenty-five. Found that his younger twin sisters, who had struggled to survive in infancy, had died together under the circumciser's knife. He left again, and never went back. He enrolled in a medical school in Lahore, spending nearly three years before getting frustrated with a losing battle to learn and subsist at the same time. Thereafter, wandered around the Middle East for a few years before moving into the horn of Africa with time spent in both Eritrea and Ethiopia. Fetched up in war torn Somalia in 1999, became a fighter employed by various different gangs, progressed into the highly profitable piracy business, which was still active in 2011, the year in which he saved me from the Toto shambles. Sinbad was there because he was hired by another Somali warlord called Shanza who had his sights on the Toto empire. He succeeded in his takeover, of course, and I don't know what happened to the Compound or any other survivors after that attack.

I never was told the name of the boat we were on. Sinbad had bought it or stolen it or fought for it - probably a bit of all three. Whichever, he was certainly the captain and in charge. It wasn't very big, and the seven-man crew were the most villainous looking cutthroats you could wish to see. There wasn't much space and most of what there was seemed to be taken up with storage tanks. They were all for fuel, Sinbad told me. He operated in support of other, much bigger pirate vessels and they all ranged a long way from home which, in his case, was the Port of Aden in the country of Yemen. I hadn't heard of either at the time but all I knew was that it took a long time to get there - something like six days and nights - during all of which I was feeling either very sea sick or in constant pain as result of my circumcision.

Over the years, I've often looked back at that strange and confusing short time. It seemed like an eternity then, but I was only a child even if in something approaching a woman's body. More to the point, I'd never before been out in the world. I knew only home of a sort - first on the beach in Cox's Bazaar for my first memories, then in the Compound with its strange mix of relative contentment with underlying fear which turned out to be not misplaced. All this meant that I never left Sinbad's side during that time of blazing hot sun mixed with the bucking antics of the boat during a rough and stormy patch. I depended on him completely and he never left me alone, feeding me with filthy, smelly water, an occasional beaker of rice and a great deal of hashish from the sordid pipe. He even held me while I squatted over the foul bucket which did duty as the only toilet or when I was vomiting over the side. Sinbad had saved me from the Compound, and he went on saving me throughout that nightmare journey. It was that which made his sharp abandonment all the harder after the boat tied up in the Port of Aden.'

My astonishment must have been apparent as Helen picked up her cup of almost cold coffee and swallowed the contents with a grimace.

'I couldn't believe it at first. He hadn't spoken much throughout the journey, but he was always there and I had come to depend on his presence and his care for me. I could not imagine going through an hour, much less a day without him. But as we sat side by side together in that grimy cabin, the boat still in the water and without any longer the noise of waves beating against the hull, Sinbad told me in his soft voice which sometimes stumbled over the Mogadishu patois that he could no longer look after me, that now I must go on my own.

I protested, of course, and clung to him, throwing my arms around his neck and breaking down in tears. He whispered a few words in reply, saying that he was exhausted through lack of sleep, that he could not trust his crew - his companions who wanted him for his money and the value of the boat ... and me for a plaything for as long as I could survive their attentions. He told me to find my way to the Refugee Centre where I would find many others who had escaped from Somalia and the Horn of Africa. Then he picked me up, carried me up onto the deck and over the side onto a rough plank of wood which rested one end on the cobbled quay. There he put me on my feet and turned away. I felt dizzy and fell to my knees. When I looked up, Sinbad had disappeared. I never saw him again.'

I could make out the glint of tears in Helen's eyes as she said this. I glanced at my watch and saw that it was three o'clock in the morning and suspected that she was becoming emotionally drained by giving me this account. We both needed a break, but she gave me a wan smile and continued by saying,

'Let me just tell you the next bit, Oliver, and then we must both rest.' I nodded agreement and she shifted in her seat before speaking again.

'I went on calling for Sinbad. I was curled up there in the dust of the quay, bawling and wailing for him. I don't know for how long but eventually I became conscious that an endless crowd of people were pushing their way past. They were pushing and shoving each other while trampling over and around me. Finally, I hauled myself to my feet and joined this throng. I shuffled forward. The heat was intense, the dust choking, I could feel my wounds reopening and the pain was crippling. I was in another nightmare. Much later, I found out that we walked and crawled and stumbled in this queue for almost five kilometres, at last passing through the entrance gate to a stockade which was the Refugee Reception Centre. Viewed from inside, the walls were as high as those of the Compound back in Moga, but these were of barbed wire, the bottom of it embedded in the rocky ground. There was no shade from the burning sun. I grovelled by the wire, pulling my robe tightly around me and its hood over my head. I could see some tents, probably not too far away but still beyond my crawling reach.

Sometime later, feeling delirious with the pain inside me and the overwhelming heat, I found by chance in my questing fingers a very small, very round pebble. It must have been filthy dirty but I stuck in my mouth anyway, remembering the trick I had learned from Sala in another life on the beach in Bangladesh. Sucking on the pebble encouraged my saliva and that did something to ease my raging thirst. Quite soon afterwards, the sun sank beneath the horizon of my view and there was relief as the temperature fell. It went rapidly from cool to cold which woke me from my fevered doze. Then I felt a movement at my feet, and I looked down to see in the full light of the risen moon a large, brown rat. It seemed as big as a kitten and it was starting to nibble at my toes, then questing upwards, sniffing at the dried blood which caked the inside of my legs.'

Sitting by Helen, I quailed at the imagined spectacle and gave an involuntary shudder. Like many others, I am repelled by rats. She saw this and gave me a slow smile.

'I understand, Oliver, but it's not like that for me. I grew up in Cox's Bazar with colonies of rats and I used to help Sala deal with them. On one occasion, I even helped him to skin and cook one! They're tough eating but can keep you alive. Remembering this, I waited for this one to crawl up to my knee, then reached down and gripped it by the neck, holding on as tightly as I could for as long as it took for the hairy body, bloated by too much food which probably included human flesh, to go limp. Then I sought and found a much larger stone - a rock really - and smashed this down on the rat's head, again and again until I was sure it was dead. I tucked the body under my robe for later and tried to sleep again. I might have succeeded for a while but then felt more movement around my feet and ankles. I kept my eyes closed, assuming it was another rat or several of them, but I was wrong. It turned out to be an angel. She was called Melanie Priest and she became my second mother. But that episode of my story is for later. It's coming up dawn and I've kept you listening too long already. I think it's time we went inside and got some sleep.'

I didn't, couldn't reply. We rose together and re-entered Tina's house. I was drained by the experience of hearing this history .... and knowing there was more to come.

Chapter Eighteen

I found it hard to rest with recollections of this remarkable account reverberating around my brain, but I must have slept because I remember waking to the sound of the shower in the bathroom which separated the two guest bedrooms. Later, I had a shave and a shower myself before joining Tina and Helen for a late lunch. We talked mundanities and it was a desultory conversation. Quite shortly after coffee, we left Tina and I drove Helen back into the City, to her serviced apartment. She was silent and withdrawn for the journey. I didn't encourage her to speak: it was obvious to me that she wanted some time alone, but she let me carry her bag in and out of the lift. As I left her at her door, she gave me a kiss and a hug, thanking me for listening. I was turning to go when she said, 'You know, Oliver, I have never told that full story before.'

I smiled but I didn't make a reply. That would have been superfluous to our understanding. Then I drove home and spent the evening on my balcony, looking at the sea.

The next few days were very busy for me. It happened that there were a great number of Secretariat matters needing my attention, most in Century but others involving the provincial Offices. Then I wanted to hear if there was further news from Rheina Blanca (there wasn't) and if Mo Odinga's enquiries were making any progress (precious little, according to Pascal Brana). I had an audience with the President who was her normal, charming self and relieved to report that her daughter Melissa seemed to be more relaxed and content. Of Luc de Houlette, there was no news from anyone.

On the Friday afternoon of that week, Helen called me. She wanted to meet again, to resume our conversation at Tina's or more accurately, as she put it, "my monologue", but, she said, 'I don't want to take any risk of being seen, least of all by my brother.'

I said immediately that it would be best, therefore, if she came to my place and that I would send Jerome to collect her. That's how Helen Priest came to visit me for the first time. It was lunchtime on Saturday the 22nd of March, exactly one week after Tina had welcomed us for drinks and a meal, to be followed much later by that long, revealing conversation.

I happened to have some smoked trout for a starter, and I was just in time to have Luigi up the road bring in lobster to be garnished with his special recipe mayonnaise. He did buttered Jersey Royals and asparagus. I had a palatable Sancerre well chilled and I opened in advance a fine Bordeaux which went well with the cheese which was all I had to finish: except for coffee - from just up the coast outside Yamoussoukro, Ivory Coast and I felt competent to brew that up myself.

Helen was looking well - her complexion glowing and her eyes bright. She was wearing close fitting grey jeans with a light wool sweater above in the colour and bearing the logo of UNHCR. The familiar *sese* hung on its gold chain around her neck.

She exclaimed at the view over the beach and the ocean from my balcony. The midday sun was quite strong, so I had run out the awning over the table which I had set for the two of us. It was warm despite being the beginning of autumn for us.

We sat down to eat and throughout that lunch we talked shop. She wanted to know what was occupying me at the Secretariat but was also happy to tell me about progress with her own project which had brought her to Millennium. For the moment, she explained to me, she was tied down by desk and research work, all stuff she could do quietly and competently from the privacy of her small apartment: there was no need to go out and she kept contact with Beatrice and spent a considerable amount of time talking to Selina in RB. Her preoccupation remained with the Uyghur immigrants there and their integration into the local community. I asked if she had similar concerns about the Rohingya people, but she believed they were more adaptable.

'It's all in my report, Oliver. I'm about halfway through now and I reckon I'll be finished by the end of next week.'

'Then perhaps we could make another date for lunch next weekend?' I suggested.

'I do believe I'd like that, thank you.'

Shortly after that little exchange, Jerome arrived to drive her home and we went back to our separate lives. Her report wasn't completed within that week, nor for two or three weeks afterwards but the promise of its imminence gave us the excuse to keep going with our Saturday lunches. With each succeeding occasion, I could feel the mutual attraction between us growing. Suddenly, the month of April was creeping past us and I was increasingly conscious that I wanted to hear more of this woman's life story - what had happened to her after the angel saviour had appeared in the refugee camp outside Aden.

Helen arrived with Jerome at the normal time on the second Saturday in April. She was carrying a canvas beach bag and from it, she produced a ring bound file in lurid green: it had the thickness of a substantial volume and at a glance, I could see that its pages were printed on both sides.

'I've done you a hard copy,' she said with her shy smile, 'so you can attack it with a red pen!'

'Can't wait', I retorted but I left the file on the side table where she had placed it.

We went out onto the balcony and Helen sat with the vodka tonic which I had ready for her whilst I fussed with the boeuf bourguignon which I had spent all morning preparing. When we started to eat, I was pretty pleased with my effort and delighted with the hefty Australian Hunter Valley red which I had chosen to accompany it.

It was a grey day, overcast and starting to get colder as we entered our winter months. The colour of the ocean matched the sky. It made for a gloomy outlook.

'I could never get bored of the view from here, Oliver,' she said, 'but it's not at its best today.'

I nodded in agreement, but she was already changing tack as she continued, 'a lot of what's in there is research,' she gestured towards the green binder, 'so spreadsheets, columns of figures, tables and the like. All very necessary in my line of work and it's well laid out and presented even though I do say so myself. But you'd be less than human if it didn't make you go dizzy before you drop off. So, here's my advice, Oliver. Start on page 202, that's where the summary with recommendations begins. Only another thirty odd pages and it's all digestible although I'm not saying you'll like it all, but I can tell you now that Selina approves .... and Arthur too. They're a bright and industrious couple, those two: you did well to recruit both of them and to station them down in RB.'

The enthusiasm in her voice was compelling as was the lilt in her soft American accent but I wasn't about to get side tracked for another week.

'Helen,' I said, 'I'll start on the whole manuscript tonight. I've no doubts about its value and I appreciate your printing it all out for me. You must have been flat out these past few weeks. But for what's left of our afternoon together, I want to hear more about you and your history. For starters, what happened after Aden?'

She sat silent for a few moments before replying. 'Yes, there is for sure more to tell you - much more. But do you mind if we go inside now. I'm getting cold and this weather is looking a bit threatening. I need to curl up before I go back down memory lane.'

So, we went in then and she did indeed curl up with her legs under her on one of my two matching sofas whilst I sat opposite her on the other. I had already got her a coffee and a glass of Port, a liqueur to which she was becoming increasingly attracted. I put an ashtray beside her and settled myself with a cigar and a large balloon of cognac. I waited for her to start speaking.

'How do I begin to tell you about Melanie Priest?' She was speaking to herself, asking a question which she had posed many times before and I could see her struggling for words as her emotion took hold. Then, quite typically of Helen, she took a deep breath and composed herself as she swallowed a large sip of Port and lit a cigarette. Then she continued.

'Part of the miracle of Melanie and Bill is that they weren't supposed to be in Aden then - not ever actually. Bill Priest was then about forty. Over the previous twenty years he had been forging a steady but unspectacular career in the US Diplomatic Service. He had progressed through the ranks as a Consular Officer, serving in a whole raft of Embassies which had included posts in Asia and particularly in South America. He was fluent in Spanish and his Portuguese was much better than average - not bad for a deep country boy who hailed from the backwoods of Oregon! Bill and Melanie got together in Caracas, he doing a stint in the US Embassy while she was there on a posting with MSF, the international medical charity. You would never have put them together. Bill was a long, thin streak of a guy with buck teeth and a lisp: Mel is short and squat and dumpy. But love is blind .... or maybe conquers all! Anyway, once together, just no one or nothing would separate them and by that time, they had been married and an inseparable team for ten years or more.

Bill had never served in an Arab country and when the chance came up to be posted to Muscat, they jumped at it, especially as Melanie had long coveted an opportunity to live in the Middle East. They had been in Oman for about a year when the refugee crisis in Yemen was building. She used her contacts and influence in the Charity Sector to gain a secondment to Aden for three months and Bill was due for some sabbatical extended leave. So, they went to live there for a short-term placement. Their accommodation was abysmal, the conditions dire and the payment minimal. But they could make a difference, make a contribution to ease the plight of their fellow men and nothing was more important to these two committed devotees of an obscure Far West Church in America.'

'But how did they find you?', I asked her, 'You must have been one of hundreds in that camp. And you'd only just arrived'.

'It was just chance, an accident and, of course, for me it was an absolute godsend. Melanie quite literally stumbled over me in the gloom of pre-dawn. I think that by then I had been there for probably a couple of days - just drifting in and out of consciousness, but that takes nothing away from my extraordinary good fortune that Mel found me and was prepared to care. So I had two angels of mercy - first Sinbad and then Melanie. Without either of them, I certainly wouldn't be here talking to you today.'

Helen sighed deeply and then propped herself up on one elbow as she searched for and lit another cigarette. She drew on it before continuing.

'This next bit won't take so long, Oliver. The Priests pretty much smuggled me out of the camp and then out of Aden. First - on that same day when she found me - they crammed me into the boot of the small car they were renting and drove me back to their accommodation which was small and hot and grubby. But it was a palace to me and became a secure home for the following two months while they worked out their contracts. I never stirred out of the place, not once. I slept a lot and thought even more. About my parents, my brother and my friends back at the Compound in Mogadishu - none of whom I expected ever to see again. I thought about Sinbad too, wondering but hoping that he had got clear to start a new chapter in his life. When I wasn't alone, Melanie took charge of me and helped me with some of my demons. She didn't need telling what had happened to me, how I was the victim of FGM. Both as a woman and as a nurse, she could and did help me with the trauma, the almost constant pain and the frequent bleeding. But of course, we couldn't go on for long with this haphazard existence. In the staff block which adjoined the refugee camp, the Priests had been allocated half a container, very basically equipped with two single beds and a couple of chairs: there was no aircon of course and it was swelteringly hot by day and by night. Basic washing facilities and latrines were a walk away. Then there was the communication difficulty. We had no common language and had at first to rely on grunts and signs to each other. It was under such circumstances that I started to learn English. But somehow, we survived and during that time I came to understand why Mel had picked me out of such a throng. In the small town in backwoods USA, where she herself had grown up, she had a younger sister who had died of meningitis when aged about twelve and there was something in my face and mannerisms which reminded her of her lost sibling.

I questioned nothing, just tried to keep out of the way, to help as best I could and to concentrate on repairing my body and mind. After three months or so of this precarious existence, the Priests' contract expired and it was time for them to return to Muscat, Oman. By then, I was able to talk to Mel in broken English and she made clear their commitment to take me with them. But I was still scared and worried. I had seen enough officialdom and lived under Toto's iron rule for long enough to wonder how the Priests could manage to smuggle me out, how the promise of a new life could possibly become a reality. In the event, it couldn't have been easier. Melanie kitted me out in a scruffy old nurse's overall - probably discarded or she may even have stolen it - and then that place and surroundings were on our side. Refugee camps are by definition pretty chaotic, people milling about sometimes lost and other times confused. I was tall enough to appear as a young adult as I walked out of the Aid Workers compound with

Bill and Melanie. We climbed on a bus together and were driven to the airport. More crowds and chaos but no one challenged us and almost before I knew it, I was being thrilled by my first plane ride. It was a bit more complicated after we landed in Muscat. I had no idea where we were or what I was supposed to do, but I could follow Bill explaining to a man in uniform, who I found out later was a Customs Inspector, that I had been ill on the plane, and they were taking me to hospital. I could see the guy's eyes glazing over as he waved us through. He was too tired and bored to question us and I would have skipped except for my guardians holding me up between them.'

I was smiling as I topped up her glass of Port. I could just imagine this effervescent teenager bouncing up and down with excitement.

'And then?' I asked, 'whatever next?'

'Well, a whole lot. But gradually, of course, over quite a time, several years in fact. But we can fast forward a bit at this point in my tale, Oliver. It was during these months that I underwent a complete transformation. I became an American schoolgirl: and I just loved it!'

'But for now, 'I said, guessing, 'you'd like to talk about something else?'

'I would, yes. You're a good listener and I do want to tell you about the rest of my background story, but you must be getting a bit weary of the monologue. And besides that, we should both remember that I'm supposed to be doing a job during my time here and that includes providing a final assessment. Have you read that briefing I left with you?'

I wasn't much surprised by how quickly she could switch from the highly personal to business speak. She was that sort of woman with that sort of personality. Nevertheless, I was anxious and diffident. We were now moving into an area of conversation which I was sure would become contentious and I didn't want to lose the intimacy which was growing between us. I took a moment to relight my cigar, then phrased my response carefully.

'Yes, Helen,' I said, 'I've read most of it but especially the summary of recommendations - as you suggested. You've been very diligent.'

'Diligent? What's that supposed to mean?'

'Just that. It's obvious how much effort you've put into it. The extent of your research is clear and most impressive.'

'Why do I hear a "but" coming?'

'It's not really that,' I was shifting uncomfortably in my seat, 'honestly, I just have trouble with some of your conclusions.'

She uncurled herself and stood up, walking towards the window and speaking over her shoulder.

'Well, I'm sorry if it troubles you but I feel it has to be said. We were asked to make the commentary full and frank.'

'Of course. I understand that but I don't see that there is any need to hurry the next stage. Nor benefit in doing so either. We should surely have some analysis and conversation first.'

'Well perhaps, if you insist. But remember that we did contract to deliver our thoughts to the President by the end of this month, ... and that's not so many days away now.'

I stared at her, dumbfounded, and finally responded to say, 'What contract is that? President Valbuena *will* get a report, but it will be verbal, from me and when I decide the time is right.'

I shouldn't have reacted so strongly, but I felt provoked by her assumption of access to our Head of State, and there was worse to come.

'I'm wondering if there are some crossed wires here, Oliver. How do you think I've come to be here in the first place?'

I felt myself floundering as I searched my memory, and then the light clicked on.

'I remember. It was just before our Christmas break here when I started seeing traffic, all of it quite routine and not very dramatic. Basically, a request from the UN, asking us to receive and accommodate a senior investigating Officer, charged with spending a few weeks in Millennium to develop a greater understanding of how our Immigration process works here. I agreed immediately: we often get somewhat similar requests from world organisations, and we like to help. Frankly, it's good PR plus it bolsters our reputation in countries where our background is still regarded as suspect. A lot of normal admin followed and then, … so did you!'

I was trying to make this light-hearted but that moment had already gone. Helen said,

'I'm here, Oliver, because your President made a formal request for help to Prosper Aguilas, the Director General of UNHCR. She first made contact on the matter weeks earlier: it was during last October I believe.

I shook my head in disbelief and amazement, but Helen didn't see that. She was still standing at the window, looking out on an increasingly troubled ocean which seemed to be reflecting my mood. Turning towards me, she said, 'I guess I better get going now. You'll need some peace and quiet to think this through.'

I called Jerome and saw her into the car and on her way back into the City. I felt very much alone without her, but I was still smarting with indignation.

It was a bad week which followed this unhappy afternoon. I started the Monday morning in a truculent mood, angry that neither the President nor a member of her staff had seen fit to tell me about her high-level contact with UNHCR. The correct thing to do was to have it out personally with her but I couldn't get a meeting with her until the Thursday morning, by which point I was seething with righteous wounds. President Laetitia Valbuena was, however, as poised and immaculately presented as ever. As we sat facing each other over coffee which she poured and dispensed, she moved swiftly to disarm me.

'I apologise most sincerely, Olty. I am truly sorry for what was simply my error - my oversight and I do appreciate that it will have left you feeling ignored and undermined. You deserve better and I blame myself, certainly nobody else. Mind you, the sequence of events and the timings were unfortunate but I'm not using any of that as a convenient excuse. Just for your interest and the record, however, I first made a personal contact with UNHCR personnel at the very end of last September, but you know how it is, the wheels of communication grind slowly in these huge organisations so it wasn't until mid-December that I had an arrangement in which I could be confident, and that was a piece of luck in itself. You'll remember that I had to make a very brief visit to London in order to meet the Prime Minister and his wife for a bit of conversation ahead of Humphrey's stay with us here in Millennium.'

I nodded at this because I certainly remembered. It had been necessary to do a lot of work ahead of this flying visit by our Head of State. The President went on,

'I should have explained things on my return, but I allowed myself to be overwhelmed by Christmas, after which, of course, you had your own priority preoccupation with the need to go to England.'

'Just so,' I said in reply, 'and thank you for your comments and explanation.' Then, conscious that I was already sounding pompous, I hurried on, 'but Madam President, why didn't you tell me sooner about your worries? I assume they stem from the concern about your daughter Melissa which you mentioned in the conversation we had just after I got back. But that was in January and now we're in April. Why the delay?'

She gave her warmest smile.

'Mostly, 'she said, 'I can blame Aggie for that.'

'Aggie? Who's Aggie? or what?'

'Aggie is Agnes. She's a very close and dear friend. We first met in Primary School in Madrid. We've never lived in the same place since those days, but we've never lost touch either. We're soulmates and confidantes. We grew up together until she fell in love with a glamorous Greek diplomat who was then the *Charge d'affaires* at the Embassy of Greece in Madrid. His name was Prosper Aguilas and now, he heads the UNHCR. Agnes and Prosper made a special trip from Geneva to meet me in London whilst I was there and we talked for most of one night together.'

'Is this about the unrest amongst young people?, I broke in to ask her, 'all the talk about trying to force a change to our Constitution?'

She sighed, saying 'Yes and No, really. That certainly was a lot of it but there was more as well. I'd better explain myself, Olty.'

'I would appreciate it, Madam President: I'm definitely getting confused.'

She laughed briefly before continuing. 'It was a short, very private visit. Hector and I flew an ordinary, commercial flight to London. We spent one night at the Goring Hotel, funded by the British Government and eating dinner with the PM and his wife, Penny. There was more conversation the following day during which we had a chance to meet the young Humphrey, just home for the Christmas holidays. In the early evening,we transferred to spend a night at the Connaught where Agnes and Prosper had already checked in.

Aggie and I left the men to dine together somewhere as they've got to know each other well over the years and had much to catch up on while we girls went to their suite for a light meal and a bottle of champagne. We talked of course, with endless news to share but a great deal of our conversation revolved around Melissa, to whom Agnes is a Godmother. I brought her up to date with my latest worries about Mel and it was such a comfort to talk to Aggie who is a sympathetic listener but also full of sensible advice, firmly expressed.

At about midnight, Hector and Prosper appeared to join us. We sat around for a further couple of hours over coffee and liqueurs, talking mostly about the possible causes of the simmering unrest among young people here in Century City. It was during this conversation that Prosper contributed information and opinions - both of which I want to share with you.

First, his analysis. Prosper has this interesting theory that in today's overcrowded world, there are three populations of displaced and abused humans who represent the greatest and most enduring challenge to his Agency and the conscience of mankind. First, there are the Uyghurs whose very existence is denied by their oppressor, China. In his shorthand, these people are prohibited from proclaiming their *RACE.* Secondly, the Rohingyas, who are tormented by the Government of Myanmar which would have them banished or exterminated. They are thus denied *GRACE.*'

'And what's the third?, I interrupted her to ask.

'That was my question to Prosper. He replied to say that in his judgement, the third group are the Bangladeshis because they are a huge and ever-growing multitude lacking a sufficient land mass on which to exist and feed themselves. Their pressing need is for *SPACE.*'

I remained silent while I digested this, thinking about my friend Edmund and wondering if he really was Sala. Eventually I managed a response.

'Race, Grace and Space. That's very pithy, Madam President.'

Her cup clicked as she put it down.

'Let's go off piste for a moment, Olty,' and I nodded, knowing that she wanted to drop the formalities.

'As you wish, Laetitia. What's this information which Prosper shared with you in London?'

‘I was surprised at first but that’s now given way to worry. He told me that during the last twelve months, our “refugee problem”, as he put it, has moved sharply up the UNHCR action agenda and that he was coming under lots of pressure to authorise an official Agency visit to Millennium. He was inclined to agree but something worried him about his immediate subordinate’s determination to make the trip himself. So, Prosper insisted that a more junior Officer should make a preliminary investigation. And that’s how your Ms Priest comes to be here now.’

She was looking piercingly at me as she spoke and I sat back in my chair to respond.

‘The senior Official being a man, his Operations Director, name of Lee van Troung?’

‘That’s correct, Olty.’

‘She’s not *my* Ms Priest anyway. I’ve only met her a few times since she’s been here. And we’ve been discussing her draft report.’

‘From what I hear, you’ve spent quite a bit of time together and seem to be getting on well.’

‘Would this be Bea, talking out of turn?’

‘Olty, we’re girls together, from time to time, Beatrice and me. So, sometimes there’s some gossip. And you are the city’s most eligible bachelor, especially since Oksana left. This lady, Helen Priest, is certainly attractive and just as certainly, she's very bright with a load of relevant experience.'

I couldn't help but smile. The President didn't know the half of it when it came to Helen's life experience. Then I was instinctively flinching from more conversation on this personal matter, so I asked her,

'How did you leave the subject with Prosper Aguilas?'

'Well, he concluded with a warning and with some very direct advice. He said he was worried by the proliferation and growing entrenchment of what he called "tribal sects" in Millennium - specifically in and around Rheina Blanca. His strong recommendation being that we should seek and exercise every possible means of breaking up these groups and influencing greater integration amongst themselves and the wider population.'

'Or what?'

'Or we're going to see increasing demand for change in the way we manage ourselves, leading quite possibly to civil unrest.'

I grunted in response to give myself time to craft some convincing retort. Essentially, the warning from Aguilas was the same as I had already received from several others: Police Chief Mo Odinga, my own deputy Pascal Brana, my good friend Edmund Ladoux. And of course, Helen herself as recognition of the need for some radical thinking was central to her written thesis.

Then the fog cleared, and I could see my way clearly, a sign I thought to get back to formalities as I said,

'Madam President, I am quite certain that you should hold your course and not be distracted by whatever else is going on here. We can and will sort that out later and as the opportunities arise but for now, well look, there can be no way that kids not yet out of school can be plotting to influence or overturn your Administration. That would be way beyond their skill set but more importantly, it simply wouldn't interest them. They're into school life - exams and games and friendships, foibles and frivolities. But not politics: all that will be for later. Which means that our young people are being shamefully exploited. I'm very alive to the threat and don't need persuading that it's genuine. But it's not coming from schoolchildren. For my money, I reckon we're up against a much older and more savvy group or groups whose agenda is a takeover - a coup if you like - but by quiet and apparently democratic means. They want to see a reduction in the voting age which would lead to a General Election at which a great army of young things would be eligible to vote and influenced - even bribed, I've no doubt - to vote for whoever is behind the current stirrings and demos.'

'So how do we respond Olty? What do I do now?' I could feel the tension in her rising, keeping time with the click of the coffee spoon which she was gently knocking on the table between us.

'Take the initiative, Madam President, that's what I recommend, and do so now. Go public with a crystal-clear announcement. Say that during the remainder of your term in Office, there will be no change to the Constitution of Millennium, no change to the voting age, simply a commitment to the principles and the programme which you embraced when you were sworn in.'

'And what reaction would you expect?'

'From the kids on the street, none whatever. I believe they'll be content to move on and get on with their lives. From whoever else may be behind all this, I honestly don't know, but it may flush them out into the open and then at least we would know more of what we're dealing with.'

'It's high risk, Olty.'

'Not higher than doing nothing, Madam President. Look at the other prospects we've got going for us that we don't want to lose. Young Corton is due here in a few months and it's going to do our prestige and reputation no good if they cancel at the last moment. More important, it now looks quite likely that Millennium will get the invitation to host the WCC Conference in 2040 which would be a singular accomplishment. We'd be the first country in Africa to achieve that status.'

WCC is the World Climate Conference which replaced the COPS jamborees in 2025 and is held annually in different cities around the planet. Nominations are held three years out and I'm hoping that we'll get the nod next year for 2040. Our chances look good, especially since we have invested so much time, money and effort into making ourselves carbon neutral. We may have just a medium size land mass and a seriously small number of inhabitants when compared to some of the world's most densely populated countries, but we are super-efficient and very committed.

I checked the time at that point. I needed to go anyway but sensed that she wanted a break, was probably thinking that she'd already said too much. But there was something else so, as I stood to leave her, I asked the question.

'Laetitia, while you were in London, did you say anything to the Prime Minister about our difficulties here?'

'The youth voting age business, you mean?'

'I do, yes.'

'No Olty, I made no mention of it, and he raised no questions.'

'Perhaps news travels slowly,' I replied, but as I made my exit, I was thinking that I was myself holding something back. I hadn't mentioned to the President the secret and as yet unexplained visit to RB by Helen's boss, Lee van Troung.

Another week went by, immediately followed by a weekend over which I played a bit of golf with Edmund, attended the Cathedral, thought about Pente and enjoyed a good lunch party hosted by Kane and Elspeth Merrick. Ulick Connor and the Clarks were there, plus Mervyn Tredinnick from whom I gathered that detail arrangements for Humphrey Corton's arrival in September were taking shape.

I went back to work on the Monday morning and was excited to receive a call on my office line from Helen. She was keen to meet again, to further our discussions on her Report and recommendations. I was just as keen, but I had a different agenda. I had simply been missing her company and honestly, the pursuit of romance was preoccupying me.

I proposed dinner that coming Friday evening and invited her to Galliardi's, an Italian owned restaurant which specialises also in French cuisine - how's that for confusing! They have live music as well over a weekend. There's a lot of history to the place: it used to be called Michel's, named by its founder who played the double bass, but he is long gone now. I offered to collect her from her apartment, but Helen said she would prefer to make her own way there. We agreed to meet at eight and I hung up to ask Bea to make the reservation.

She was wearing a plain black dress, sleeveless, contour cut to frame her slim body with the hem line just above the knee. Her lustrous hair had been cut so that it fell to barely brush her shoulders. Her neat feet were encased in what looked like the same black pumps she had been wearing on the first evening we met at Tina's. The familiar *sese* was secured between her breasts by a heavy gold necklace and was accompanied by a gold, star shaped pendant. Her fingernails were unvarnished and she was carrying a discreet clutch bag as she was ushered graciously by the proprietor, Emilio, across the floor to my table which was set in one of the alcoves away from the quartet which was softly playing. She looked enchanting, giving her shy, slightly mischievous smile as I rose to greet her.

Over drinks, menu choice and then dinner, we talked shop. I told her of my interview with the President, we went on to her dossier and her ideas and suggestions as to how we might influence a deeper and more productive integration of the immigrant communities in Rheina Blanca.

When we had coffee and liqueurs in front of us, Helen shifted tack with typical candour, saying,

'Oliver, would you like me to resume an account of my early life?'

'Very much indeed.'

'Well. I believe I had got to the point of telling you how I came to arrive in Muscat and became an American schoolgirl?' Her raised eyebrows begged the question, but I simply nodded in reply.

'We were there for about three years until Bill Priest's contract came to an end but during that time, just so much happened to me and for almost all of it, I have so much to thank the Priests. For a start, they had a pretty comfortable house there - a bungalow in the US Compound. Mel took me shopping and I was kitted out with western style clothes, accessories, toiletries. I could have a bath or a shower whenever I wanted, could turn a tap and see water come out of it. I ate regularly and learnt to enjoy a hamburger - even a hot dog!

I was enrolled into the American School, swiftly becoming fluent in English and competent in some European languages as the school was open to other expatriate nationalities. I learned fast ... and enjoyed it. I played a lot of sport, becoming pretty damn good at tennis especially. I developed socially, making good friends and enjoying high days and holidays.

'Quite a metamorphosis', I remarked, smiling at the happiness of her memories.

'Complete in every way: and the security of feeling. I was grateful for all the comforts of life - things I had never known before. But what was best of all was the feeling of belonging. I was the Priests' daughter, and I was at home.'

'And what happened next? Why did you move to the States?'

'Mostly because Bill's tour came to an end. But that wasn't all of it. I didn't know at the time, I wasn't told, but while in Oman, he was diagnosed with Prostate cancer. It wasn't too serious to start, but enough of a worry for them to decide that he would take early retirement, hope that continuing treatment would keep the condition in check while we moved back to the US and he looked for a job outside the Consular Service. Meanwhile, his profession was a real help because Bill knew all the ropes and procedures, the right access to the right authorities. So, by the time we came to fly out, I had already become their daughter by adoption and had my own Passport. I was an American citizen and in myself, happily unconscious of my past, never giving a thought to my brief time in Cox's Bazar or to my longer stay in Mogadishu. D'you know, I had by then almost forgotten my parents and was hardly ever thinking about my brother Sala. I seemed to have a clear vision in mind as to the next chapter in my life so that when we arrived outside their modest house in the little township of Hulett, Wyoming, it looked just as I had expected.'

'How old were you then?'

'Sixteen. That was anyway best guess as Mel and I had worked it out for my Passport application while we were still in Muscat.'

'So, you were still in full time education?'

'Very much so, yes. I was enrolled in the local High School and resumed life much as I had come to know it in Oman. Same syllabus, same subjects, same sports - tennis was still my best - oh and drama: that was new for me and I really took to it. I so enjoyed the acting and the dressing up for it. Of course, the surroundings were quite different and so was the climate. I never got used to the cold and even now, living in Geneva, I still miss the year-round heat which I grew up with. But as for friends and fellow pupils, I soon mixed in with them and quickly got absorbed into the new routine. After all, Oliver, we're all adaptable at that age. Didn't that work for you too?'

'Yes, I suppose.' But I didn't want her to lose the thread, so asked her immediately,

'What about after that? What then?

'Then, I went to college. To University on the Campus of Stanford in California. That was a very big moment as it meant leaving home and being on my own for the first time since Mel had found me in the refugee camp. I was eighteen and a half, quite presentable as an American girl but inside, very conscious of my background as a penniless waif from the coast of Bangladesh via a warlord's stronghold in Mogadishu. That taxed my self-confidence and I had some trouble settling in to Uni life while the whole process took another big knock at the start of my second year at Stanford when Mel visited unexpectedly to tell me that Bill - her Bill and my Bill - had succumbed to his prostate cancer and died very suddenly at home in Hulett. I was devastated. This gangly, buck toothed, soft-spoken American had become over the years such a caring, calming influence that I was distraught at the loss of his considered sentiments and quiet advice. Of course, I was being selfish. If Bill had been important to my life, he was everything to Melanie and I was overwhelmed by the bravery of her self-sacrifice in making the long journey from Hulett to tell me in person whilst carrying the heavy burden of her own distress. Her resolve and determination were enough for both of us to pick up the pieces and carry on.'

There was a pause then and a break in her account. I signalled to our waiter, asking him to move our drinks and bring us fresh coffee to a table in the courtyard. I felt that

Helen would like to smoke, and I knew that I wanted my after-dinner cigar. When we were settled there, with the little fountain gurgling beside us, I asked her,

'And what after Stanford?'

'Then came Harvard,' she replied. 'I did well at Uni and came to enjoy it enormously. I majored in languages and won high grades. I succeeded in the women's tennis - second team - but did best in the mixed doubles. I did a lot of drama and had a starring role in an obscure Ibsen play. Best of all, I made some very good friends and have stayed close to most of them. I wanted to forge a career with an international organisation and fancied doing a course at the Harvard Business School but knew I couldn't afford the time or the money necessary. But getting home to Hulett from Stanford, I found from Mel that dear Bill had been putting a little money aside from his Pension from the day we got back from Muscat until just before his death. So, I applied, was accepted and immersed myself in that high pressure work environment over the following year. With that qualification, I had not much difficulty in getting a job with the United Nations in New York City, staying there for a further three years until the chance came up to switch to UNHCR in Geneva. That was in 2030 .... and here I am now!'

Helen finished by lighting another cigarette and saluting me with her glass of Port.

'And what of Melanie?', I asked as I relit my cigar.

'She seems indestructible, Mel. She's still in Hulett, still the same house, still working in the Hospital but not full time, now. And still visiting Bill's grave there once a week. She has good friends, caring neighbours and the respect of the community. She's still game to travel as well: she's been to visit me in Geneva on several occasions and I'm sure she'll come again.'

'And if I may ask, Helen , your own social life?'

She smiled, saying 'I thought you'd get around to that question!' After a pause, she resumed,

'Well look, at Stanford and Harvard and as a single in the big Apple, I've always been lucky in the people I've met and in the surrounding social circumstances. I like clubs and pubs and bars and parties. I'm naturally inquisitive and gregarious. I'm a social animal. I'm straight hetero. I find men attractive, and I like being attractive to them.'

Looking her in the eyes, I inclined my head in agreement at this, but she just went on, 'but I've never been a great success on the dating scene because I arrived at that stage of life as already damaged goods because of what I went through in Toto's cellar outside Mogadishu. What was done was not finished - the bomb saw to that - but even worse, it was botched. My inside workings never recovered properly throughout schooldays and Stanford. I had Melanie to talk it through with and any number of highly professional medics and gynae's to examine me and advise but ultimately, I had to have a serious operation before I left for Harvard. I had a full blown hysterectomy plus they took out some other bits whilst they were at it. Since then, I could not conceive and I've never been able to have sex, at least not with a man. I've tried with a woman and that repels me, so I've had no joy with the dating game. I've just had to accept that I can't make love and find fulfilment.'

I shifted in my seat, quite uncertain as to what response I might make but Helen hadn't finished speaking.

'So, the bottom line, Oliver,' she concluded, 'is that I enjoy your company and your conversation. I find you attractive and I'm very ready to sleep with you, but you'll have to understand that's about all I can do. It's your call.'

So, I called for the bill and we drove home together, back to my apartment overlooking the beach, the only thought in my mind being that I was in love for the first time in my life.

Looking back now - as I do too often - I am consistently amazed at how easily Helen and I fitted together. Fundamentally, we had little in common except for a mutual attraction. Very few of us could claim to have survived a childhood and upbringing like hers whereas my own had been happy and predictable, almost boring in its normality. In all our conversation over the last few weeks, we had established that she was, naturally, quite firebrand, and resolute in her determination to challenge the injustices of the world but also realistic in accepting how little she could accomplish on her own to change them. In contrast, I was cautious, reluctant to be drawn into controversy, content to be the competent administrator, a safe pair of hands in anything approaching a crisis. As soon as we got home and climbed the stairs to enter my apartment, she went straight through to the balcony. It was a warm night, unusually so for our autumn month of April. I poured a glass of Port and took it out to her, with a balloon of Armagnac for myself. She lit a cigarette and I allowed myself another cigar. We stood side by side, wordless as we gazed over the quiet ocean and savoured the stillness of the night.

The moment was broken by the dull gleam of the *sese*, ever present on her chest and now trying to summon her attention. Helen flicked a finger at it and the soft light disappeared.

'The message service will tell whoever it is that I'm not at home. And that's true. I'm not,' she said as she turned to face me. It was a signal to us both but as we moved together, it was more into contented embrace than blazing passion. That started to change for me, of course, as soon as I felt the contours of her body and nuzzled her neck to pick up the scent of her Givenchy. Even then, there was no real urgency in either of us, just a certainty of what was meant to be. I was picking at the buttons on the front of her dress when she said,

'You're very calm, Oliver. I'm not sure if I'm being undressed or unwrapped.'

'Is there a difference?'

'Certainly. Undressed is seduction. Unwrapped is a donation: and I'm not available for charity.'

'Well', I said, 'you're a worthwhile cause for me and I revere you for it.'

'Reverence?' I like the sound of that.' And then. 'Let's get on with it.'

But even then, there were a few more minutes of playfulness and badinage before we were both finally naked and in bed together for the first time. I would never hold myself out as some lothario and I do confess to one disastrous and short-lived assignation that was fuelled entirely by lust but generally, I have been very lucky in my relationships with women and my affairs have been as much matters of the heart and companionship as about carnal imperative. I knew instinctively that things would be different with Helen, but I wasn't at all prepared for the process of education which began almost immediately.

Our Millennium skies are never quite dark and there was a fine, full moon that night, so I was able to lie there and study her with appreciation. She had a fine, strong body, the colour of café au lait, the contours and muscles in her arms and at her shoulders rippling gently to give the impression of translucence.

I couldn't see clearly the colour of her eyes, the deep violet which had so attracted me from the first, but the high cheek bones and strong jaw line spoke to me, as did the small, firm breasts with their much darker nipples. Her mischievous smile played at the corners of her mouth as she lay there quietly, watching me admiring her, seeing my rapt attention slide down her body, passing over the taut, flat tummy to rest on the lush thicket at the junction of her slim thighs.

She reached up, snaking an arm around my neck and pulled my face down to hers. We kissed and this time there was real passion in the meeting of our lips and mouths.

My arousal was immediate and intense. In my mind, I was trying to stay calm and considerate, but my body was in a state of primeval force as I threw a leg over her and grabbed with one hand at her breasts. I just wanted to feel myself inside her, surrounded by her, possessing her.

But with a strength which surprised me, she pushed back against me, and I found myself flopping down, my head on the pillows as she eased herself onto one elbow and looked down on me, her other hand playing gently with me as she started to speak.

'If we are to be lovers, Oliver, there are things - more things - which you need to know about me, matters which dictate terms and conditions. If you are able and willing to accept these, all well and good. If not, I shall entirely understand, and we will have to move on with our separate lives: it's happened to me before and more than once.'

'I'm listening,' I managed to blurt out, 'and trying to concentrate but if you don't stop doing that to me, I'll explode.'

‘That’s exactly what I want you to do.’ So she continued, with subtle delicacy, and I did.

Later, she carried on talking as if there had been no interruption.

‘Now then’, she announced, ‘if I’m to go on talking, I simply must have a cup of tea.’

She didn’t wait for a reaction from me, just immediately bounced out of bed and walked straight through into the living and dining area of the apartment. I started to hear the kettle boiling and the angle was such that in the subdued moonlight, I could see in the full-length mirror which is mounted on the wall of my bedroom her naked body with a one hand resting casually on the kitchen worktop as she waited for the water. It was an arresting and an erotic vision.

Soon, Helen was back placing a mug on the table by my side of the bed, then stalking round - all long limbed and tempting - to puff up the pillows on her side before climbing in and sitting up, cradling her mug in both hands as she sipped at it. I reached for my own, wondering how she knew how I liked it, strong with a sweetener, and as I turned to face her, pulling a pillow up around the back of my head, I couldn’t help but smile.

‘What’, she asked me.

“Well, here we are, a first love making encounter, so we should be consumed in passion, yet we’re sitting up in bed together like some stately, established couple. And anyway, I thought you Americans drink only coffee?'

'You can thank my mother for that. Mel loves her tea, and we drink it by the gallon at home. And in case you're wondering how I know about your favoured brew, you can blame Beatrice. But she'd be delighted to see us here like this. She's been matchmaking since the day I arrived in Century.'

'Don't I know it! But look, Helen, you obviously want to talk and unless it's business which is off limits with you looking like that and feeling better, I'm all ears.'

'OK, ... but it's more tell than talk.'

'Whatever', I said, just get on with it', and I stretched out my hand to circle the breast which was nearer to me. She brushed it away and sat up straighter.

'Just concentrate, Oliver!'

She continued without a break, speaking in honeyed tones but still in the straightforward, fluent monologue which was her style.

Chapter Nineteen

'You've already heard enough about my beginnings, my experience in Mogadishu and on that boat. I'm not going to revisit those lurid details, nor say any more about my rescue from the refugee camp by Bill and Melanie. We'll fast forward now to Hulett, Wyoming and my last year of High School which was before Bill's death and the only time of stress between Mel and me when I was feeling teenage rebellious and she was struggling with me. It was this which led to my first sexual experiment and my partner was a full year younger than me. He was called Nathan Willard, he was big and bold and boxed for the school, so we snuck off one afternoon and did it in the barn of his father's smallholding just outside town. Nathan was attractive in looks and character, but the encounter was a typical teenage disaster. He was short on practice, patience and finesse while I had no idea what I was doing. So, it didn't take long and was a messy business, made worse by my bleeding profusely which put him in a complete panic. The episode was not repeated.'

Helen took a big gulp of tea, then kept the mug cradled in her hands as she continued.

'While I was at Stanford, there was more choice and more opportunity. During those years, I had about half a dozen liaisons. I won't call them affairs because none of them lasted beyond one bout, and all left me feeling disillusioned and despairing. I loved the social contact, all the fun and the flirting. I enjoyed being attracted and attractive. I delighted in the build-up but when it came to the carnal act, I was hopeless. It was always excruciatingly painful and left me feeling abused and inadequate. It seemed to me that I'd had enough of sex without ever starting.'

She turned away from me then but only to put down her mug on the side table. She snuggled up companionably and ran a hand over my chest as she went on.

'After Graduation, I went home for three months to spend time in Hulett with my mother.'

'You mean Mel?', I interrupted her.

'Yes, of course. Since Oman, I've never thought of her except as my mother. She's amazing really. She continues in robust widowhood, content to be on her own but at the same time completely involved in that small, rural community. She retired from working in the hospital a long time back, but she still lives a happy, healthy, independent life. Mel's now seventy-five and has many years left in her, I hope and expect.'

I nodded and she picked up her theme. 'Throughout what was left of my childhood and my adolescence, Mel had this amazing instinct of when to engage with me. This time, it took a whole month. A month of immersing myself again in Hulett places and people. Then, one evening after supper when we were sitting together on the balcony and Mel was asking me quite casually about social life at Stanford, friends, boyfriends, activities. I started to talk then, and it all came out. Mel was herself a one-man woman, she never looked at another guy after she met Bill but as she said to me with disarming candour, “not many of them looked at me either. I had qualities to offer but not looks. I was never sexy.”

That said, she was no prude either. She had expected, hoped even, that I would get into relationships while I was at Uni and do some experimenting. She would have been quite content to see me involved with another girl if that took my fancy, which it didn’t then and never has. But as we talked that evening, she could tell that this was about something else .... and I could tell that she wasn’t entirely surprised. Of course, Mel knew everything which had happened to me, and she had considerable general medical knowledge. Even so, I was startled when she came out with it and said, ‘so you don’t enjoy sex, Helen, is that the heart of the problem?’

I replied that I thought it was more the case that I physically couldn’t and that set us on a course of much more intimate conversation and a search, together, for medical help which eventually led me to the door of a distinguished gynaecologist in Phoenix. He was a lovely guy, born of German Jewish parents, studied, graduated and practised in DC where he established his reputation amongst the elite and wealthy ladies. He was a gentle, infinitely patient man with great expertise and experience who eventually tired of Washington weather and moved to the heat of Arizona. That was their loss and my gain. After much consultation and investigation, he operated. He was so moved by my background story that he made no charge. I was three days in his smart clinic and then I went home to Hulett, determined that I could go on to start a whole new phase of life. I was relieved to have the operation behind me, quietly confident of the success from the reconstructive surgery which had been performed. Time would be needed, of course, for things to settle down so on my arrival at Harvard Business School, I kept to myself and concentrated on the work which was high pressure and challenging. But three months into the Course, hooked up with another starter there, a Canadian man, called Bill ironically. We got on from the first and I felt an immediate urge for him so was content to be tempted into his bed, confident that it would all go well. It didn't.'

She looked up at me then, just a brief glance which seemed to be a plea for understanding. I couldn't give her that, so I clasped her to me in sympathy, but she pushed away to sit up straight and rearrange the pillows behind her. Then she went on talking.

'I left Bill immediately and went back to my own room. I called Mel and had a long talk with her, sparing her no detail of everything that had and hadn't happened during the episode: talk about a brief encounter,' she said with a wry smile. 'Then, encouraged by Mel, I gave myself all of that day to think over what she had said and to reflect on what the gynae had told me during my stay at his clinic. In a nutshell, that was that my problem could be as much or more mental as physical, that he had done all he could for my body and if that wasn't enough, I should try and find help for my mind. So, cutting this long saga a bit shorter, I embarked on a journey amongst eminent psychiatrists, therapists, consultants, the whole nine yards of experts and theorists. Mel came East for a while, and we spent ten days doing the rounds together. At the end of it all, the consensus of advice was to confirm the view that I'm stuck with an affliction which is in my mind and that nothing is likely to change that. One woman I consulted described it in a way which struck a chord. She encouraged me to think of it as a phobia, like some people have for spiders or snakes or the wide-open spaces. In my case, it's sex and I start to feel pain before a man comes near me. It's something I just must live with. And it's tough because, basically, I have a romantic nature, but you can't have much romance without sex.'

I could sense rather than see the tears in her eyes as she jumped impatiently out of bed and went off to boil the kettle again, her lighter rasping as she lit a cigarette. After a minute or so, I went after her and we stood together, hand in hand like Adam and Eve, drinking our tea and looking out over the ocean.

That bittersweet occasion set the pattern for our lives over the next few weeks. It should have ended our relationship before it became established and that's what I would have expected. Normally, I'm quite a selfish character: I guess most men tend that way and, at that point, I had enough going on in life without sparing time for someone who was irretrievably hurt. But that isn't what happened.

After a while, we shared a gentle embrace, got back into bed and slept soundly until the dawn broke, curled up together like spoons facing first one way and then the other. As I awoke, I was conscious of feeling deeply rested, at peace with myself and with this woman with whom I was finding a communion, albeit more of the soul than of the body.

Later, Helen joined me in my normal walk along the beach. As we were returning to the apartment, we passed Troy who had Absalom with him, and I was able to introduce her to both of them. It already felt as if we had been together forever.

Chapter Twenty

But it was time to go back to work. I knew that I was going to be busy over the next three months, perhaps more. I didn't know for how much longer Helen could stay in Millennium, before her job would call her back to Geneva and I simply didn't want to think about that prospect. So, without really planning it, we fell into an easy, comfortable pattern of life as we progressed through our autumn and winter months. There was more wind than normal and a few spectacular storms when we witnessed a frenzied ocean from the calm of my balcony: there was a little less daylight, but dawn kept coming up as usual.

Helen held onto her apartment at No 23, spending most weeknights there before coming to join me on a Friday evening. But she also spent time in Rheina Blanca, once a whole week at the beginning of May and when there, she lodged with Selina and Arthur Baine. She was tight lipped about what she was doing there, promising me a full presentation in due course but not until she was ready.

In the meantime, there was a full agenda for me at the Secretariat. Much of it was routine and I spent hours in my office with Pascal Brana, poring over teething problems with our new IT network. But there were exceptional matters as well: our experienced Administrator in the Northeast, in Zebra Province, died in a car wreck in early June and I was there for a few days to attend his funeral and to confirm his capable deputy as a permanent replacement. To the South, in Leopard, there were more encouraging signs of ingress by large game, and I stole a day to see for myself the passage of another procession of elephants. In the City, however, and in RB, a calm seemed to be descending.

I had regular visits from Mo Odinga. He would bounce around in his chair as he told me all the detail which amounted to a confirmation that the student revolt had died a quiet death and it seemed that those fanning the flames had gone with it. He had further good news as well: the spate of minor disturbances and break ins had declined back to normal levels and repairs to the *Dawn* were almost complete. I was happy to accept these reassurances but somehow, they continued to trouble me.

I paid my regular weekly visits to the President. She was as ever gracious and welcoming, clearly relieved that her daughter Melissa was back to normal, worrying more about her grades and boyfriends than the voting age. Laetitia Valbuena's preoccupation was now on the Government Budget for the new year which for us begins in July, and looking further ahead, on arrangements for the arrival of Humphrey Corton in September.

I played three or four rounds of golf with Edmund Ladoux. Over a Clubhouse supper after one of them, he told me that he retained his concern that there was more serious trouble brewing but he wouldn't elaborate, perhaps because he was distracted by his affair with an alarmingly good-looking young man who had recently arrived from Egypt. I saw Tina once and Hugh & Alexa Dundas on several occasions - marvelling that all three seemed as healthy and composed as ever.

Meanwhile, Helen was very busy herself. A strong bond had developed between her and my PA, Beatrice Kebir. They spent a lot of time together, a good deal of it on gossip and jokes at my expense, but also on the serious business of developing Helen's work programme. This was focussed on Rheina Blanca, so she spent much time there, flying down to the Coast as her schedule dictated.

One week towards the end of July, I went with her and at my suggestion, we took the bus down there, a long but comfortable journey which gave us the chance of conversation whilst Helen could see some more of our country. I took the opportunity to ask if she was much in touch with Geneva and her boss, the elusive Lee van Troung.

'D'you know, Oliver, it's quite odd,' she replied, lounging gracefully back in her Premium Class chair as we rolled almost silently down the long, straight highway, 'I send a voice report every week and I get an acknowledgment,' and she tapped the *sese* hanging round her neck as she spoke, 'but nothing more than that. No demand for more news, no query about my return date and absolutely nothing from LvT. I'm not complaining as I love being here and with you, but the absence of pressure is a new experience for me.'

We left it at that as we were just pulling into the Halfway House which is a large truck and bus stop where we were to have lunch and when we continued on, Helen was sleepy and nodded off for most of the remaining journey whilst I reflected on the changing pace of life - all panic and alarm one moment, complete peace and calm the next .... or was it coming just before another storm?

There was a welcome surprise waiting in RB. Mervyn Tredinnick was there and with him was Royce Harrison, the second Personal Protection Officer of whom Mervyn had spoken to me. Royce had just arrived in Millennium, out from London and Mervyn was taking the earliest opportunity to introduce him to the Rheina Blanca Yacht Club and its Diving Centre where Humphrey was expected to spend a good deal of time.

We got together in the hotel for dinner that evening, and we were joined by Arthur and Selina Baine. Royce made a strong impression from the outset. He stood rather below average height and was of slender build, but he moved with a sinuous grace. If Mervyn was the bull elephant, Royce Harrison was a striking leopard.

We took a table in a corner of the dining room so we could talk freely without attracting attention. I started by asking Arthur for his assessment of developments since we had puzzled together over the brief appearance of Lee van Troung.

'It remains a mystery, Olty,' he said rubbing his head, 'Generally, things have been pretty quiet down here since I last had a chance to talk to you, and that was at Tina Fullerton's place back in February. There's been no further sign of the little Priest fellow and definitely not another visit from Mr van Troung. I have been keeping half an eye on those two houses - the one in Malaika and the other in Quartermain but there's been nothing particular to report around either of them. And we've had no disturbances or unusual gatherings. There have been more Council Meetings, of course, and I've had one of my guys attend all of them, but the agenda in each case has been routine with no interruptions.' Arthur paused here and rubbed his head again. He went on, 'There is one thing though.'

'Tell me,' I said.

'You remember I told you that when the four *vouyou* types picked up de Houlette from the Council Meeting, they were driving a big black pickup and I took note of its number?'

'Yes, I remember.'

'Well, I've seen that vehicle around town on a few occasions since and others on my team have spotted it also.'

'So?' I asked him, 'if it's legal, what's the significance?'

'Oh, the truck's road legal, OK, and properly registered to another address in Quartermain. It's not the vehicle that stands out, it's the driver.'

'Go on, Arthur,' I said to him.

'Well, whoever the guy is - and the driver is certainly the owner of the pickup - he certainly cuts an impressive figure, an absolute man mountain. He stands over two metres in height and is broad with it. Dark and swarthy, long black hair, softly spoken, lithe and quick on his feet. You wouldn't want to meet him in an alley on a stormy night. I couldn't find anyone amongst my contacts to give him a name: everyone seems to know him as simply "the Uzbek". Not to be argued with.'

'But we've nothing against him?', I asked.

'No, we haven't. No criminal record, no complaints against him, no neighbour disputes, nothing obvious.'

'So where's the problem?'

'Olty, I don't know that there is a problem, but you asked me for an assessment, and I can't leave the Uzbek out of it. Call it a cop's gut feel if you like. I just have the sense that there's something simmering here in RB and that he's a part of it.'

I felt instinctively that Arthur was holding something back and I had an inkling of what it was but in company around the dinner table, this wasn't the moment to pursue it, so I said,

'OK. Let's move on to other things. What are your impressions so far, Royce?'

'I'm happy,' he spoke up immediately in his Caribbean drawl, 'I like everything I've seen at the Yacht Club and in the Diving Centre. With care and attention to detail, I don't believe there'll be a difficulty in providing proper security for Humphrey while he's here.' And then he added, 'I think I'm speaking for Merv also.'

Tredinnick just nodded assent from his place at the table.

I asked, 'What about the communities and their interaction? Any progress on that?

Selina Baine took over. 'On the face of it, Olty, not much change. The Uyghurs and the Rohingya people tolerate each other but there's still mistrust between them, and they don't mix. I must say, however, that it's been a great help having Helen down here on her visits during the last couple of months. We benefit from her experience in other parts of the world and her communication skills are excellent. She's been extremely active amongst both communities and has managed to start a Women's Group which embraces both cultures and strives to get over the language difficulties. And Helen has a new idea which is both exciting and a big challenge.'

With this introduction, Selina looked at Helen to continue and I was conscious that amongst this group, the Baines were alone in knowing the extent of our relationship, but Helen adopted her professional mode and fixed me in the eye as she spoke.

'To achieve some harmonisation between the two ethnic groups, we need to concentrate on the younger generation, specifically on the mid teenagers who will be near to leaving high school. What do they have to look forward to next? They - and especially the girls - want more and different to the expectations of their mothers and grandmothers. They don't want to be saddled with a lifetime of kowtowing to their menfolk and raising kids. They want more learning and education, the chance to build careers and to play a real role in society. But as things stand today, they have little chance of that. A girl finishing school in RB, or a boy come to that, will really struggle to go on to University in Century and locally here, there is just one Technical College in which the courses available concentrate largely on trades. So, you will have a future supply of plumbers and builders, but precious few doctors or lawyers.'

Helen sat back in her chair as she finished by saying, 'What Rheina Blanca needs is a university.'

Instinctively, I moved into cautious, Civil Service mode, saying in response,

'In principle, I can see the potential benefits, but you can't just conjure up such a development out of thin air. The implications of cost and administration are enormous.'

Selina took to the stage again. 'Yes, Olty, we appreciate that and know that it will take time and effort. But it's the dream and the aspiration that's important here. We need desperately to get the objective onto the Government agenda. And we can't do that without you!' She gave me her most winning smile as she hurried on to say, 'also, Olty, it's Helen's thought that we should start small and build up gradually. There's a conference room in the Town Hall which is seldom used and could accommodate a dozen students for lectures. We were thinking just a single course in the Humanities to kick things off, borrowing a professor from the Century campus to come down here on a weekly basis.'

She tailed off at that, glancing at Helen for encouragement and I was about to play for time with some holding comment when our waiter appeared to summon Arthur to the phone in the hotel reception for an urgent call. He got up and moved away in his ponderous style, returning just a few minutes later to announce, 'It was the hospital. Harvey Mueller died an hour ago.'

This news reduced our table to an immediate silence. For Mervyn and Royce, it meant nothing as they had never met Harvey. For Helen, it meant more as although she hadn't met him, I had spoken often to her about this significant man, a solid pillar of the Government administration here in RB, much respected and relied upon by his immediate boss, Police Commissioner Odinga and equally admired by me. Mueller had been the first to identify with concern the influx into his city of Uyghur and Rohingya immigrants with their instinctive preference for self-isolation. He had voiced his growing anxiety before the stomach cancer had been diagnosed.

But it was the Baines who were most obviously troubled by this dire news, for all that it had been expected for some days: Arthur, because as Mueller's No 2, he was now in the firing line to take over, albeit temporarily, and he would worry that he wasn't ready for it and Selina, just because she was there to support her husband.

We all hurried through the remainder of our meal without speaking and then adjoined to the hotel bar for our coffee and drinks. This gave me the opportunity for a quiet conversation with Arthur, expressing my absolute confidence in his ability and total support until Mo Odinga could get down here from Century to spend time with him. After this, Arthur squared his considerable shoulders and went off into the night to see Harvey's widow, Helga. The rest of us had a nightcap before bed, Helen and I going to our separate rooms to preserve discretion although we got together behind her door thirty minutes later.

During the next two days, we spent more time together and with Selina, assessing the practicalities of establishing a basic university course in the room at the Town Hall, the plan being to welcome twelve students to start in September. I remained a bit sceptical but couldn't see the harm in experimenting and conscious that there was little cost involved. So, I signed off the project and flew back to Century on my own, returning briefly the following week for Harvey Mueller's Funeral. By then, Helen had moved to stay with the Baines. She and Selina were flat out working on the details of the proposed Course and about to start interviewing potential students, so I left them to it and went back to my desk in the Secretariat, accompanied by Mo Odinga who had installed Arthur Baine as the new Rheina Blanca Police Chief.

Chapter Twenty-One

By then, it was the month of August, and we were past mid-winter. Not that you notice much difference in our climate except that the days grow a little longer and we sometimes get storms and heavy mist coming in off the ocean. Helen had spent an entire week down in RB and I was yearning for her return on the Friday evening. I picked her up myself from the Domestic Terminal at the Airport and we had dinner at Galliardi's before heading into the weekend alone in my apartment, a blissful time of slob, talk and love making with no one to disturb us. She was delighted with progress on the Uni project, especially as they had found the right man who would be available to come in as Course Tutor for the first year which would begin in late September.

On that Sunday afternoon, Helen and I went for a longer than normal walk along the beach. We had reached almost to the Dundas house before we turned for home, but we were still talking, reviewing progress and making plans as we approached my apartment building. On a whim and just to make a change, I suggested that we walk round through the car park to the front door. As we came nearer to it, I noticed a familiar looking car parked in one of the bays. It was a small, innocuous looking hatchback, Korean made I think, and I knew I had seen it before. As I was about to remark on this to Helen, the driver's door opened, and the tall, slender figure of a man climbed out and stood there, motionless by his car. It was Edmund Ladoux.

I felt Helen touch my elbow as she whispered that she would go on ahead and wait for me in the apartment, but he interrupted her. 'Please stay for a minute or let me come with you. I'm here to see my little sister again .... after so many years.'

We stood together for a second or so, frozen in shock and silence, before Helen left my side and stepped forward, her arms open and he had to stoop to return her embrace.

'Oh, Sala', she said, 'why has it taken you so long to recognise me?'

'It hasn't', he replied, 'I knew you from the first moment I saw you again in the restaurant that lunch time, but I was afraid, I suppose. Afraid I would be rebuffed because I wasn't there for you in Mogadishu at that time of crisis.'

I could see that Edmund was deeply affected and weeping silently, so I suggested that the three of us went inside. I grabbed a bottle from the fridge - a white Burgundy - and carried it with three glasses onto the balcony. When I filled and handed one to Edmund, his hands were shaking so much that I had to steady it until he was seated. By then, Helen was puffing on a cigarette, her gaze fixed on her brother.

'Tell me, Sala,' was all she said. He made no reply for what seemed like an age of waiting before he shrugged his bony shoulders and began to speak.

'Really, you know, I simply can't talk for long now. The enormity of this moment is too much. I have convinced myself over so many long years that this would never happen – that I would never lay eyes on you again, that I had lost you forever in that moment when the bombs went off and destroyed that cellar and every living soul in it. And now this. Seeing again my precious little sister as a grown and beautiful woman. I hardly had the courage to come here today. I'm glad that I did but the confirmation will take time to absorb.'

And so it was that the three of us just sat there in total silence for the next twenty minutes or so, simply sipping at our glasses and lost in individual thought. Helen smoked continuously, once getting up to stand at the balcony rail as she looked down on the beach. Edmund - or Sala - couldn't take his eyes off her while I concentrated on resisting the temptation to light up a cigar. Eventually, the spell was broken by Edmund as he rose to his feet.

'I'm going to leave you two in peace now,' he said, 'but I'll be in touch with you, Shishuke, very soon and we'll get together to talk.'

I sat silently, taking my lead from Helen who didn't try to stop him as he went out and presently, we heard the front door close and shortly afterwards, the sound of his car as he drove off. Helen came into my arms then and we hugged each other as we tried to come to terms with the shock that Edmund's sudden appearance had generated.

Over the following three weeks, I had to share Helen with her brother, and I must admit that I resented this. I had come to prize her presence so highly that the loss of her companionship hit me hard. It wasn't that she disappeared entirely: she did spend one or two nights with me but most of her time while she was in Century was based on her apartment at No 23 where she could and did make herself available to her brother Sala at all times of day and night, according to his whim and willingness to talk. During the middle week, she spent two days in Rheina Blanca, occupied to overflowing with the final preparations for opening the first Term of the new University but throughout all this, I suffered with the knowledge that Helen was so near to me ... yet so far.

However, as we moved towards the end of August, Helen rang me to announce that she wanted to spend the last weekend of the month with me. I was very happy to arrange for Jerome to collect her from the city in the early evening of the Friday, so she was with me in time for dinner. We didn't talk much during our meal and not at all about Edmund. We spoke of other things, enjoyed the food which I had chosen from my normal caterer and the wine from my cellar. Then we went to bed and made love.

I shall always remember Helen's passion that night. She was both loving and uninhibited. With patience, dexterity and determination, I was able to help her to achieve a climax and she, of course, had not much difficulty in seeing to me. When eventually we fell asleep, it was entwined together and with the shared whispers of a couple who had come home.

In the dawn we walked on the beach and then, after breakfast, we sat and talked throughout a long day, mostly in the sitting room but for a while on the balcony when the spring sun was shining. I shan't attempt to repeat the conversation verbatim. It was anyway mostly another monologue as Helen compressed into one account all the history which her brother Sala had been telling her but inevitably, there were pauses and backtracks, to say nothing of my questions and interruptions. So, it's good that I'm able to tidy all this up and present now a chronological summary of how Sala became Edmund over many years and episodes.

Obviously, it's a miracle that he survived that explosion in Toto's cellar room and then lived for a couple of days under the rubble that covered him. Having finally wriggled free, finding that he could still walk and talk and breathe, it's less surprising that he managed to survive. The scavenging skills which he had developed as a boy on the Bangladesh beach came swiftly back to him and although there were no tourists to be found in Mogadishu, he found sanctuaries and somehow, just enough food and liquid to keep himself going. He spoke to no one and kept well clear of the Compound. It was clear that the new Warlord was paranoid about his predecessor and that all who were discovered to have survived the violent takeover were being despatched - generally by public stoning.

Sala couldn't tell Helen for how long he existed like this. It was certainly for weeks rather than days and could have been months. His only objective was to stay alive and hope for better times to come. He slept wherever he could on the beach and instinct drove him to walk north, into increasingly inhospitable country which offered the benefit of isolation. He veered West, away from the sea and closer to the lonely coast road which carried very little traffic but featured the occasional truck stop at which he could forage for something to eat, almost anything liquid to drink and if he was lucky, some cast off clothing or shoes. At one point, he stowed away on the luggage rack of a bus but fell asleep and was discovered at the next halt where he was lucky to be just given a beating and thrown out into the dust of the parking area. Eventually, Sala walked into the City State of Djibouti. He reckons it was then sometime during the year 2012. He has always quoted his birth year as 1989 so that would have made him about twenty-three years old.

Djibouti was a thriving, bustling place in which Sala could find security in anonymity. More to the point, he could find work in the Port where international shippers were always short of labour and asked no questions about the provenance of their staff. He was able to find a room to rent cheaply and within a month or so, was enjoying the most settled way of life he had known since Bangladesh.

Edmund stayed in Djibouti for more than a year, supplementing his established pattern of life by gaining some education at a French Missionary School in which he did cleaning work in exchange for tuition. By the end of this time, he could read and write as well as take an informed interest in the local and international politics of the day. Without knowing it, he was becoming an intellectual and developing his own philosophy which was broadly sympathetic to the doctrine of communism. He lived each day as it came and no longer thought of his parents, his sister or the few friends he had made in Mogadishu. He presumed them all to be dead and they were certainly that to him.

But his own soul was restless and on an overnight impulse, as he explained it to Helen, he left Djibouti, crossing the land border into Ethiopia without difficulty and travelling west to Addis Ababa where he put down some roots and stayed for about a year. Then the wanderlust took hold again and he moved on into Sudan, but Khartoum, the city, the politics and the repression held no appeal for him so after a month or so, he travelled north into Egypt, rapidly losing himself in the culture and the chaos of Cairo.

But attracted though he was by the lifestyle of the souk and the press of multi-ethnic humanity which reminded him of his time in Djibouti, Edmund found that he couldn't settle in Egypt. Helen told me that, from the many exhaustive conversations with her brother which concentrated on how his history had evolved, she came to understand that he was, above all else, driven by his own isolation, the loneliness which afflicted him even when squashed together in crowds of noisy fellow travellers. He had always to rely on his own company and it was this sense of permanent solitude which kept him moving and at that time, his instinct always directed him West. So, he continued his journey, first and with some difficulty through Libya which was dangerous and inhospitable amid their civil war which recalled Somalia, then through Algeria in which conditions for travel were hard and testing. His sights were set on Morocco and the City of Rabat which his imagination assured him would provide the peace he sought but then he stumbled almost by chance on Tunisia and when he alighted from the wheezing old bus in which he was travelling, he knew that Tunis could become the home he had been seeking. Sala was instantly addicted to the sights and sounds and smells of this compelling city, its long history redolent with romance and intrigue. He was so fascinated that he spent almost all his first day there wandering aimlessly but in great contentment. Come the evening, he rebuked himself because he had not given a thought to finding accommodation, so on impulse, he turned into a cheap traveller's hostel thinking to spend a night there or maybe two at the most while he looked for work and a room to rent.

The hostel was very cheap and offered only dormitory sleeping arrangements for single males. That was good enough for him and he was happy to carry his backpack to a corner bed. Across the central corridor from him was a skinny, lightweight Asian looking fellow who held out a hand in welcome and gave him a shy smile. This was the young Lee van Troung who was to become such an influence in his life.

Lee was then already working for UNHCR but had himself been in Tunis for less than a month. The Mission there was extremely small, and Lee's responsibilities were ill defined, leaving him with plenty of time for diversion and mischief. In all of this, he involved Sala without delay and it's probable that they became lovers almost immediately.

Helen compressed the next part of her brother's history into the short time it took us to walk to and from my log on the beach one morning. She didn't attempt to be accurate over dates, but she could tell me that between 2013 and 2015, Sala followed Lee van Troung on brief visits to no less than five different African nations. It seems that they went from Tunis to Abidjan, Cote d'Ivoire and from there to the Central African Republic, then to Tchad, Liberia and finally Mali but not forgetting a very short stop in Dakar, Senegal but that was apparently just for sexual diversion amongst the lady boys on the beach. I asked Helen how they could have afforded the cost of travel and accommodation. She was surprised by my question.

'Oliver', she told me, 'The UN is not very competent or disciplined as an organisation and I know how LvT would have been able to play the system. He would have been on the books in Tunis, a salaried if junior member of staff and he would have been able to simply turn up in all those other places and present himself as a bona fide member of the establishment and the UN family. That would have got him somewhere to stay, enough to eat and the illusion of some working purpose of being there.'

I shrugged. 'OK, so that might have done for him but what about Edmund trailing around in his wake?'

'No problem there either. I can just hear Lee explaining that he was a new recruit - a trainee on work experience. LvT is nothing if not persuasive and convincing.'

'A good bullshitter?'

'Precisely. But you haven't asked about his motives for all this country hopping. I'm sure myself that he was always on the lookout to make mischief and make money and the more of either or both, the better.'

The darkest part of the tale came next. Towards the end of the year 2015, the two of them together flew into Port au Prince, Capital City of the Republic of Haiti. They swiftly immersed themselves in the sea of UN personnel already established there, found themselves lodging and work of a sort with the UNHCR Office which had been long present in this, one of the most impoverished and violent cities on earth. Most of the United Nations Task Force on the ground were designated Peacekeepers, nationals of various countries, there to ensure order and some stability amongst a population which had suffered long and hard under repressive and autocratic regimes. The specific responsibility of UNHCR was to help the dispossessed and homeless who had flooded into Port au Prince from the countryside and other urban centres throughout this unhappy country.

As has been well researched and documented over the years, the desperate poverty and living conditions combined to produce a behavioural cesspit in which foreign charity workers and UN personnel acted disgracefully to abuse countless native Haitians who were crying out for help. There was widespread cruelty, exploitation, enforced prostitution and sex slavery. The great majority of the UN guilty were to be found amongst the Peacekeepers but the universally recognised Blue Beret was worn also by UNHCR staff and Lee, with Sala, took full advantage of the anonymity it provided.

They were there in the city for almost two years, growing richer and more comfortable as time passed. Sala persuaded himself that he was due some good fortune after all the deprivation of his youth but couldn't reconcile his conscience with the inhumane treatment to which he was a party.

Lee van Troung could not resist the compulsion of his own nature and sexuality. He organised a 'party', bringing a dozen cronies into the squalid, dingy apartment which Sala was sharing with him. During a night of drinking and drugs, Lee introduced four small boys, aged about five or six years old, who had been bought or stolen off the streets of the violent city which had ceased to recognise any hint of civilisation. One by one, these little boys were gang raped and snuffed out - strangled in the agony of their abuse with their pathetic little bodies thrown out of the window onto the mean pavement below.

The whole performance so excited LvT's depraved senses that he immediately proposed another and similar horror. It was then that Sala became Edmund: then that he knew he would go mad if he did not immediately tear himself away from this slight Asian with the winning smile which had first befriended him way back in Tunis. He grabbed his few belongings and vanished into the grimy murk of another Haitian dawn.

Helen had wept openly as she told me this over Sunday evening supper at our little restaurant on the beach road.

‘I tell you, Oliver, it took Sala hours and quite a few visits to me in No 23 to confess this and honestly, I just couldn’t believe it at first. I simply could not comprehend how this man and the boy he used to be, the same person who was my brother, my guardian who carried me on his shoulders along the sand at Cox’s Bazar, how could he have become so debauched into such evil? Eventualy, I had to accept that he was telling me the truth. And I hoped that the confessing was cathartic. But I couldn’t and can’t get over the horror of hearing that.’

It was only later, after we had returned to the apartment, that she was able to continue and that was easier because she went on to give me a straightforward, much abbreviated account of how her brother had gone on to find a new life for himself.

‘We all know how much the world has been changing over the last twenty years or so, Oliver, but even so, some of the things which Sala had to tell me came as a surprise.’

‘Such as?’ I asked her.

‘Well, the whole process of personal identification and travel for starters. Today, anyone travelling from one country to another carries proof of identity on a mobile device or a *sese* like mine’, and she touched the pendant hanging round her neck, ‘and as you know, that carries the story of who you are, where you were born and when, your gender - fluid or not - and your medical history. But back then in the two thousand and teens, we all relied on printed passports with hazy photos, written documents of one sort or another.

It was incredibly easy for Sala to assume another identity. He simply stole it. It seems that there was another guy, an American from Arkansas working in Port au Prince for a medical charity. Sala had met him a few times and knew where he was living. The man was white but suntanned, about the same height and with a similar slight build: much the same age. Sala went to the Portakabin in which he was being accommodated during working hours, broke in, found and took his passport. That was when he discovered the guy's name. Edmund Ladoux from Little Rock, capital city of the State. He was apparently unmarried and without dependants. During a brief as possible invasion of the man's privacy, Sala found no note of a home address but that didn't trouble him. He went straight to the airport and bought a one-way ticket to Miami. He had no difficulty either in leaving Haiti or arriving in Florida, USA. He had plenty of money, almost all of it dishonestly acquired during his meanderings in the wake of Lee van Troung. All that mattered to Sala was that he had escaped the control of a malign influence and he set about building himself a new life. And in this, he was successful. After about a year in Miami, he went north and east to settle in Philadelphia where the arts and culture scene captivated him. He took a small but comfortable apartment in the city centre and studied all hours to qualify as a Paralegal. Eight years on, he was well established both professionally and personally when he came across one of your government advertisements inviting qualified individuals of good character to apply to become citizens of Millennium. He arrived here in Century City in October 2025 and says that, as Edmund of course, he first met you sometime during the following year. I guess that was ten years ago?'

I just sat there for a minute or so, twirling my glass between my fingers and pretty much lost for words. Finally, I smiled at her and said,

'I suppose we're lucky that either of you is still here - let alone both.'

She returned my smile, and we left it at that, going to bed early and feeling emotionally drained. Tomorrow was another day, with Helen on the early flight back to RB and I had a heavy schedule in the Secretariat.

Chapter Twenty-Two

Normally, I sleep very well if not for long as I'm a habitual early riser but two nights into that week, I woke suddenly in the early hours, about 2 am I guess, and lay there for a few minutes wondering what had disturbed me. I was alone in the apartment with Helen in Rheina Blanca until the Thursday but anyway, I knew it wasn't thoughts about her or work which had broken into my sleep. It was a noise. I concentrated on remaining motionless until I heard it again: a slithering sort of click which I recognised immediately as the sound the latch on my front door makes when you push it home to lock.

I like to hear the waves and I've never, since childhood, liked the dark so I always go to bed with the window open and the curtains drawn back. There was moonlight in addition, so I had no difficulty in making out the figure moving gently from the doorway into the hall towards my side of the bed. This was not Helen, and it could not be Troy who has keys to the apartment. It was a large, tall man and in a fluster of rising panic, I reached for the storm torch which sits by my bedside. I was much too late.

Whoever it was pushed me back flat against the pillows, a hand against each of my shoulders exerting an enormous strength which left me powerless. Then came a prick which could only have been a needle slid into my left bicep and a guttural voice whispered in my ear, 'Stay out of this and stop interfering'. Then everything went black and blank.

I don't know for how long I was unconscious. Obviously, it wasn't a matter of minutes, but it can't have been for hours. I could see it was broad daylight and something about the sound and smell of the sea made me think that it was about eight or half past in the morning. I wanted to look at my watch, also to scratch my nose which was itching infuriatingly. I discovered that I couldn't do either because my arms were trapped by my sides and my legs also were refusing to move. At first I thought I was hit by some form of paralysis - a stroke maybe - but then that voice came back to me and I made the connection. My assailant had done more than just put me to sleep. Little by little, I put things together. I could flex my fingers, wiggle my toes, turn my head in both directions, but not very far. The itch in my nose was being caused, it felt, by dust or maybe some sort of fur but I couldn't raise a hand to dislodge it. I could see alright and by squinting painfully, I could make out that the fur was a deep auburn colour. I knew I recognised it and then it hit me. It came from the large rectangular rug which my mother had given me following the only visit she had been able to make to me here in Millennium before the dementia had claimed her. I could hear her saying, 'This is a lovely apartment, Olty, but you need something to soften that huge sitting room.' She had returned home and sent me, at enormous cost of transport, the equally huge and heavy rug which lay between the sofas and under the coffee table.

But it wasn't lying there now. It was rolled up on my bed and I was inside it. It was both a strait jacket and a shroud, large and heavy enough to imprison me whether or not there were also straps around it. This thought process started a panic in me which, at first, I could not control. I struggled and fought to get free, shouting, screaming, swearing. My claustrophobia made me catatonic.

I went on battling until sheer physical exhaustion brought about a small measure of calm which encouraged me to think. I was still breathing, so I was still living. I could see and smell and hear. Surely Helen or someone, anyone would come into the apartment and find me, trussed up and helpless. That very thought started me fighting again and it took every mental effort I could muster to make myself lie still and think: 'You're still alive,' I kept telling myself, 'Be patient and wait.'

These few words became a sort of mantra which I kept repeating to myself. Over and over, sometimes in my head, sometimes speaking out loud, even shouting. Eventually, I don't know how long it took, the effect was to make me drowsy, and I nodded off, only to snap awake again with a jolt of realisation that I was trapped in a tomb and that started me fighting and panicking again. This process of blind terror inducing impotent struggle, followed finally by some calm as I repeated my few words of comfort, seemed to be on an endlessly repeating loop. I don't know for how long I was lying there on this merry go round from hell, but it must have been for some hours as the new day advanced and I could see sunlight creeping through my bedroom, could hear the sound of waves breaking on the beach as the tide receded.

I was startled by a sudden, soft noise. The front door was being opened. It was just as it had been at the start of this nightmare. I flinched in my tomb. Was the same assailant returning to finish me off? I was muttering to myself again, 'You're still alive...' when I heard scuttering on the bare floor and a heavy weight landed on top of the rug which enclosed me. A hairy face thrust itself into my cheek and realisation dawned. Absalom the Alsatian had arrived.

It turned out that Troy had been walking on the beach, normal route, normal hour. He told me, with normal language difficulty, that whilst he noted my absence that morning, he didn't question it. There were more than a few mornings when I couldn't make it - generally work related commitments. He kept calling Absalom to him, but the big dog wouldn't respond. Instead, he ran off to the apartment building and started scrabbling at the entrance. Eventually, Troy followed him and used his own passkey to open my door, very quietly and with diffidence in case he was disturbing me. He might well have thought that Helen was there with me. Then Absalom pushed past him and sprang onto the bed, starting to worry at the couple of straps secured around the rug which encased me. Between them, they freed me in seconds, and I breathed a mighty sigh of relief.

An hour or so later, Mo Odinga appeared in haste, and we sat over a cup of coffee to talk.

Mo said, 'This was a warning, Olty. I guess we can say you were lucky it wasn't worse, but it must have been scary.'

'It was certainly that,' I replied, 'but a warning of what?' I was trying to keep the tremor out of my voice but conscious that I wasn't completely succeeding.

'Whoever broke in last night wasn't *vouyou*. They're all smash and grab. They'd have knocked you about to deliver a message. This was more subtle. And confident too. We'll run the rule over the apartment now - check for prints and anything left behind. But I'm pretty damn sure we'll find nothing, no clue as to the identity of the person/people who attacked you. No, this episode was carefully conceived to fire a shot across your bows, tell you to keep clear and mind your own business.'

'Yes, Mo but warning about what? Jesus,' I expostulated, 'what the hell is going on here? The fire on the *Dawn,* the voting age business, the phony priest, the oddball visitor to RB. Are all these just messages, more warnings? How is the Government meant to react? What should I be telling the President? Is there a crisis building? Or what?'

Odinga shrugged his broad shoulders as he leant forward in his chair. He paused before giving me his reply, stabbing a sausage forefinger at me to emphasise his advice.

'You've got to stay calm, Olty, while we work to sort this out. Short answer to your question is that I simply don't know. I'm guessing and wondering just like you are. But also, I'm worried that whoever it is and whatever it's about, they're going after someone in your position of influence. So, for now, just stay safe. Use all the security you've got in this apartment, don't open the door unless you know who's on the other side of it. I'll step up patrols in the area and let's keep in close contact. Ring me whenever you like.'

Shortly afterwards, he was gone, and I was left trying to relax and to get my life back into some sort of order. I showered, shaved and dressed. I couldn't eat and didn't attempt any breakfast. I called Jerome to collect me, and we drove into the city in silence. I didn't want to talk to anyone about this incident, but I was yearning for Helen's return.

It happened anyway that it was a busy time in the Secretariat. There had been an increasing number of reports that poachers were operating in Hippo Province, and I was anxious to get an update on the situation and to know what we were doing about it. Then Pascal Brana wanted to talk to me about his concern that he might have discovered an accounting fraud in Flamingo, our smallest Province situated in the extreme Northeast and late in the morning, Beatrice told me that the President had called a meeting in her Office that afternoon to hear progress on our application to host the Commonwealth Heads of Government Conference in Rheina Blanca in 2038. Bea announced also that the Ambassador from Bangladesh wanted to talk to me ahead of a formal visit she had requested to see President Valbuena. I found myself snapping at Beatrice when neither of us could recall the name of the lady from Dhaka and Bea looked at me reproachfully as she withdrew. I realised that I was pent up and nervous, affected by my ordeal of just a few hours previously and unable to talk about it.

Abruptly, I left the office and spent thirty minutes or so walking around the City Centre, pausing for a while to sit on a bench in the small park which surrounds the Cathedral. I knew that I had to pull myself together and hold on tight until I could talk this thing through with Helen. At the same time, I was conscious of the fact that I was bad at this. I might have brain power and position, but in character, I am ill-equipped to deal with personal threat. I got up and wandered on, returning to the Secretariat building via the Cloisters and wishing that Pente was still there to give me comfort and advice.

Things improved during the afternoon, and I was able to function better during the President's meeting despite the presence there of Edmund Ladoux in his capacity of legal counsel. I looked at him, wondering to myself if he knew, if he had been involved, responsible even? I forced myself to carry on and concentrate. That worked but I still felt drained when the time came to go home.

On the drive back out of the city, I felt stronger and sat up front alongside Jerome, chatting to him about the game in Hippo Province and a bit about European football. But as he left me outside my apartment building, I felt a lurch of apprehension. I knew I was scared, frightened by the prospect of the night alone, unnerved by the thought of another break in at dead of night, conscious that I hadn't followed Mo's instruction to set the complicated alarm system.

Then a stab of real panic hit me as I made out a shape in the gloom of my under-cover parking bay. I was on the point of turning to make a run for it when I checked myself, recognising who was there. The diminutive figure of Troy rose from squatting on his haunches and throwing away the stick of balsa wood he was chewing, he sauntered towards me, followed as always by Absalom.

Troy gestured towards his sleeping mat lying on the concrete and with his fighting sticks under his arm, he climbed the stairs to my apartment and waited for me to unlock the front door. He went in front of me, walking through all the rooms before returning with a seraphic grin on his face.

'All clear, Boss,' he muttered, 'but we stay here tonight.' Then he trotted back inside, leaving me standing there at the door of my own apartment. I could hear him at the kitchen island, then the sound of running water and after that, I could feel as much as hear the sliding door onto the balcony being opened. He called and I found him standing out there, the scruffy bit of rug he sometimes carried over his shoulder now lying on the balcony tiles and next to it, a mixing bowl he had found and filled with water. He whistled then and almost immediately, Absalom appeared, going straight to lie down on the rug, ears pricked for further instructions. With sign language and a very few words in his awkward, stilted English, Troy made clear his intent. He was to sleep down in the garage while the dog would stay with me on the balcony. And that's how it worked. After some bread and cheese with a couple of drinks, I took a shower and fell into bed. I have never slept so well, Absalom never stirred, and we had no visitors. As dawn broke, I heard a discreet knock at the front door and there was Troy, appearing to take the big dog for his morning walk while I shaved, dressed and had some breakfast. When Jerome arrived to collect me, they were back together downstairs and clearly planning to stay for the day. That was Wednesday and the pattern was repeated that evening and the next but on Friday when I got home from the office, Troy and Absalom had gone. To replace them I found Helen who had arrived from RB on a mid-afternoon flight and was starting to do something about dinner. I was ecstatic to see her standing there, her arms open wide in welcome.

It's a surprising trait of human nature - at least for some of us - that an episode of crisis produces a reaction of silence and introspection rather than a voluble outpouring of emotion, although I suspect that Helen knew instinctively that I was struggling to control myself as the memories of my time in that carpet kept nudging at me. Also, of course, she had news for me, but we talked of other things while sharing a simple cold supper and a bottle of Moselle. It wasn't until we were in bed later, her warm naked body comforting me with her head resting on my shoulder, that she produced the bombshell which she announced in a soft, quiet voice.

She said, 'LvT has been back in Rheina Blanca.'

I jerked upright, dislodging her head onto the pillow and looked down on her, feeling myself trembling and unable to control my hand properly as I switched on the bedside light.

'What?'

'Just as I say, Oliver. My boss, nominally, Lee van Troung came back to Millennium last week and spent two days in RB.'

'Well, for God's sake,' I blurted out, 'I mean bloody hell.' I knew I was gabbling but I couldn't stop myself. 'Did you see him? Did you talk to him? What's he doing here, what does he want?

'No, no and don't know', Oliver, but look,' she said, laying a hand on my arm to restrain me as I was about to spring out of bed, 'this is a shock and not pleasant news, but you've simply got to stay calmer.'

I should have stopped myself from turning huffy but I didn't, snapping at her, 'It's all very well to say that but you haven't been through my experience this week!'

Helen was of course equal to that jibe and fixed me with her steely look as she responded, 'That's not worthy of you, Oliver, you may remember that I've been through quite a bit of my own over the years.' That brought me up short but before I could voice an apology, she went on, 'Stop your tantrum and get back into bed while I make us a cup of tea. Then I'll tell you more.'

Later, sitting up in bed side by side, she continued. 'Arthur Baine told me two evenings back while I was having dinner with him and Selina. His team have been keeping a lookout and one evening they spotted the same big black pick up outside the same house in Malaika. They hung around expecting it to maybe go on to the other place in Quartermain and it did but not before loading up with four passengers, one of which was LvT. The driver, of course, was the huge guy they call the Uzbek.'

I interrupted her, 'How did they recognise him?'

'Easily. Arthur has issued a copy of Lee's passport photo to all his people and told them to be especially watchful.

'But why this week?'

'That would be Inspector General Odinga. He called Arthur just as soon as he left you here after you were discovered. Mo ordered maximum surveillance for a week, but it only took a day.'

I had recovered my composure and was thinking all this through when I glanced towards her and saw tears glistening in Helen's eyes.

'What's this? Is there more?'

'I'm afraid there is', she said dabbing at her face with a tissue, 'Sala was with him.'

'Oh God, Edmund, the bloody idiot,' I exploded, 'what's he doing for Christ's sake? He'd promised to have nothing further to do with van Troung.' Then I rounded on Helen to demand, 'How d'you know this? Did you see them together, talk to your brother again?'

She shook her head, replying impatiently, 'No, no, nothing like that. I only know this because Arthur found out and that was by chance. They followed LvT and found that he spent a couple of nights at the Intercontinental. Arthur thought to check, just to be thorough, and saw that Sala took a room just down the same corridor …. and for the same two nights. As for being in touch again, Oliver, I guess Lee acts like a drug on him. He simply can't make himself do without.'

'Well,' I said, 'whatever it is, we've got no answers but now we've got more questions and they all revolve around finding out what's going on here. Did Arthur say any more?'

'Not much. He was obviously pretty shocked himself. So was Selina. She and I were having a very busy time of it with the Uni course getting established, but we did talk, of course. Then, before she went home and I left to come back here, Arthur appeared to tell us that he thought he knew how LvT had arrived in RB …. and departed.'

'Go on,' I urged her.

'Well, it seems that he has a girl Constable who covers some of the rural district outside the city boundaries but still within his district. She is known for being painstaking, not to say nosey, and she has in her patch the old grass airfield called Four Winds. Have I got the name right?'

'You have,' I said, 'I remember the days when it was the only way into RB by air. But that was years ago.'

'Anyway, this girl told Arthur that she called in to chat to the guy who runs the flying club there and he showed her a little four-seater something with long range tanks fitted which had skipped in from the south somewhere and was staying a couple of days. She went back later that same evening, hoping to learn more but it had already gone again.'

There was silence between us for a minute or so. I sat back against the pillows, thinking deeply. I was suddenly feeling calmer and clearer in my mind. We needed more help and brainpower on this, and I wished I could consult Edmund but that was now out of the question. I had to assume that he was in the camp of the enemy, whoever that was and whatever its intent. I needed to assemble our own war party and there was no time to waste.

Helen and I seemed to know instinctively that we had to leave it there, at least until the morning and the start of another week. I drew her to me, and we made love, as always as best we could. Then we slept.

Chapter Twenty-Three

On Tuesday, 9th September, the Panel assembled at 9am. We met in the Long Room at the Secretariat, so called because it is just that and because it offers comfortable space and all the appropriate audio visual kit. I took the Chair at about 8.30 so I was there to welcome attendees as they arrived. Beatrice was on hand with me, checking that notepads and carafes of water were in place. The seat to my immediate left was reserved for Hugh Dundas, our *eminence grise* and still astonishingly adroit of mind for a man who had just passed his ninetieth birthday. The others could choose their own spot. We started promptly and I was pleased to find myself relaxed and reasonably confident. In these surroundings and with this sort of an agenda, I was back in my comfort zone.

I set out the stall, saying that we were here to assess the likelihood of facing a security emergency. I presented a synopsis, covering the various episodes which had occurred during the year to date and detailing our concerns about the unexplained visits to Rheina Blanca, the clandestine calls at the suburban houses, the unidentified giant in his black truck, but emphasising that we didn't know what, where, when or why. My own priority task was to coordinate the available data, sift opinion and report to President Valbuena. I would therefore appreciate contributions from all present at this meeting, but we must be both precise and concise. We had no time to waste.

Following this introduction, I invited Hugh to speak first: he didn't disappoint me.

'Let's sum up.' He started to speak in the familiar, quiet tone which was exact but unhurried and commanded attention. Looking down the long table, I could see at a glance that he was already holding their concentration. 'We have a young priest of doubtful authenticity who is playing Pied Piper to the youngest in our society, the most vulnerable who are on the cusp of adulthood. Our second largest urban population, Rheina Blanca, is the focus of an interest which may be seeking to unite or to divide its two significant ethnic groups. There has been unrest and minor criminal activity over the last six months throughout the greater area of Century City. We have the evidence of petty troublemakers inciting misbehaviour amongst younger citizens and there has been one serious incident of an assault on a senior member of our national management team, namely our Secretariat Director Oliver Aveling.'

Hugh paused as a murmur ran through the room: this was news to most of those present, but they did need to hear it. Then he continued.

'Millennium is indebted to Ms Helen Priest who came here by prior arrangement on an extended visit representing a significant United Nations Agency. I have seen her interim report and I fully endorse her initiative to establish a University in Rheina Blanca. Quite apart from this activity, Ms Priest has been able to confirm for us the identity of Mr Lee van Troung who is her immediate workplace superior. It is also now proven that Mr Troung has paid two recent, short-term visits to this country, both to Rheina Blanca, neither pre-arranged nor announced.'

With a nod and a smile in her direction, he went on to say less formally, 'It has also been a surprise to learn that Helen is related to our own Edmund Ladoux. She is his sister, but they were separated as children under distressing circumstances and have been reunited only during her visit to Millennium.

Finally, by way of introduction, it seems that Edmund and van Troung know each other well, having shared experiences in other African countries well before Edmund arrived here in Century City.'

The subdued murmur around the table was now turning into a background buzz as attendees stared to talk to each other. Hugh Dundas held up both his hands and was rewarded by an almost instant silence as his age and authority were respected. He finished by saying, 'I am myself persuaded that all these things are in some way connected and that Government action should now be taken as a matter of urgency to clarify and confront whatever threat may be emanating from them.'

This was an emergency meeting of the Panel, called at short notice so I was not surprised that there were some absentees. Some Members can't make it, even for the regular Meetings which we hold on the first Monday of every month except for January which gets complicated by the New Year holiday season. At any other time of the year, there may be alternative commitments which must also take account of the travel time to and fro the farther flung Provinces. But I was pleased that Kane Merrick was present. He represents Century North, so hasn't far to come and his Panel Portfolio is for Agriculture and general Exports but on other matters, he speaks with a measured and articulate voice. For this debate today I'm sure Kane will be an asset. Ken Sanchez has arrived from Buffalo Province, Ken is a safe pair of hands, handling everything concerning Transportation on our Panel ... and that includes both goods and people.

From Rheina Blanca East, Jessica Jessop is here. Jess arrived in Millennium from Florida, USA, with the First Fleet and understudied Hugh Dundas until his eventual retirement. I know that Tina Fullerton doesn't care for her, but I suspect that's because she resents Jessica's prodigious intellect. She's our Panel Member responsible for the nation's finances and like Hugh before her, she seems to me to do a miraculous job, with that rare ability to both appreciate the big, international picture whilst keeping a steely grip on the detail at home. But Jessica is in her early sixties now and looking forward to retirement. We will shortly have to worry about identifying her replacement.

By tradition, the Panel Members sit to the left of the President's Chair, in which I am installed today, so they may look out over the gardens and the last of them attending this morning is Distance Okuyu who is our current Member for Health. Distance was born in Douala, Cameroun, the son of an émigré Frenchman who sent him as a child to Toulouse for his education - school, university and thereafter medical college. He flourished as a bright and assiduous student but rarely returned home to Africa so his family gave him a suitable nickname which he couldn't or wouldn't shake off. Distance came to us in Millennium about seven years ago and lives outside Tamalourene in Giraffe Province. He's very dedicated to his work as Medical Director of the Hospital there and as a valued Panel Member. It must have taken a considerable effort for him to be here today.

We invariably have additional attendees at Panel Meetings - people who have specialist knowledge to contribute or maybe particular accounts to present. They sit in a line on the opposite side of the endlessly long table, each place with its own audio system, connection for whatever device, carafe of water and storage space. Today, we have been joined by seven such. First to my right is Helen, then Mervyn Tredinnick but not Royce Harrison who has already gone back to London and will not return until he arrives with young Corton later this month. Next to Mervyn sits Maurice Odinga, next to Mo are Arthur Baine and Selina from RB, then Fergus Carradine and finally, Denzil Tremayne.

Fergus was the military commander who secured the success of the invasion in the year 2000 and as Millennium settled into some sort of order, he became our first Panel Member for Development, giving him a very wide brief for many different projects with more than enough variety to satisfy his initiative and imagination. But he's well into retirement now, being in his late seventies and he passed the Development baton at the last Election to Constance Demidenko, an extremely capable woman who lives in our central Kudu Province and hails originally from Kazakhstan. Constance doesn't do military, so Fergus Carradine put another arrangement in place before he stepped down.

Millennium doesn't have a standing army. We have no air defences of any kind and at sea, we depend for the protection of our fishing fleet on two converted trawlers which we bought from Malaysia. For our peace and tranquillity, we have come to rely on the international reputation we have worked over the years to win for being a welcoming, caring, and prosperous society. But Fergus Carradine did develop a modest insurance policy for us because before his retirement, he created a militia which is a permanent fixture although it is about thirty percent manned by part time reservists. The force is located at Camp Cougar, some fifty kilometres East of Century City and is well equipped in basic weaponry, transport and especially communications equipment. During the past twenty – five years, the Militia has only been called on to fight some bush fires, to provide a guard to welcome visiting dignitaries from overseas and African countries and to be in evidence on important national occasions such as the swearing in of a new President. It has a fine military band, but I don't know where the name of their barracks comes from: unlike the marching soldiers, it seems out of step!

The Militia is commanded by a full time Officer, a Brigadier retired from the Welsh Guards in the UK, and this is Denzil

Tremayne who came here with his pretty wife, Claire, and their two boys. Denzil is now the first to make a contribution, raising his hand and I invite him to speak.

'Mr Chairman', he said, being quite old school in his form of address, 'from the synopsis provide by Hugh Dundas, it would seem that Edmund Ladoux is central to all this. May I ask why he isn't with us now?'

'A fair question, Denzil,' I replied, going on 'He'll be here any minute. I guess he's just been delayed.' As I finished, I glanced at Beatrice, sitting on my left and taking notes. She would be writing up the Minutes of this session and she looked up now to comment.

'I've spoken myself to Mr Ladoux a couple of times this morning, Brigadier, and he will certainly be attending but gave me warning that he might be unavoidably detained for a short while and therefore a little late.'

Tremayne nods his understanding, and we move on with Kane Merrick who is keen to engage.

'Olty,' asks in his deep, booming voice, 'what are you hearing from Mbwenye? Is all quiet down there?'

Kane is putting his finger on a vital location and he's right to ask the question. Mbwenye is the principal town of Flamingo Province which is our smallest by population but also accounts for most of Millennium's wealth. It is here that our oil industry is centred, drawing exceptionally high-grade crude from the Tamalou Trench which is about 100 kms offshore in the Atlantic and filling tankers for export from the deep-water port facility at Mbwenye. A high proportion of the town residents are expatriates on medium term contracts and many of them are American Nationals, vastly experienced in oil exploration and extraction. Reserves from the Trench are expected to last for another forty years or so, but the timeframe keeps moving out as world-wide demand for crude oil diminishes in the face of ever mounting efforts to Go Green and save our planet.

Mo Odinga responds to say, 'Nothing unusual to report, Kane. No disturbances during the last couple of weeks and I believe the maritime traffic is moving to schedule through the port.' He glances at Ken Sanchez as he speaks and Ken, sitting opposite, nods in agreement and comments, 'I confirm, Olty, all on time and going to plan.

'So's the money'. This from Jess Jessop. 'I saw the Receipts Report just before coming here and it's all up to date.'

I can see Distance Okuyu waving a pencil at me and I'm about to invite his comment when Jessica continues. 'May I just add,' she says, tapping her finger on the table which is her habit when she has something to emphasise, 'Personally, I don't buy any connection between the phony priest, the student demos and the acts of sporadic violence, as in torching the *Dawn,* random robberies and the assault on you, Olty. The latter could be a threat, but the young people shouting the odds couldn't lead to anything happening in a hurry - even if they did get what they say they want.'

Kane Merrick came in immediately. 'I hear you, Jess, and I'm inclined to agree, but with my younger granddaughter involved, I'd like to hear the constitutional position spelt out by Edmund: as soon as he can stir his stumps and get here.' The acerbic tone was typical of this burly guy, nevertheless I could agree with him.

I turned back to Distance and gave him the floor.

'It's been a while since I was in Rheina Blanca, he said, 'six weeks at least, but from the daily reports I get, the infection rate of the latest Virus strain is rising there and pretty much all the cases are amongst the Uyghur population. I'm wondering if this could be significant?'

From across the table, Selina Baine responds. 'I've asked myself the same question, Distance, but I really don't think so. Regular inoculation is proceeding according to the national programme you put in place last year and none of the cases reported recently have had a serious impact: I mean no hospitalisation at all and if we're speculating about some attempt to spread disease amongst one section of the RB population, what would be the point of that?'

Alongside her, Arthur assumes his Policeman's gravitas as he chips in to say 'Selina's right. If there's a threat to be faced, it's not going to build up gradually, it's going to burst without much warning. I'm concentrating on information - using all our best contacts in the Rohingya and Uyghur communities but I'm not getting much back. My prime sources aren't drying up on me, it's more that they don't seem to have much to say. We're continuing discreet surveillance on those two houses, the ones in Quartermain and Malaika, but there's been nothing further to see, no more clandestine visits, not by the priest or van Troung or anyone else. Even more frustrating, that big black pick up seems to have vanished off the streets and with it, the huge guy they call the Uzbek.' Arthur rubbed his bald head as he concluded, 'there's *something* going on down there, I'm bloody sure of it but I can't see its shape … or judge its direction. At least not yet.'

Hugh Dundas intervened again at this point, commenting in his soft but commanding voice.

'Whilst we continue to wait for Edmund, whose contribution will, I'm sure, be valuable, could we hear now from Helen Priest? Our best collective guess is that Mr van Troung is behind or at least connected to whatever it is that may be a threat and apart from Edmund, it's Helen who knows him best.'

Hugh's spontaneous choice of words served to emphasise our paralysis as a group. We simply didn't know what we were up against. He was also underlining the cost of Edmund's absence, so as Helen pulled her chair closer to the table and prepared to speak, I whispered to Bea by my side, asking her to pop out of the room and continue to chase him up.

Helen looked directly at Hugh as she started to address us, then letting her eyes travel around the company as she progressed. She started to speak.

'I've been with UNHCR for close on ten years now and Lee van Troung was there long before me. So, I've got to know him well but gradually and much better since he and I both got promoted. Lee is now the Operations Director of the Agency and I work directly for him.

We all call him LvT. That's for one obvious reason but also because the abbreviation suits his style. He's very direct, full of energy, keen for a challenge, always looking for a solution to a problem rather than an analysis of its cause.

Lee has a first-class brain, he's articulate in four languages, he has a bright and welcoming personality and a reputation for getting things done. I enjoy working with him and admire his accomplishment.

We don't mix much socially, and he likes to keep a certain distance between himself and his staff. He's openly gay and lives in a swanky apartment located in the heart of the fashionable *quartier Paquis* in central Geneva, close to the beach and with a fine view of the towering *Jet d'eau.*

Overall, he's a hard character to read but I've always had respect for LvT, that is until I've heard some of the things my brother Edmund has told me about him. And honestly, I have no idea why he should have been paying unannounced visits here without telling anyone - myself included.'

As Helen sat back in her chair, I could sense that Hugh, Kane and Jessica all wanted to put further questions to her but before I could invite the first of them to speak, I heard the door open behind me and imagined it was Beatrice returning with more news of Edmund. It wasn't, it was Pascal Brana bending down to whisper in my ear.

'The President sends her compliments and regrets for disturbing the Meeting, but she needs to see you urgently, she's waiting in your office now.'

Naturally, I excused myself immediately and found Laetitia Valbuena pacing the carpet nervously, up and down in front of the windows.

'I'm sorry to interrupt, Olty, but you need to hear this - all of you do. I've just taken a call from Prosper Aguilas at the UNHCR. He says that after a day trying to locate Lee van Troung, his staff got into his apartment in Geneva and found it completely empty. No sign of him or any of his belongings, no clothes, pictures, photographs, papers. Nothing … and of course, no indication of where he's gone.'

'But we know where he's gone. He's here in Millennium, probably somewhere in RB.'

'That's the point, Olty. He's here to stay. He's not going back this time.'

I gazed at her, temporarily lost for words. Finally, I asked her, 'Did he say anything else? Prosper, I mean.'

'Not much, too shocked himself, I guess. But he did add that the Federal Police in Switzerland has a Warrant out for van Troung's arrest, should he try to sneak back in. But why would he? Olty, we've simply got to find this man. Go back into your meeting and share this news. We need our best brains and experience to be united on this.'

She turned on her heel and left my office.

I was greeted by a buzz of conversation as I re-entered the Conference Room, but it subsided as Hugh Dundas held up his hands. I remained standing as I gave them the President's news, then resumed my seat as Maurice Odinga was the first to speak.

'We must step up the search immediately,' he said, turning to Arthur Baine alongside him, 'hotels, boarding houses, restaurants, museums, galleries, the lot. And raid those two houses also. We don't need a discreet surveillance now. We're responding to an international request for help.'

As her husband was nodding his big head vigorously, Selina Baine broke in to ask, 'What about the black pick up and the big guy driving it? the Uzbek? Should we be looking for him too?'

'Certainly' re-joined Mo, 'the two of them are connected, that's for sure.'

'But are they?', the question came from Hugh Dundas in his calm and measured tone, 'I'm not so sure myself. I think we may be dealing here with two quite separate concerns.'

I noticed that Distance Okuyu had his hand up and I nodded at him.

'I believe I may know this Uzbek. I noticed him during my last visit to RB, amongst the congregation at Holy Ascension Church in the city centre. He's too big to miss!'

'You've never mentioned this before.' It was almost an accusation coming from Arthur, immediately across the table from Okuyu.

'Well, I didn't know before that you had any interest in him. But I can tell you all that aside from his size, this man is unusual. He appears to be a Christian, he certainly took Communion that Sunday morning and there are very few Christian Uyghurs in the world, even fewer amongst those now living in Millennium.'

'Did you talk to him, Distance?', I asked.

'No, I didn't. I had to go straight on to the Hospital, checking records.'

I nodded my understanding. He's very conscientious, Distance, and likes to stay aware of recent arrivals into our communities for those who may have brought infectious disease with them.

Next to contribute was Ken Sanchez, saying that he would start looking for small plane arrivals into the many grass strip airfields we have throughout the country - a long shot as he acknowledged but better to leave no stone unturned in the efforts to locate Lee van Troung.

Then Kane Merrick wanted his say, volunteering to have his people look out for passengers on their bus services but

Kane suggested also that Denzil Tremayne might consider deploying some of his Reservists down to Rheina Blanca on a watching brief. Fergus Carradine expressed his agreement, and I could see Denzil taking note.

Jess Jessop interposed here, saying, 'I think Hugh's right that we shouldn't be assuming connections until they're proved. This Uzbek fellow. Can't we at least find him and start asking some questions. It sounds like he must stick out from the crowd.'

I felt the need to inject more urgency into this discussion and raised my voice to comment. 'We need to agree on an action plan before we break up. And there is something else. It's only a few days until Humphrey Corton is due to arrive and we must decide if we should ask to delay his visit.'

Hugh asked, 'Is there a suggestion that he may be a target, Olty?'

I looked towards Mervyn Tredinnick for an answer, and he responded immediately, his sing song Welsh lilt full of confidence.

'At least I have a bit of good news. You may not all be aware that we did receive reports some time back that Humphrey might have been fingered for a kidnap & ransom attempt but that threat has been discounted recently. I heard from my colleague, Royce Harrison, only this morning that the Cortons have just returned from a week's summer break in Crete where they arrested a local thought to have been behind this rumour. So now, my outfit in London, the VIP Protection Squad, is content with all arrangements as they stand, and Royce will get here with Humphrey on schedule - the 24th of September.'

In the lull which followed, Denzil Tremayne stood up and addressed me, 'Chairman, if I may be excused at this point, I need to start organising the detachment to move out to Rheina Blanca. They should be in place by this evening.' Whilst speaking, he looked down at Fergus for approval, but Carradine spread his hands in a clear message of "it's your call." I nodded at Denzil who picked up his tablet and made to leave the room. I was about to sum up, asking Bea to note the action points, when I noticed Helen raise her hand, so I invited her to speak.

'This is for you all', she began, 'but it's in support of the point just made by Mr Dundas because it's to do with the possibility that Lee van Troung is operating on his own and to his own agenda.

First, I need to ask how many of you are familiar with the *Omniverse*?' She looked around the company and saw that only Selina and Jess Jessop had raised a hand. Helen continued, 'Well look, briefly stated, the Omniverse is successor to the Metaverse which was invented and established in the early twenties. The Metaverse, you'll all remember, grew out of an ever more sophisticated Internet and in its most developed form provided the user with a three-dimensional experience within an entirely computer-generated environment. That's why they called it *Virtual*

Reality and it went to the extremes of allowing you to own land, build houses, trade in an invented, crypto currency.

Much more recently, *Meta* has morphed into *Omni* because this has added another dimension. In addition to a virtual world of vision, sound and ownership, you can now create your own senses of smell, taste and passions. As an *Avatar* or player in this make-believe world, you can, in privacy or in company, live a life in parallel to your human existence and no one can or need know anything about your unshared imaginings. In this capacity, the Omniverse has usurped the Dark Web, allowing people possessed by perversions to indulge their evil fantasies unchallenged and undetected.

Now, from what my brother had told me about his time with LvT, it would seem that the very latest technology is providing him with just the opportunity he has needed to escape from the real world into the fairy tale existence which permits and encourages his gross behaviour.

So …', Helen finished, 'I think it's possible that he has come here not to threaten, still less to invade, but simply to escape before he was found out.'

There was a short period of silence as her audience sought to digest this bombshell explanation, then Hugh asked her gently, 'could you tell us, Helen, a little more of the sort of behaviour of which you believe he is capable?'

'I could, yes, but I won't: at least not for the present. That information would be more accurate and better expressed coming from my brother and I think that his absence so far is explained by his extreme reluctance to give witness. But he must do so and without further delay, so I suggest we now redouble efforts to contact him.'

I wound the meeting up at that point and we agreed to get together again the following day, same time and place but hopefully including all the other members of the Panel. For now, it was agreed that I, with Helen, Mo and Arthur, would go in search of Edmund Ladoux.

And that's just what we did. But we couldn't find him.

Chapter Twenty-Four

The four of us left the Secretariat just after noon, I having delayed only to ask Pascal Brana to give the President an update. Once outside the building, we split up. Odinga and Baine went off to Police HQ to see if any fresh information had come in, from either and both of Century City and Rheina Blanca. Helen and I climbed into my official car which had appeared by magic with Jerome at the wheel. He explained as we set off that he had been summoned by Beatrice who told him that we would want to go first to Mr Ladoux's apartment, and she was right in that assumption. Lunchtime traffic was heavy, but we sat in silence for the twenty-minute journey to the rather shabby apartment block to which Edmund likes to retreat for his isolation and no doubt it gives him discretion for some of his seedier assignations.

There was no sign of him around, and no response to our repeated hammering on the door. I couldn't see his little car in the park either. We drove back into town, pausing briefly at The Club and then at a couple of bars which I know Edmund favours but he's not to be found and the staff in each place tell me that he hasn't been there today. Back in the car, Helen and I look at each other and she says wryly, 'Pretty obvious that he never intended to join the meeting this morning. Sala's hiding out and doesn't want us to find him.'

'Probably.' I said and then I asked, 'What sort of place would he choose, to be alone. With space and time to think?'

Without hesitation, Helen replied, 'Oh a beach, that's for sure. He was always out on the beach in Cox's Bazar.'

'Like outside my apartment?'

'No. Rainbow's too populated. Too busy for Sala.'

I leant forward to speak to Jerome, asking him to take us next out to the Golf Club which would give us access to the normally deserted and almost private Banana Beach. And at the extreme northern end of it, we found him or rather, what was left of him.

In deference to his established, fastidious style, the small pile of clothes was neatly folded. Suit trousers, jacket, plain white shirt, a deep maroon tie, black lace up shoes in one of which his wristwatch glinted in the afternoon sun. There were no underclothes.

Helen stood there for a long time, saying nothing but contemplating this sad bundle of a life. Finally, she found words.

'This was Sala', she said, 'that's obvious and I know he won't be coming back. When I was a little girl in Bangladesh and he took me onto the beach after a bad day, perhaps when he had been having an argument with our parents - and that happened often enough - he would say that when it all became too much, he would swim out up the track of the moon, as he put it, and not come home. That terrified me as he was not just my big brother but my guardian and guide. Sala was my sun and moon, so I would start to cry, and he would pick me up and comfort me, promising that it would never happen. But now it has.'

We stood side by side for a while, looking down on this sad remnant of a life, absorbed in our respective thoughts of a dependent childhood and an adult friendship. Each had meant much and now deserved mourning. Looking back, it's significant that neither Helen nor I were moved to summon help in a hope of finding him still alive. Instinctively, we both recognised the finality of the message he left with his neat pile of clothes. That was his statement of intent and there was to be no doubt as to how thoroughly he completed its execution. Helen remembered him as having been an exceptionally strong swimmer as a boy and he must have gone a long way out as the ocean never gave up his remains and nothing was ever found of him.

But Edmund left more than a suit and shirt behind. Helen had me drop her at No 23 as she wanted to be alone for that night. So, I didn't see her until the Panel resumed its crisis meeting the following morning but earlier, just after my dawn walk, she rang to say that she had found waiting in her apartment a letter from her brother Sala, delivered through the post box, composed in his pedantic style of English language and written in his careful, spidery hand. I never did see the letter, but she gave me the gist of it over the phone and enhanced this with more detail when we were able to be alone together later in the day. Evidently Edmund had supplied his sister with a lot of the history of how Lee van Troung had discovered him in Millennium about five years previously. It's still not clear how but probably it was a matter of pure chance with LvT monitoring international media and Edmund becoming quite high profile in his government work here. Anyway, finding him was one thing and that was followed by extreme pressure that he should provide help to Troung, help under many varied headings for his plans to leave Europe, abandon his job at UNHCR, seek to put down roots somewhere remote and south of Rheina Blanca, some hideaway in which he could have his cake and eat it, giving full rein to his aberrations whilst also participating in all the Omniverse has to offer. This insignificant looking man was, or rather is, capable of evil which knows no bounds. He orchestrated the pretty ridiculous youth vote fiasco with de Houlette but just for mischief and his own warped humour. He encouraged closer contacts between the Uyghur and Rohingya communities when his real purpose was to drive them further apart. Worst of all, he promised Edmund that he was creating a "cataclysmic disaster" which would forever expunge our new country's reputation, but he refused to specify what form this was to take. He threatened my friend with exposure of his past misdeeds during the years they spent together and the price of avoiding this fate was simply to do exactly what he was told.

I listened carefully to all Helen had to say, of course I did, and I did my very best to comfort her, but the truth is that we were mourning two different people - she a boy who had been her guide and comforter during childhood and early adolescence whereas I had lost a mature friend who had left us much too soon. Edmund was a man of exceptional quality with the promise of so much more to come in his lifetime. The tragedy of it for me was my conviction that if he had only shared his troubles and distress, I could have persuaded him to abandon his precipitate action. His death was suicide, that's for sure, but I've never been convinced that he meant to do what he did. I'll never know if I'm right.

The Panel Meeting reconvened the following morning. I started proceedings at 9am sharp, addressing the same attendees excepting Denzil Tremayne who was with his Reservists. I gave them the news although all had already heard it. There were comments of sympathy for Helen but not of understanding: none of us could offer that. She sat silent throughout, composed but tired and drawn. By ten o'clock we were through talking with the agreed conviction that we could do no more now than redouble the effort to locate and apprehend Lee van Troung. I undertook to circulate a summary Minute to all Panel members and to call a further crisis meeting as soon as there was more news to share. With this, we broke up and went our separate ways. I was relieved to overhear Helen tell Bea and Selina that she would remain in Century for the rest of the week, then returning to RB to resume work on establishing the university course. After that, she and I went home together.

The following day during our early morning beach walk, I asked Helen if she would let me read her brother's letter for myself. I was looking for any further nugget of information as to his motives and what caused him to take his own life. She had no difficulty with the principle of my request but by then it was too late. She had burnt it, determined to keep the best of him alive in her distant memories of childhood. She explained to me as we walked together, hand in hand,

'Most of what he wrote was sloppy stuff, Oliver, lovely and meaningful to me, but still sloppy: he addressed me as "*shishuke*" which means baby in our Bangla language and from that, I knew he was just turning the clock way back in his head as he rambled in reminiscences about our childhood days on that far away beach, writing about what was and what might have been, then going on to finish with some barely legible paragraphs about his pride in me and his shame that he had let me down. It distressed me and I knew that I didn't want to read it again. I just wanted to remember him as I had known him in another life all those years ago. But there was an enclosure in the envelope. I kept that and you can have it because it means nothing to me, and I doubt it's of any importance.'

Probably, she was quite right. When we got back to the apartment, Helen rummaged in her handbag and produced a single sheet of paper, a bit less than foolscap in size and by now rather grubby and creased. On one side of it, there was a pencilled drawing, quite faint and with a couple of corrections. It seemed to depict the outline of a vessel: not a ship but the sort of water pot you will see being carried on the head by people, particularly women, in parts of Africa and countries in Asia. Underneath the drawing were scrawled the words written in English by Edmund's crabbed hand which I recognised. "The promised land".

That was all there was to see. I gazed at it for some time but could make nothing of it. Finally, I put the piece of paper in a drawer of my desk, and we went through to sit on the balcony, watching in silence as the ocean rolled in.

Chapter Twenty-Five

During the next few days, I tried to get back to work, mostly from home but with two trips to the Secretariat. Helen spent some time in Edmund's suburban apartment, absorbed in the sad duty of going through the detritus of a life. No news came in regarding LvT or any other development. Then the weekend was upon us and on the Sunday morning, Helen flew down to RB, planning to stay for all the following week.

I spent a long Monday in the office, working late with Pascal and Bea but when Jerome dropped me home late that evening, something continued to nag at me, some recollection which I had trouble in pinning down until I recalled what President Valbuena had told me about her visit with Hector to London before Christmas and the conversation they had with Prosper Aguilas. Inspired by a thought, I rang the Dundas household and asked if I could arrange a visit to talk to Hugh. They offered me lunchtime on the following day, Tuesday, and with Helen away in RB, I was happy to accept. I was happier still on arrival to find that Alexa was with us and, at Hugh's initiative, Cogs Carradine.

Delilah met me at the door with her normal affectionate welcome and showed me into the sitting room. After warm greetings and some fruit-based cocktail, we had a very light lunch before settling over coffee in their covered veranda. It was a calm, mild day and the ocean was quiet.

'What's on your mind, Olty?', Hugh opened the conversation with a question which I recognised as carrying his insistence on a measured and articulate response.

'I'm still looking for motives,' I said, 'and I need some help.' Then I continued by telling them about the letter which Edmund had left behind for Helen. As I was speaking, Alexa poured coffee from the tray which Delilah had placed in front of her, and she started by passing to Hugh the mug of herbal tea which he favoured. As I was finishing, Alexa commented as she passed a cup of coffee to me, 'Poor Helen. I can understand her emotions in all of this.'

In the pause that followed, Fergus Carradine intervened to ask me, 'Olty, I appreciate that the fact and the manner of Ladoux's passing are upsetting but I don't see how they bear on the question of who or what may be threatening our national stability.'

Fergus had never much liked Edmund, probably because Carradine was fundamentally homophobic. Nevertheless, he was right to pull me up: I had asked for help, and rehearsing the circumstances of Edmund's death was not going to contribute.

'Sorry, Cogs,' I said, 'I've been straying off the point. The reason I'm asking for your thoughts arises from a conversation which the President had with Prosper Aguilas, head of UNHCR, when they met in London some months ago.'

Hugh Dundas put in immediately, 'I didn't know anything about that. Was this trip reported to the Panel?'

I shook my head. 'Nor did I at the time, Hugh. It was a private, personal visit made by the Valbuenas just before Christmas and was for only a couple of days, principally for them to spend a short time with the Prime Minister and his wife, also to meet young Humphrey ahead of his visit to us here in Millennium and his course at our university.'

'But surely, Olty, that's still Government business. Why weren't we at least kept informed?'

This conversation was not going well. I could sense agreement with the sentiment from Alexa as she cleared her throat and from Fergus as he noisily returned his cup to its saucer. I needed to move on with my response.

'Point taken, Hugh, but I had no prior warning, and I was at that time myself in England following my mother's death. Anyway, it seems that our President has been a close friend of Mr Aguilas' wife Agnes since childhood days in Madrid and they were concerned to talk about Melissa Valbuena, who is a godchild of Mrs Aguilas and was for a while apparently falling under the influence of that Luc de Houlette who, you will recall, was a concern to us all back then. The two couples met by arrangement, stayed in the same London West End hotel and talked of family matters. After that, conversation between them turned to world politics and the global refugee crisis which, it was agreed, is both growing and apparently incapable of resolution. According to Laetitia Valbuena, Aguilas acknowledged that his Agency's most pressing problems revolve around the Uyghurs and the persecution they suffer at the hands of the Chinese, secondly the Rohingyas who have been and continue to be tormented by the military government in Myanmar.'

Alexa broke in here to ask, 'Is the UNHCR worried about the populations of both origins who have come to live here in Millennium?'

I turned to look at her as I replied. 'Yes, they are, but specifically their concern is that almost all the immigrants to our shores of either background choose to settle in Rheina Blanca and nowhere else in the country, yet, generally speaking, they keep to themselves and don't mix.'

'Not with each other or not with anyone?' Alexa persisted.

'Look,' I said, 'we don't have anything like what you could call ghettoes - not anywhere in Millennium, including RB, but at the same time it's undeniably the case that throughout the city, you'll find areas or suburbs in which almost the entire cast of inhabitants are Uyghur in origin, other places where they all seem to be Rohingyas. And on the rare occasions when they mix, they tolerate each other but they don't bond.'

'Olty,' remarked Fergus as he steepled his fingers together in a gesture which I recognised as a defining habit, 'are you saying that in Rheina Blanca - but nowhere else in the country - there is some threat of violent discord between sections of the populous, even the possibility that one faction will try to evict another?'

'There are two points there, Fergus,' I replied. 'First, it's true to say that this whole matter is, for us, concentrated in just one place. In no other Province, city or town throughout Millennium do we have this separation and possible clash of cultures and background. The problem, if it is that, is exclusive to Rheina Blanca.

But that's not unusual. In the UK, the first immigrants from the Caribbean all tended to settle in the same place, even more the case for arrivals from the Indian sub-continent. And of course, from Africa. Check out where in England the majority who were expelled from Uganda so many years ago ended up.'

'The same goes for the States,' put in Alexa. 'You must be old like me to remember it, but the famous old musical "West Side Story" proves the point. Sorry, Olty, I'm interrupting!'

'And frankly, Cogs, no I don't think there's a risk of fracture along tribal lines or provenance. That's mostly because the two groups have such different agendas. The Uyghurs, even those now securely established here, are forever looking back over their shoulders at the Chinese who persecuted them so cruelly and for so long, essentially trying to deny their very existence. That's why Prosper Aguilas sums up their psychological problem in one word. RACE. They believe that despite all the continuous pressure to be subsumed as an integral part of the Chinese multitude, they stand apart with their own distinct character, language and history. They are, in their own right, a People, ... a RACE.

'For the Rohingyas, it's different but similar. They too have been abused and bullied, but also banished. They've been told not just that they aren't wanted but that they simply don't exist, so in Aguilas speak, they've been denied GRACE.'

You've all heard something of the apparent difficulty in influencing these disparate peoples towards greater integration and at least there is more encouraging news here. The initiative, suggested by Helen Priest and now being driven forward by Police Chief Arthur Baine's wife Selina to establish a new university in Rheina Blanca, does look promising. It's as yet in its infancy but the amount of interest and enthusiasm so far exceeds all that we had hoped to see and seems to be drawing together not just potential students from both communities but, significantly, representatives of a younger generation who are not in thrall to the prejudices of their parents and grandparents.

I broke off at that to finish my cold coffee and to wonder briefly what reaction I might have provoked. It came swiftly. Hugh passed a hand over his face in what struck me as a weary gesture. I knew that he and Alexa were in the reasonable habit of taking a nap in the afternoon and I was conscious that this conversation should not extend to the point of taxing his energy too far. But his voice was clear and firm as he pointed a finger gently towards me and enquired,

'I do recognise the talents and experience of Ms Priest but equally, we have to bear in mind that she's an employee of the United Nations and not a citizen of Millennium. But tell me, Olty, what do your subordinate colleagues have to say?'

'Commissioner Odinga and the RB Police Chief Arthur Baine are agreed that there is no current risk of anything approaching civil unrest down there, but they do retain considerable concern about the identity and activity of the giant Uzbek fellow, of whom you heard Distance Okuyu make mention at our Meeting.'

Now Alexa came back, saying with a wry smile, 'so to keep the rhyme going, we now need a name to put to the *Face*!'

'Oh, very good, Alexa, 'I chuckled with her. 'I like that and you're not far out but the word used by Prosper Aguilas when he was telling the Valbuena's about the third group of refugees which is causing him so much worry is SPACE. His anxiety centres on the entire nation of Bangladesh, a sovereign state which has a huge and growing population, yet further swelled by the tide of Rohingya escapees from Myanmar, and an insufficient land mass to provide for them all, especially because too much of it is subject to extreme weather conditions which result in flooding and the destruction of foodstuff crops.'

'We don't have a large number of immigrants from Bangladesh, do we?' enquired Fergus.

'No, we don't,' I responded, 'and ironically, those that are here are established right across our country: you find Bangladeshis in almost all our Provinces, more often than not working in some area of agriculture.'

'So, what's the significance of this to our conversation here this afternoon?'

'It concerns Edmund. I have a theory about the underlying motivation for his suicide and I want to bounce that off you because it might relate to the problem we're grappling with.'

'Then let's hear it'. Hugh's interdiction was immediate.

'OK.' I took a breath and began my summary. I wanted to keep it succinct, which is Hugh's way, but still complete.

'Edmund, and his sister now known to us all as Helen Priest, did not start life in Somalia. Both were born in Cox's Bazar, Bangladesh. When Edmund was a young teenager and Helen little more than a baby, their parents took them to Mogadishu at the instigation of a man whom we may call a warlord.

'Somalia?', Fergus interjected with emphasis, 'at the end of the last century. *Really?*'

'Yes, really Cogs,' I answered him, 'amazing but true.'

'Keep going, Olty', Hugh instructed, I want to hear where you're going with this.'

I continued, 'This little family of four - there had been other children but none had survived infancy - in effect had voluntarily bound themselves over into slavery. They entered this man's huge compound on the outskirts of Mogadishu and started on a life of complete subjugation, being fed, watered and housed but nevertheless denied all freedom of movement, expression and choice. Edmund would have been then about eight or nine, Helen no more than four. About ten years later, their lives were changed again amidst great drama. Their slave master, known as Toto, was deposed by a rival warlord who orchestrated a violent attack on the compound which had become home for them. A savage bomb blast destroyed the entire building in which all four members of the family were located at the time. The parents died at the scene, along with many others including Toto himself. Helen was undergoing physical abuse but survived with life changing injuries.'

'You mean she was being raped?', Alexa demanded to know.

'Worse, really. They had just started FGM on her.'

'Oh Jesus, that's bestial', said Alexa in almost a whisper as she lapsed into a shocked silence.

I went on. 'Helen survived, if only just. She was rescued by one of the assailants, whose real name she never discovered. He got her out of the collapsed building and away out to sea on his pirate boat. She imagined that her brother Sala, who we all knew as Edmund, had been killed in the blast. After a rough journey, the boat tied up in Aden where the pirate left Helen, telling her to seek refuge in a refugee camp. Some time later, she was discovered there by a volunteer nurse called Melanie Priest who, with her husband Bill, took Helen to their heart. They cared for her, protected her and eventually smuggled her into the USA, where she became an American citizen - a schoolgirl, then a university student, finally an up-and-coming employee of the United Nations, in which capacity she came to us here in Millennium. Finding her brother still alive and living among us in some prominence was a huge shock to both of them, however welcome.'

'So why didn't Edmund tell us?', Fergus wanted to know. 'Why did he kill himself?'

'I agree, Olty,' said Hugh, 'What more can you tell us?'

'Obviously, I'm guessing here, 'I replied, looking at all three of them in turn, 'Edmund said nothing to me and although he left a note for his sister, I didn't see it. But the circumstances bring me back to that theory of Prosper Aguilas. You'll remember that he spoke to the President of Race for the Uighurs, Grace for the Rohingyas and Space for the Bangladeshis?'

They nodded at me in unison as I continued. 'Edmund Ladoux, the man, and Sala, the boy/youth cared deeply for the land of his birth and the desperate circumstances of so many millions of his countrymen who labour in squalor to sustain a life of limited quantity and practically zero quality.

And all because they don't have enough room - hardly to survive and certainly not to improve.

I can tell you - but at another time, I suggest - how Edmund survived the attack in Mogadishu, how he kept himself alive in the weeks afterwards, how and where he travelled and sustained himself during the following years, most significantly, how he came to fall under the enduring influence of Lee van Troung who is the malign character in all of this. Because, you see, it's my belief that the reason he took his own life was simple disappointment. I'm convinced that all the puzzles we've been trying to solve - the torching of the *Dawn,* the mobilising of young people over the voting age business, the random robberies around the city which have perplexed Mo Odinga - all these had Edmund in the background, planning, cajoling, encouraging. On top of that, when I asked for his opinion over a lunch months ago, he suggested that I consider if some person or outfit was intent on mounting a coup. He even had the cheek to point a bit of a finger at Mad Max Merrick: he must have been laughing up his sleeve at me all the while.'

'So, Olty,' Hugh was determined to keep me focussed, 'if all those things were just distractions, what's your theory on the real agenda?'

I paused for a moment before looking him in the eye as I replied, 'Honestly, Hugh, I don't believe there is an agenda. I've come to believe that we've all been jumping at shadows, that there is no grand plan lying in wait to threaten us in Millennium. But there is a bit more to say in support of this theory.'

'Then let's hear it.' Hugh's scepticism was apparent: Fergus was looking down at his steepled hands: Alexa remained silent but looking doubtful.

'Hugh,' I said, 'you'll remember well that twenty odd years back, there was much talk around the world about the Chinese land grab in Africa?'

He nodded and I continued, 'it's true that China put people on the ground and invested small fortunes to acquire political influence across this continent - God knows we had them trying to trample their way in here, didn't we? But what's much less recognised is how the Indian sub-continent has been buying its way into Africa over the last ten or twelve years.'

'Olty's right about that,' Fergus contributed, 'India started it years ago, just after we got here, so in '04 and '05, using state money to buy land in what used to be in the middle of the twentieth century the East African Federation - so today Kenya, Tanzania and Uganda. Delhi acquired the properties through nominees and used the food produce to help sustain their own mushrooming population at home. It's still happening today and what they don't keep for themselves is sold at very useful profit to the markets of Europe and the States, daily plane loads of cut flowers and the like. Later, they moved into less attractive country, even parts of southern Sudan. A decade or so afterwards, Pakistan embarked on a similar strategy but concentrated on the Sahel and former francophone countries in West Africa and even areas of Zaire despite the risks of local conflict and very hard operating conditions.'

'Very instructive, Fergus,' Hugh broke in with his fingers steepled together again, determined to keep us concentrated, 'and interesting, but let's stay with the current conundrum.' Then, turning to face me again, his question, 'where does this lead you, Olty?'

To answer, I handed to each of them a copy of the insignificant looking piece of paper which had been enclosed with the letter left for Helen by her brother.

'I almost discarded this', I told them, 'I could make nothing of it. But then I thought that Edmund couldn't have stuck it in the envelope by chance, not on a whim. It had to have some meaning, so I kept staring at it from every angle and suddenly it hit me. We're looking at a crude map here and it's a rough depiction of the ranching land in our central highlands. This is the property here in Millennium built up by Kane Merrick and now owned by him and his family.'

They were all silent as they studied the drawing. Then Alexa was the first to respond, furrowing her brow and squinting through her spectacles as she said, 'Yes, I can see it now. It looks like an African water pot, but it could indeed be a map, showing the deep, wide belly of the Merrick land … and there at the top it narrows to the spout which is that dam they constructed in the north of their property.'

Now Hugh and Fergus were both nodding their agreement as I went on, 'I didn't copy the other side but on the reverse of the original are written just these three words, "The promised land."

I waved this in front of all three of my audience as I continued, 'The writing is definitely Edmund's and my theory of what he meant by it is this. Helen has recorded all he told her about his meanderings across the north of Africa following his escape from the compound in Mogadishu. He had time and the inclination to share all the detail with her during their conversations at her apartment in No 23. So, she knows and can recite from memory the where and roughly when her brother went but particularly how he came to meet Lee van Troung for the first time in a travellers' hostel in Tunis. And after that, how he fell progressively further under Troung's evil influence as they went on together, moving through more countries in Africa, always sponging off the UN infrastructure, until LvT's whimsical leadership encouraged them to swap continents and saw them settle in Port au Prince, Haiti. It was from here that her brother finally broke loose, sickened by Troung's literally murderous aberration and Edmund went on, stealing the identity by which we knew him, to educate himself in the USA and to establish the lifestyle which he relinquished to come and join us in Millennium.'

I paused here and glanced around my audience of three before resuming with my conclusion.

'I don't know quite how or when Lee van Troung found him here and nor does Helen, but it seems certain that the old compulsion reasserted itself. Whatever LvT wanted, our Edmund would do his best to provide. And why? Simply because he was trusting in a promise which was probably vague and certainly without structure or logic, but it centred on the assumption that Troung was going to take control of our country, or at least a large part of it, following which Edmund was to be gifted as his reward the means of fulfilling his heart's aspiration which was always to resettle his childhood's community, bringing a new life to the droves of have-nots and dispossessed amongst whom he had started his own deprived life in Cox's Bazar, Bangladesh.

We will never understand how the Edmund we all knew - that cultured, deep thinking, intelligent man - could allow himself to be so deluded, but we have none of us lived through such an upbringing as he experienced, nor been exposed to such damaging pressures.

And as for Lee van Troung? He must be a pronounced schizophrenic, a Jekyll and Hyde, capable of considerable achievement in his professional work for the United Nations whilst at the same time immersed in a dark world of complete make believe. He must, in my view, be found and exterminated or at least confined for life. But I don't believe he represents a real threat, except in his own twisted mind.'

I could see immediately that the three of them were inclined to accept my analysis but typically, it was Hugh Dundas who put his finger on the point, saying, 'but we must still worry about to whom else he has made a promise.'

Very shortly after that, we broke up. Fergus said that he wanted a walk on the beach, and I went home, happy to leave Hugh and Alexa to their afternoon siesta.

I felt buoyed up by the conversation and its conclusion, so much so that I drove myself to the airport at the end of that week on the Friday evening to meet Helen off the last flight of the day from Rheina Blanca and we stopped for a light supper on the way back so I could talk her through every detail of my analysis and the ensuing discussion. She was relieved at the outcome but had one reservation.

'You're right in what you worked out, Oliver, I'm quite sure of that. But we still need to find LvT. I won't be able to rest easy while he's still unaccounted for.'

I nodded my agreement. 'I know that, and I understand. We must widen the net and I'm going to start by convening a full Panel Meeting just as soon as it can be arranged. We need all the help we can get.'

We then spent a blissfully relaxed weekend, hardly stirring out of the apartment before Jerome collected us both early on the Monday morning and dropped me at the Secretariat before going on to the airport for Helen to fly down to RB. She was bubbling with excitement at the prospect of completing plans for the university.

Chapter Twenty-Six

Here in Century, the full Panel could not be assembled before the Thursday of that week, which was the 25th of September. All those who had attended the first emergency meeting were present and in place for 9am that morning, plus also Constance Demidenko who was responsible to the Panel for Development, a fairly general title which covers a wide range of topics and initiatives and also Prudence Dan, born in Singapore and now carrying the Panel Portfolio for Education. She had been much involved with Helen in pushing forward with establishing the university course in Rheina Blanca. The only Panel Member still missing was Cyril Ramaposa, a native of Botswana in charge of the Resources brief, but I wasn't expecting him as I knew him to be still recovering from open heart surgery and unable to fly in from Rhino Province in the Southwest.

I opened the meeting with a full summary of the background and a reminder of where we had left matters at the conclusion of our first session. Then I went on to report the tragic death of Edmund Ladoux, providing further information on what we now knew to be his background, his relationship to Helen Priest and his close connections with Lee van Troung.

At this point, I laid out before my audience my own theory of what had been taking place, making clear that I had already shared this perception with Hugh, Alexa and Fergus Carradine. I was looking at Hugh as I announced that they were inclined to accept my proposition and was grateful that he both nodded and voiced his agreement.

Then I told them all, 'Yesterday evening, I gave a full brief to the President, and she is going to join us this morning to give you her own view on the single matter which is the subject of our meeting now.'

The planned timing worked out well. It was then approaching 9.30 and right on cue, Pascal Brana opened the double doors to allow Laeticia Valbuena to enter. She walked up to take her position at the head of the table, and I stood aside, moving around to my left to take the chair which had been occupied by Denzil Tremayne before his departure for Rheina Blanca. The President remained on her feet to address us.

'Thank you all for being here this morning,' she began, bestowing a warm smile on us all, 'Olty has talked me through our current circumstances in great detail. There is nothing I can add to that except to say that I have been as baffled as everyone else by the strange events of the last few months. The fire on the *Dawn,* the activities of the suspect priest ... and I don't mean you, Helen.' That drew a polite chuckle from her audience as she resumed.

'Then we have had a bit of student unrest, rather random robberies throughout Century, diverged communities in Rheina Blanca although that is not a new phenomenon like the other happenings, unexplained and unexpected visits from Geneva, finally, most recently and tragically, the death by his own hand of our much loved and valued Edmund Ladoux.

I do understand why most of us have, both individually and collectively, sought to find an explanation which also provides a link to bind together these apparently unconnected episodes. But I'm now personally convinced that there really isn't one and I have accepted Olty's rationale which I know he has already shared with you. It's comforting to know that Hugh, also, is in accord.

That said, we must now do everything we can to locate and detain this man Troung. We no longer suspect him of plotting to disrupt Millennium, but he remains a liability. He's now the subject of an International Search Warrant and we can be certain that he's hiding himself somewhere within our borders. I look to you, Mo,' and she emphasised her instruction by pointing at Odinga who braced himself in his chair and bowed his head in acknowledgement, 'I look to you to lead our charge in this. You have the authority now to use all and every one of our resources to track him down. We need him in custody as a matter of the greatest urgency.'

The President paused here and looked around all of us before she proceeded.

'Now to conclude, we really must move on. Our country has some great opportunities in prospect, and I don't want us to stint in effort to make the most of them. It's now certain that Millennium will be invited to host the Commonwealth Heads of Government Conference in 2037 and if that goes well, I believe we can expect a State Visit before the end of the decade. These events will cement our position as the leading light of Africa, and I'm committed to doing all I can during the remainder of my time in Office to make sure they happen. And before any of that, indeed in the immediate future, we have the educational visit of the British Prime Minister's son, Humphrey, who is due to arrive in about two weeks' time, so that should now be our focus. So, thank you for your time this morning and let's now all pull together.'

The President didn't invite comment or questions. Having issued instructions and a clarion call, she turned on her heel and left us.

There was little more to be said and within five minutes, I had closed the Panel Meeting. I saw Helen leave the room with Bea and Selina, while I adjourned to my office accompanied by Mo Odinga and Arthur Baine. We spent a couple of hours together, brainstorming how we could get more feet on the ground in the hunt for LvT. My own gut feel said that he wouldn't now be found within the city limits of RB, that he was much more likely to have found some point of refuge in remote countryside – and there was plenty of that down there. Arthur disagreed, quoting the old adage of *where do you hide a tree?* Answer, *in a forest.* Mo Odinga told us that we had to look everywhere and tasked Arthur with making sure that all his officers and all the Militia Reservists now deployed down there under Denzil Tremayne had a photograph of van Troung and were, between them all, visiting every house and farm, every office and factory, boarding public transport, stopping people in the street and at roadblocks, asking everyone in the hope of getting a lead.At Arthur Baine's suggestion, we finished by doubling the manhunt and adding the big Uzbek as a person wanted for questioning. We didn't have a photograph, but Arthur had a clear vision of the guy he had seen collecting de Houlette from the Town Hall months earlier and his sheer size might well jog memories. We knew his vehicle – the black pick up – and even had its registration number although it was likely to have been changed long since. As Arthur reasoned, finding the Uzbek could well lead to finding our main target and he went off to work with a police artist in creating a drawing which could be circulated amongst our searchers.

My working day ended with a huge headache but the consciousness that I could do no more now but wait for news. So, I swept up Helen who was still cloistered with Bea and we went together home to Rainbow Beach. I felt very grateful to the President. She had made a good job of a precise and concise summary of how matters stood. She had been quite clear in how she wanted us to proceed. Above all, she had taken the responsibility and I admired her for that.

Chapter Twenty-Seven

Helen remained in Century for the following day, returning to RB on the Sunday evening. I went with her, thinking I would likely be of more help to Arthur there than by staying in the Secretariat. I was impressed by the work that Denzil Tremayne had been doing. He had caused to be produced a huge map which covered all of one wall in Arthur Baine's spacious office at Police HQ in Rheina Blanca. The map detailed all the buildings in the metropolitan area, showing every house in every street, even bus stops and gardeners' sheds in the parks. Outside the city, it extended over a radius of forty kilometres, noting every farm and agricultural building, every rural house and place of business. To complement this, Denzil had designed a rolling report which was being constantly updated in real time to show which of his team had visited which property in town or country and when. This degree of thorough surveillance really encouraged me, and I returned to Century full of optimism that we were on the verge of a breakthrough. I had been conferring with Mo Odinga every day and reporting by phone to the President each morning. All of us just kept going.

I could hardly believe that at the end of that week, we had nothing to show for our efforts. There was not a trace of Lee van Troung and by then Denzil's teams had been round the entire course twice and had even visited some places on three separate occasions – all without result. The man had vanished off the face of the globe. There had been one promising sighting of the Uzbek, in a shopping mall in the middle of Mbwenye but the target turned out to be a perfectly legitimate American citizen, an oil man from Alabama on a contract for six months at our oil shipping terminal. He was the right size for the Uzbek but spoke the wrong language in the wrong accent. We weren't really looking out for him but there was no sign either of the priest, de Houlette.

By then, the date was 3rd October and other pressing matters were starting to impact the search mission. The new University of Rheina Blanca opened its doors for the first time on the 8th of the month, a Wednesday. The timing was later than foreseen, but the delay was inevitable given the other pressures. The President flew down from Century for the day to lend weight and give a blessing to the project. She gave a short and well-judged address of welcome before handing over to the Principal to greet the first students. There were only twelve for that opening term and they stood in a self-conscious group, but their smiles and the cheers of their families and friends were more than enough to prove the value of this initiative as I stood to one side, beaming my own pride at Helen's accomplishment.

Then, early in the following week, Humphrey Corton arrived from London on a normal direct flight, accompanied by his personal protection officer in the person of Royce Harrison. In a deliberately low-key event, President Valbuena met him at Century City's Heaven International Airport and took him straight to Millennium House, her own official residence where he was to spend the next few days acclimatising himself and seeing something of the city, particularly the Century University Campus and the accommodation into which he would be moving at the start of the academic year. Before that, he would travel to RB with the President and would there receive an official welcome to our country, at the same time inspecting the Diving Club and its impressive facilities where he was expected to spend a considerable amount of time during his time with us. The date for that occasion was set for Thursday 30th October, and I flew down the evening before to spend the night discreetly with Helen in the hotel, then to be on hand to assist the President as might be required.

That Thursday dawned in a blaze of Spring sunshine which promised a perfect day for the occasion. Shortly after 6am, I rode out to the Diving Club in a Police car, accompanied by Arthur Baine. On arrival, we were met by Alexander Chivengo, an immigrant born in Russia who had been managing and developing the Club over a period of nearly ten years. Alexander is very well regarded and on this auspicious day, he was obviously highly charged but took trouble to show us over the interior of the new Club building which had been completed only two months previously. Then we moved outside to inspect the arrangements for the official opening.

Jack Kirchoff was, as always, in charge of our ceremonial. We greeted each other warmly and he showed me how he had struck a fine balance for this occasion between the grandiose and the informal. On the broad green grass sward in front of the Diving Club building, a dais had been erected and on this was placed a simple podium. The tarmac approach drive from the main road divided about a hundred metres short of the Club Entrance, one arm leading to a spacious car park. Jack told me he was expecting about two hundred spectators, most arriving in their own vehicles but there were to be several buses. In front and to one side of the building, an area had been cordoned off so that onlookers could stand behind for a full view of the proceedings. Next to the dais, the military band, which is a unit under the command of Denzil Tremayne, would be stationed. The musicians had already arrived and were starting to set up their positions as we watched. Club staff in their distinctively coloured track suits were busy sweeping and tidying. There was a general hum of activity and anticipation, yet still another five hours before we were due to start, however Jack told me that the band wanted time to practice, and the audio system had to be tested. He was busy with detail, so I left him to it and Arthur's driver drove me back to the hotel to shower, shave, breakfast and change. It was seven am.

Chapter Twenty-Eight

Four hours later, I was back again, now in my official car and driven by Jerome who had brought it down from Century the previous day. I was accompanied by both Helen and Beatrice in the rear seats while I rode up front. We were all togged up for the occasion, Helen in a silk trouser suit of powder blue which approximated UN colours and set off by a wide brimmed dark grey hat. She looked very glamorous, and I told her so. There was time for her and Bea to take in the setting and to peer inside the entrance to the new building before we were escorted to our seats by one of Jack Kirchoff's team.

It was then some time after eleven and the ceremony was set for twelve noon, so we had the opportunity to look around us. In front, some hundred metres away, the new building looked down on the crowd which had already formed behind the heavy rope barricade and was being swelled by fresh arrivals with every passing minute. Children were being pushed gently forward up to the rope so they could have an uninterrupted view and at one point, a collection of wheelchairs for disabled visitors was marshalled. There were quite a number, so they formed two or three rows. A subdued chatter of excited anticipation ran through the growing crowd of spectators. At regular intervals, a uniformed member of Denzil Tremayne's Reservists stood facing the onlookers.

The dais was an oblong platform, raised up and approached by steps on both its shorter sides. At its front centre stood the speaker's podium which carried two microphones and between them, an autocue screen. Behind the podium were ranged three large and ornate chairs, one each for the President, her husband and Bishop Moses Chirungu who would close proceedings with a Prayer of Blessing. I had already urged him not to expand this into an impromptu sermon. There had been some debate amongst us as to whether Humphrey should remain on the dais after he had delivered his words, but we had been firmly advised by Mervyn Tredinnick and supported by Royce Harrison that his father, Prime Minister Edward Corton, was emphatic that this would be overplaying his hand, so we did as we were told.

On either side of the platform in an extended horseshoe shape were arranged comfortable but less imposing chairs, facing the crowd of onlookers. To the right, these would be occupied by Members of the Panel – which would turn out in full force today – plus a place for Hugh Dundas who had been regarded as Father of the Nation ever since the death twenty years ago of my grandfather, David Heaven. On the other side, there were seats for the lesser brethren: local and national dignitaries including the Mayor of Rheina Blanca, Arthur Baine as Police Chief, also Mo Odinga and others from Century City plus a few from further afield. I was included in this group and had managed to arrange for Helen to be near me.

We took our seats which were identified by a tastefully printed programme of events, headed by the date, Thursday, 30th October 2036, and the name of the occupant. Mo Odinga was to my right, immediately next to the presentation dais, to my left, chairs for Royce Harrison, then Humphrey, then Arthur Baine and beside him Selina with her sister Beatrice Kebir next to her and then Helen. The platform loomed over us so that I couldn't see to the other side of it but sensed that Panel Members were assembled and seating themselves. Mo whispered to me that Hugh Dundas had arrived the previous evening unaccompanied by Alexa who had decided against making the tiring journey down from Century.

Jack Kirchhoff patrolled behind us, ceaselessly checking for details and Mervyn Tredinnick stood like a statue behind Odinga's chair, his eyes sweeping over the scene. The sun shone, the light breeze played with the national flag mounted on the diving club building, the band played melodiously. As far as I could tell from my position, all was in place, and we were good to go.

I glanced at my watch: about five minutes to twelve noon and on cue, the band struck up with our National Anthem as the Presidential Limo turned off the main road onto the access drive to the Club. From my chair, I couldn't see inside at this distance and through the armoured glass, but I knew that the President, her husband Hector and Humphrey Corton would be in the back seats with Royce Harrison riding alongside the driver, Sam Hodgson.

Sam is a native of Solihull in the UK and arrived in Millennium with the car, a stretched body Range Rover, now over twenty years old which had been pensioned off from the Royal Mews by King William shortly after his accession on account of its unsuitable petrol power and we had grabbed the opportunity to buy it for a modest price. It still looked magnificent in its deep maroon colour, worth every penny for such an occasion as this, even if it had guzzled a fair few litres just getting here from the airport.

Sam brought the car to a stately halt outside the building and Royce hopped out to open a rear door. The President emerged first, followed by Humphrey and Hector Valbuena. We all stood as the band played again the National Anthem. The crowd fell silent, the wheelchair brigade motionless and the line of watching reservists at attention.

Alexander Chivengo and Jack Kirchoff stepped forward with a formal greeting, then Jack led the party across the grass to the dais. Humphrey was looking around with a lively interest. He was a little above average height, quite a stocky build, sensibly dressed in grey trousers with a well-cut blue blazer. He held himself erect and seemed relaxed as he exchanged a few words with Alexander.

We remained standing as they reached the steps and climbed the few steps to the platform. The President led the way and Humphrey held back to allow Hector to follow her before he ascended and stood at her side as she started to speak. The cameras and microphones of the International Press were rolling. As we had anticipated, there was plenty of global interest in this event. Laetitia Valbuena spoke with her accustomed fluency, without hesitation and without notes. She held attention without prolonging formality. Her message was one of warm welcome to Humphrey Corton but she managed to garnish it with a reinforcement of Millennium's standing in the world, our standards, accomplishments and aspirations. I had formulated a good part of this brief speech and was pleased with the way it sounded. Then it was Humphrey's turn.

He stepped to the lectern and said his piece. It was well judged and well delivered. He didn't say much, but he didn't need to: he covered all the right bases - thanks to the President for her welcome, how much he was looking forward to his time at our University, also to participating in events here in RB at this "magnificent new diving club". Above all during his time here, he would enjoy meeting the people of Millennium. He spoke in a strong, clear voice and unusually for an eighteen year old, he didn't hurry. I was sure I would not be alone in being favourably impressed.

Humphrey finished, gave a polite nod to the President and skipped down the steps from the podium. He walked confidently to his chair between Royce and Arthur Baine. I bent forward to reach across Royce with a handshake of congratulation. That's when my world changed forever.

Even now, at a distance of over fifteen years, the trauma of the following few minutes is so imbedded in my memory that my instant perceptions replay in my mind like a constant film sequence which I would like to erase, but never will.

I sense a commotion in the crowd and whip my head back to look.

The wheelchairs of the disabled are being disrupted. There is shouting amongst the spectators.

Two rows in, a man stands up from his wheelchair. He doesn't need it. He's fully functional. He's huge. He must be the Uzbek. He's fooled us. Where do you hide a tree?

He pushes forward, scattering wheelchairs around him, overturning one. Cries of alarm and protest. He jumps the rope cordon, sweeping aside a girl Reservist who raises her hand to him.

The Uzbek is running at us, arms punching, legs like pistons. He's a terrifying sight, made more threatening by the balaclava which covers most of his face.

There's a crunching, cracking explosion to my right. Mo Odinga slumps in his chair. I look up at the podium but can't see it through enveloping smoke.

Royce Harrison dives to his left. Is he attacking young Humphrey? Is he in this too?

I spring to my feet, staggering with a sudden pain in my leg. I hear a noise like a swarm of bees buzzing past my head.

Mervyn Tredinnick steps past me, coming from behind our row of chairs.

The huge guy is now almost upon us. He's brandishing some sort of sword - a weapon anyway and I see the sun glint on its blade. His eyes from behind the mask burn with fury.

Past me, he overruns Royce prone on the ground and his big feet in their trainers slip as he turns. He charges again, screaming in passion and in front of him now stands Mervyn, rock still, legs apart, arms outstretched, weapon in both hands. There's no hesitation. Tredinnick fires twice and the big Uzbek collapses backwards, splayed out as if crucified. I can see the hole in his balaclava, right between his eyes. The earth seems to shudder with the impact of his body.

Mervyn Tredinnick steps round him, gun in one hand while the other grabs at Royce Harrison's collar. He heaves him away to reveal Humphrey who immediately struggles to his feet, gulping and trembling in shock as tears course down his young face. He's apparently unharmed, at least in body.

The immediate aftermath lasts several hours, the full enquiry as many months. We were fortunate to have suffered only three fatalities: the Uzbek, of course, Royce Harrison and most significantly, President Laetitia Valbuena.

After Humphrey's few words on the podium, she had stepped forward to the microphone to speak further about the Diving Club and to declare the new building officially open. The bomb exploded immediately beneath her feet and eviscerated her lower body with devastating effect. Then there were serious injuries to others. The President's husband, Hector, was saved by being blown backwards off the podium, breaking an arm, a leg and several ribs as he hit the ground. At my side, Maurice Odinga was blasted by the contents of the bomb.

It was filled with ball bearings and some rusty nails as well as the explosive, so Mo bled extensively over his best dress uniform. I couldn't see him from my position, so found out only later that Hugh Dundas, seated at the extreme end of the row of Panel Members on the other side of the podium, was so shaken by the blast that he suffered a mild stroke which was to leave him with a shuffle and slight speech impediment for the short remainder of his life. Helen, just a few chairs away from me, was extraordinarily calm and was occupying herself with bringing some comfort to Humphrey until she saw me clutching at my leg and came over to give me a hug.

Noise and activity were everywhere around us. I was impressed by Denzil Tremayne, signalling forward the ambulance which had been stationed behind the crowd and simultaneously using his *sese* to call for more from the city hospital. Then instructing his girl sergeant, his second in command, to organise the body of Reservists to start moving the body of onlookers away and back towards their cars and buses in the parking area. Jack Kirchoff wandered past me in a daze of shock.

Mervyn Tredinnick upturned a chair to place it over Royce Harrison. I was to find out later that he had been hit in the back of the head by a fusillade of the ball bearings. Royce had moved with lightening speed to provide the protection which was his profession and had paid for it with his life, snuffed out in an instant.

The remains of the podium were scattered over the grass. I tried to move behind the debris to see the state of the

Panel Members and found myself limping painfully. It wasn't serious but my leg was bleeding, my trousers torn by one or two of those ball bearing bullets which had made the sound which I had heard as buzzing bees.

I felt a guilt then which has never left me. I had reviewed the evidence and decided that we didn't face a threat from Lee van Troung. I had been wrong and Hugh Dundas right. Danger had been lurking in his wild promises - not just to Edmund but also to this unnamed Uzbek.

Shock can take effect to reflect the character and there were examples before me. Kane Merrick was stomping around, swearing quietly and looking for a target to punch. Jess Jessop was still in her chair, head bowed and scribbling on the back of her programme. Ken Sanchez bustled to and fro, Fergus Carradine stood, gesticulating as he talked to Denzil Tremayne. Between them, they had moved fast. An ambulance was already standing there with doors open as the crew started to load Hector Valbuena and there was a plain panel van next to the groundsheet which covered the remains of our President. It distressed me to see her handbag lying there, white but discoloured by streaks of blood.

I stood there for a minute, surveying the scene of devastation and tragedy before limping back to my original position. Two Paramedics were treating Mo Odinga and further away, the young teenager was seated in his chair, hands clasped together in his lap, shoulders shaking and tears coursing down his face. Mervyn Tredinnick took a firm grip on my arm and spoke quietly as we stood together.

'Olty, I need to get Humphrey out of here. I'm going to commandeer the Presidential car - that Range Rover along with its driver. We'll drive through the night to get back to Century without stopping except for fuel. Plus, we need to leaven the mixture of company for him, so I'm going to take Beatrice too. We'll make it OK. The vehicle's armoured and I've got more weaponry inside in case there are any more mad dogs roaming.

I nodded dumbly. He didn't need permission and I wasn't going to argue. Bea appeared and knelt beside Humphrey in his chair. They talked for just a few seconds and then moved away towards the Diving Club Building. I noticed that Sam Hodgson had already started to move the car towards our group and Mervyn left me, moving to overtake Bea as she shepherded her charge.

Then Arthur Baine appeared with Selina beside him. She said, 'I'm going into the Club to find a quiet spot from which I can ring London. Downing Street needs to be informed before this news of all this starts to break.'

'Quite right', I said, 'please do exactly that.'

'I'll go with her,' said Helen as she walked over to join us, 'and I'll wait for you inside, Oliver.' I just nodded my thanks to both of them and turned away to help in any way I could.

I spent a further three hours at the scene, all of it in the company of Arthur Baine. The paramedics had gone with Mo Odinga to hospital. Before leaving, they reassured Arthur that Mo's injuries to his right arm and leg were serious but not immediately life threatening. Then I got together with Arthur, Jack Kirchoff and Denzil Tremayne for an impromptu conference, the four of us grouped on chairs which had been occupied by members of the Panel. We agreed that Denzil would remain on site, using his Reservists to secure the entire area pending the arrival from Century of a forensics team which would include Lenny Williamson, the engineer who had examined the *Dawn* back in January. The major responsibility for Jack was to formulate and execute a policy for handling announcements to the Press. Reporters and TV crews were already starting to appear, and I encouraged Jack to make it simple and honest. Yes, there had been a horrifying attack resulting in the death of the President, but our VIP visitor was unharmed. No, we did not yet know the motivation, nor the identity of the assailant who had been confronted and killed. Regular bulletins would follow, and Jack would return to the capital forthwith to oversee these from his office there.

As we talked together, sharing traumatic memories and listing all that needed to be done, the afternoon remained sunny and the weather balmy: it made for a sharp and sorry contrast to the carnage we had witnessed. I left them then and re-joined Helen in the Club, from which Arthur arranged for us to be driven back to the hotel. We packed up and caught a late flight back to Century. We were back in the apartment by nine that evening. I felt physically exhausted and emotionally drained.

Chapter Twenty-Nine

In the days that followed, I threw myself into as much work as possible, finding that the effort dulled the pain. Life and the activities of national government administration had to go on and there was no shortage of things to do. Helen was preoccupied with some teething problems at the new university in RB and a week after the Diving Club, she flew back down there for a few days to help sort them out.

Meanwhile in Century, I kept a close eye on how things were going for Humphrey Corton. I was helped by Beatrice who had formed a close bond with him on their long drive up here after the bomb. She stayed near to him as he embarked on his course at Century University, settled into his accommodation and started to make friends among his fellow students. I found out only later that she had numerous telephone conversations with his parents, reassuring them that their son was demonstrating great resilience in the face of distressing memories. Mervyn Tredinnick helped in all of this and was always at hand but took a step back when Royce Harrison's replacement arrived from the UK.

Bert Hankers could hardly have been more different to his predecessor. He was shorter, much more sturdily built and his broad cockney was in marked contrast to the Royce Caribbean drawl. Bert had no affinity with water and, as he told me, could hardly swim a stroke, but he was dedicated to physical fitness, had been a talented amateur boxer and with his infectious good humour, he made for stimulating company. And he was immediately committed. He and Humphrey quickly established the habit of going weekly to the Diving Club in Rheina Blanca, usually by air on a day return, but once taking the coach service so they could see more of the country.

Under the broad heading of "Incident Aftermath", a title I disliked but couldn't conceive of better, progress was slow and grinding. A Commission of Enquiry had been appointed under the effective leadership of Fergus Carradine who was ensuring that we did all we could - interviewing everyone, following up on every possible lead, reviewing every detail - to establish what had led to the fateful day and to allocate responsibility for the assassination of our President. We were reaching conclusions, but still lacking proof positive and worse, no trace had been found of Lee van Troung, nor of the little priest, de Houlette.

I was happy that Maurice Odinga was making a recovery. He had been released from hospital pretty swiftly, but the injury to his right leg meant that he could move only with an awkward, crab like gait and the arm was almost useless. I could not believe that he would return to full time duty as Police Commissioner but judged it best to leave him to make that decision for himself and to tender his resignation when he was ready.

I was also concerned for Hugh Dundas. He had not been touched by the blast, but all the circumstances had taken their toll and Alexa reported privately to me that she was worried for him. He was losing weight and retreating into himself. Given Hugh's age, I thought he might well be losing his appetite for life and wished that Pente was still around to give us all his uncompromising brand of comfort.

On the first day of December, Monday 1st, I was at my desk in the Secretariat working on holiday arrangements for Christmas and the New Year. Around mid-morning, Bea came up to me with my mug of coffee and with a request. 'There's a guy in Reception, Olty, asking to see you. He doesn't have an appointment, of course, and he didn't ring in first. I haven't seen him, but Colleen is on duty at the Front Desk. She's pretty reliable and says he seems OK. He's been through the checks and the scanner, all fine and now he's just sitting there waiting to find out if you'll see him, just for a few minutes, he says.'

I sipped at the coffee, blowing out a breath and frowning. I had a lot going on and could do without interruptions. Walk ins like this are unusual and I suspected this might be a Press commentator of some kind, but it would probably be better to confront than avoid.

'He's given a name?', I asked Bea.

'Yes, he has. He's got a card'. She handed it over, normal sort of size, plain white with writing in black and just a name: *Afzul Iqbal*. It meant nothing to me but I shrugged and asked Bea to fetch in the visitor. She reappeared shortly and stood aside to let him enter my office. I rose to greet him and asked Bea to organise coffee for us in the window seats overlooking the garden.

'Good morning, Mr Iqbal, how may I help you?'

He was a tall man, spare in build and looking a bit grizzled as if life had shown him some rough edges. He was neatly enough dressed in cowboy blue jeans and shirt, large black boots which could do with a polish. I put his age at mid-fifties, but he moved with the lithe fluidity of a much younger man. As we sat down on opposite sides of the coffee table, he gave an attractive, lopsided smile and opened the conversation.

'Thank you for seeing me, Mr Aveling. I regret that my English is very poor, but your secretary tells me that you can manage other languages?'

He was speaking French and I replied in kind. 'French is fine for me, Monsieur Iqbal, others possible but harder. Tell me why you're here.'

'Of course. It won't take long. I arrived in Millennium only yesterday and I have booked to start my return journey this weekend.'

'And that's to where?', I asked him.

'To Djibouti. On the other side of this Continent. The Horn of Africa.'

'Yes, I know where to find it. Have you always lived there?', I asked him, wondering about his name.

'Oh no. I have lived in many places, but I was born in Afghanistan.'

'In Kabul?'

'Quite close, but in another world. I grew up near to Mogala, about fifty kilometres north of Kabul and south of Jugdulluck. That's Gilzai country, harsh, hilly and remote.'

I didn't want more geography, so I asked him again, more abruptly, 'So why here? And why now?'

'I'm looking for an American woman, now called Helen Priest. I believe she lives with you when she is in Century City. I'm here on behalf of an old friend of hers - Michaela who lives in Mogadishu, Somalia. Can you help me please?'

I was rocked by this announcement, standing up instinctively as Bea arrived with our coffee, signalling to her to serve the Afghan while I moved away to ring Helen. There was nothing to be gained by delay.

I keyed her number and held the visitor's card in front of me as I waited for Helen to pick up. The Afghan held out a hand to distract me, saying as he did so,

'Mr Aveling, she will remember me as Sinbad.'

I was astonished, of course, this name taking me straight back in memory to that momentous first conversation on the terrace of Tina's house when Helen told me about her ordeal in Mogadishu and subsequent escape from Somalia at the instigation of the man now sitting before me. It seemed beyond belief but somehow, the very look of him seemed to confirm it.

Anyway, there was nothing to be gained from hesitation, so I kept the call ringing.

She eventually answered with an apology. She was sitting in on a tutorial at the University and would have to get back to me.

'Make it quick, please', I said and hung up. I turned back to Sinbad and made some small talk as we waited. He told me that he had been in the country for just a few days and that he was staying at the Vacation Inn, a perfectly respectable, second division hotel, conveniently located not far from our City Centre.

Then Helen was back, using her *sese* to make it a vision call and I could see she was still sitting in a lecture room. I told her who was with me and there was quite a pause before she passed a hand over her eyes and said with incredulity, 'What are you saying, Oliver? It can't be Sinbad. That's just not possible! Let me look.'

I turned my phone towards him, and Sinbad helped by moving his position, first giving her a full-frontal view, then turning to present his profile and highlighting the long scar on his right side which ran from the temple to the jaw.

Helen's reaction was immediate. 'I'll catch the first flight I can get on, 'she said, 'keep him with you.'

I called for Jerome, and we took Sinbad with us as we drove out to the Airport and met the plane inbound from RB.

He and I were standing in the concourse of the Domestic Arrivals building when Helen walked through, wheeling her small travel bag. I glanced up at Sinbad, standing beside me and could see he was much affected, brushing away tears as he opened his arms to her. Helen stood motionless for a few seconds before hugging him fiercely, then giving me her winsome smile.

The three of us moved out of the Terminal doors to find Jerome with my official car drawn up to the kerb, ignoring the parking restriction. I ushered Helen and Sinbad into the back seat while I joined Jerome up front and asked him to take us direct to The Painted Garden which is a large and spread-out restaurant close to the Airport complex and much less than full at that Monday late lunchtime. We sat at a round table, shaded beneath an acacia tree, ordering soft drinks and something light to eat before starting in on conversation. We spoke in French, Sinbad in his deep, guttural voice and heavy provincial accent as he told us what had brought him here. Or rather, who. The connecting link was, of course, Michaela.

Sinbad started by telling us about her. She had remained living in the Compound in Mogadishu for the twenty-five years since Helen had left. Of the six children she had born, four had gone out into the wider world while the youngest two, both girls, had stayed with her. Like their older siblings, they had been conceived at the behest of Toto but not fathered by him.

Sinbad had returned to Moga about fifteen years ago and he now lived with Michaela. They had met by chance while he was roaming through the Compound buildings, many of them still collapsed and abandoned following the explosions in which he had played a part. The warlord who had usurped Toto still ruled the roost but had established a more benign regime which had enabled Michaela to eke out an existence of sorts. Sinbad had found clerical work in the recently created UN Mission for Assistance and Stability. This was a far cry from his earlier days as a buccaneering pirate, but it gave him a modest income in dollars and the two of them found comfort in each other. They talked of times past, often dwelling on that day of horror and bloodshed and this led them to share their different memories of the young girl whom they could identify only as *shishuke* – Sala's name for his little sister.

Sinbad then told us that the guy who had replaced Toto, had less bulk and brawn but much more brain than his predecessor. He cultivated contacts within the UN Mission who helped to secure his position and to keep US Dollars rolling in. A very few of these he gave to Michaela to pay for the cleaning and laundry she did for him and his household. This work gave her access to Ferdie's house, naturally the largest and best appointed in the Compound, and she was permitted to help herself to some of the magazines and periodicals which littered the dwelling, many being devoted to United Nations news from around the world. Michaela couldn't read, of course, not in any language, but she had a sharp eye for places and people.

'Still has', said Sinbad ruefully, 'and she spotted me immediately as one of the gang which raided and bombed the Compound to oust Toto. 'Anyway', he went on, 'one day she showed me a UN internal gossip mag which had a feature on new recruits to the Organisation. It included a photo of a group standing with a senior looking boss lady who we later found out was Juanita. And in the group was one young woman. Looking at her, Michaela said to me immediately. 'She was the girl who was being cut that day when the building blew. It was her that you carried out and took away on your boat. Aren't I right?'

Sinbad continued, 'I looked and looked, eventually decided that she was right. I could see the same shy smile which I recognised …. And I'm looking at it again now.'

Helen smiled at him now, saying 'that's an old photograph.'

'Well,' he said, 'we're all older and that does go back a long way. It must be nearly fifteen years since you and Michaela started corresponding - with me as scribe.'

'You're exactly right, Sinbad, it was back in 2021 that I got the first E Mail from Michaela and was wondering how she managed to find me, to recognise me and still more how she had been able to write a message. Now I know and I'm grateful to you for putting us in touch again. During the final months of my childhood, she was like another mother to me, but with big sister advice.' She paused before continuing, 'Now tell us, what's life like now in Mogadishu?'

'It's tough still, Helen. Tough and hard and sometimes dangerous. You must be always on your guard, watching out for the desperadoes, the riff raff, the *vouyou* as I think you call them here: small gang people always on the lookout for something to pinch or for a bit of trouble to keep themselves amused. Ideally for both at once. But apart from that, life is easier than you would remember. There's more food, more shops and the markets from which you can buy essentials, even more electricity more often. Oh, and the sun still shines!'

'So, what brings you here now?', asked Helen, changing tack.

'I'm here because Michaela sent me. And she paid most of the cost of the travel through her savings squirrelled away over the years. She has been just desperate to get a message to you.'

'And that is?'

Sinbad shifted in his seat but did not reply as he leaned forward to accept the cigarette which Helen was offering him. When they were both smoking, he directed an unblinking gaze which alternated between Helen and me as he concentrated on his response,

'This will surprise you,' he began 'but since Michaela and I have been together, we have both converted to the Christian faith. It's been a gradual thing and we don't shout about it but it's a belief which has helped us to make more sense of our past and to give us more confidence about whatever the future may bring. She likes me to read passages from the Bible to her and she is particularly drawn to the teachings of St Paul. About two months ago, we were studying the Acts of the Apostles and she went into some kind of trance when I read out the excerpt in which Paul has a vision, seeing a man call to him, saying "Come over into

Macedonia and help us." A few hours later, while we were sharing our evening meal, she said to me, 'That's what I want Shishuke or Helen or whatever she now calls herself, that's what I want her to do: come here and help us.'

There was a long silence between the three of us after this announcement from Sinbad. Finally, Helen lit herself another cigarette and inhaled deeply before responding to him.

'Let me think very carefully about this, Sinbad. You will know better than anyone that I have had a lot of contact with Michaela during the months I have been here in Millennium. As you say, you are the scribe, and you know all the correspondence between us. She has been of much help and comfort to me, especially over the loss of my brother, Sala, whom she seems to have remembered vividly. So, I would like nothing better than to see her again but at some point, I must return to Geneva, and I really do want to complete the establishment of the university in Rheina Blanca. Then there is Oliver here, with whom I have shared so much and don't want to leave. I must think.'

She broke off abruptly and the silence returned before she resumed to ask, 'What are your plans now? When do you need to go home again?'

'I'm due to leave this weekend,' he said, 'my flight out is early on Sunday morning, but it will take me two days of travel to get home. As you will know, there is no direct flight from here to Mogadishu.'

I nodded at that and put in a comment. 'That's true, but perhaps you could stay a few days longer?'

'I could, Mr Aveling, but I would rather not delay. Michaela is nervous of being alone, even with her daughters around her and her health is uncertain these days.'

Helen asked him, 'Is she suffering from something, Sinbad?'

'Nothing specific, no. But she's more than ten years older than you and has lived all her life in a rough city and a country in which life expectancy is still only mid-fifties. She has cause to be anxious and I like to spare her that so far as I can.'

I glanced at Helen and could see that we were both moved by the sincerity and compassion of this guy - himself a survivor of tough times and perilous circumstances. It would have been this thought which prompted Helen to ask him, 'and what about you, Sinbad? Where have you been and what have you done since that day in Aden?'

'I've kept moving and travelled far and wide,' he replied, smiling as he accepted the cigarette she proffered. 'I left Yemen on foot - or at least the Port. I had no choice after my crew mutinied and attacked me. I knew they were going to, so that's why I kicked you out. My lot were upset by the way I had drowned that little shithead, Chico – the skinny guy with the wispy beard who tried to rape you, even in your condition at the time and I expect they were wondering which of them I would get after next. My boat was pretty valuable, so they assaulted me in a group, beat me senseless and gave me this knife scar', he fingered the side of his face as he spoke, 'so I just bummed around, doing a bit of paid work here and a lot of thieving there. At some point much later that year, I managed to make it back home to Afghanistan, but I found my family all dead and gone. I wasn't welcomed by the remnants of the tribe, so I took off again and finally fetched up in Djibouti where I found work and a place to live. I learned the language - that's to say French - and went back to working on boats. But the days of the coastal pirates were gone by then and I thought it was time to learn other skills, so I enrolled on a computer course run by the French Medical outfit, MSF. It didn't cost me anything and it gave me a qualification. I stayed in Djibouti four years before deciding I would have another look at Somalia. Once in Mogadishu, I went to revisit the Compound and almost immediately bumped into Michaela. We got talking and a week later, I was living with her and working at the UN Mission. I've been there ever since.'

The time was approaching mid afternoon by then, so I paid the bill and Jerome drove us to the Vacation Inn, leaving Sinbad for the night and arranging to pick him up again in the morning. That set the pattern for the week. Helen didn't return to RB and together, we showed Sinbad the sights of Century City, eating lunch and dinner at different spots every day. He was good company and very appreciative, remarking in wonder at buildings and features of the life going on around us which were so alien to him as a citizen of Mogadishu.

Each evening of that week, after we had left him at his hotel for the night, Helen and I would go home to the apartment to sit on the balcony overlooking the beach, drinks in hand, cigarettes for her and a cigar for me as we talked, often late into the night and lulled by the sound of the surf. There was much to discuss.

On the Wednesday evening - or to be precise, at 2am on the Thursday morning, I asked Helen to marry me. She responded immediately, saying. 'Do you really mean that, Oliver?'

'I do.' And then I amplified and added, 'Married or not, I just want you with me. We have found a communion together, of body, mind and soul. I want to nurture and develop that, growing ever closer as we grow older.'

There was a look of longing in her eyes as she replied, 'I'd like that, Oliver, I really would. I want to find a place to call home.' I could have leapt off the balcony with the ecstasy of that moment and I leant forward to kiss her gently. Shortly afterwards, we went to bed to find rest in great contentment. Later that morning, we went for our normal walk on Rainbow Beach before breakfast and then collecting Sinbad from the Vacation Inn. There was excitement in every step of our walk - the thrill of planning and anticipation.

Nevertheless, Helen was organised as ever in her thinking. As we rounded the turning point of that log in the sand, she said,

'I'll take the first plane down to RB tomorrow morning, Oliver, but only for one long day. I owe it to Selina. We're just about at the end of our first term and there are a few details to go through. But more than that, she'll be thrilled with our news - so will Arthur come to that. Then we can have a last day with Sinbad before seeing him off on Sunday for his journey home to Michaela.'

'Hang on a minute,' I said smiling and delighted at her exuberance, 'what message are you going to give him to take back to Mogadishu. Are you going to turn down her request to go over there?'

'No, Oliver, I can't do that, and I won't. I will go there, but just for a visit and not quite yet. There are other things I need to do first. I must go back to Geneva, to resign my job and pack up my things there. Perhaps there'll be time for me to sneak over the border and see Juanita in France. After that, I'll hop over to the States and spend some time with my mother, Mel, in Hulett and then I'll come home to you. All that will take a couple of weeks or a bit more but then I can make the trip to Mogadishu from here. Maybe take you with me?'

'Let's see', I said to her, 'first things first.'

We'd had a long day, a late night and a fair amount to drink so we cut that Thursday a bit short, spending time in the Central Market which Sinbad seemed to enjoy as he marvelled at the range and condition of produce on offer. We left him at his hotel, agreeing that he would amuse himself on the Friday while Helen was in Rheina Blanca, and

I did some catching up with things at the Secretariat. Saturday would be our last day together and I planned to drive out to Tina Fullerton's place so Sinbad could see something of the bush country outside the Capital.

And that's pretty much the way it went - at least until we got to the Saturday evening. Apparently, Sinbad enjoyed walking around the city centre for most of Friday, impressed by the order, the cleanliness and all the signs of prosperity which he found in sharp contrast to the conditions in Mogadishu. Helen had a successful day in Rheina Blanca, celebrating with students and overwhelmed by the congratulations of Selina and Arthur. For myself, I spent some productive hours at my desk, working with Pascal Brana before sharing champagne with a gushing Beatrice. Bea was obviously thrilled with the news of a union between Helen and me, taking full credit for her matchmaking!

We started early on Saturday morning, immediately after our beach walk and a hurried breakfast. I had intended driving myself, but Jerome insisted on chauffeuring us, so we collected Sinbad from the Vacation Inn and then taking a circuitous route, seeing some of the Merrick grazing land before the Grenadier snarled its way through bush tracks to arrive at Tina's sometime after noon. We were given a warm welcome, an excellent lunch and more celebratory champagne before leaving with a firm promise from Helen that she would come calling on Tina as soon as she was home to stay.

'Don't let me down, girl or I'll fuckin' come looking for ya!' was Tina's parting shot as she stood on her drive in another multicoloured kaftan, waving furiously.

Jerome drove us directly back into the city, but the weekend traffic was heavy, and I was beginning to think that we should go straight for dinner and an early night. I knew that Sinbad's first flight was scheduled for 8am and that he was in for a wearisome journey as he had insisted on returning the way he came, which meant north to Algiers via Nouakchott, then a series of short hops along the North African coast before flying south into Djibouti which he knew so well and thereafter a bus to Mogadishu. It sounded agony but was, he assured me, very good value for Michaela's money. As we were sitting in traffic, Helen surprised me by asking if we could make the time to visit the Cathedral.

'I'm sure we could,' I replied, 'but why? Is this for Sinbad?'

She grabbed my hand impulsively. We were sitting together in the back while Sinbad rode up front, chatting to Jerome. Helen said, 'No, Oliver, this is for me. I want to light a candle for Sala, for my brother.'

I squeezed back but made no reply. I could understand.

Chapter Thirty

Jerome parked in the Cloisters and the three of us got out, leaving him to stay with the car. We walked round and entered the Cathedral through the cobbled Square, passing the ornate fountain there which gurgles a ceaseless welcome. We went through the immense double doors to be engulfed in the gloom of the cavernous building, pausing for our eyesight to adjust from the bright sunlight of the early evening.

Pente Broke Smith had told me long ago that our Cathedral was built in colonial days and modelled on the famous Church of Saint Sulpice in Paris. It's nowhere near as big, of course, especially not as tall but at least it's perfectly symmetrical and not lop sided. It's famous also for its grand organ, the largest in Africa if, again, not the size of the instrument in Paris which it was designed to emulate, yet the structure echoes its inspiration, the organ with its loft and balcony perched way above the High Altar and approached by a narrow, circular staircase.

Helen and I left Sinbad to wander while we progressed up the Chancel, pausing to select the longest and slimmest candle I could find in the display rack. I passed it to her, and she used her lighter, waiting for the candle to flame and settle before she returned it to the rack. Then I stood still as she advanced right up to the altar rail and knelt for just a few seconds. As she stood again, I was moved to see her brush away a tear, but she was smiling as she walked to re-join me.

'Thank you', she said putting her hand out to me, 'I'm very happy to have done that.'

We turned together to retrace our steps towards the entrance doors. I couldn't see Sinbad but knew he would find us when he had finished his tour so that we could walk back together to Jerome and the car. I found myself loitering as Helen and I passed the two Confessionals which stand just inside the entrance to the Cathedral. On impulse, I stooped to peer more closely at the heavy wooden lattice work which encases and divides the two small chambers within - one for the Supplicant and the other for the Priest hearing Confession. I was startled to make out a seated figure within the first enclosure. It was motionless but I could see eyes there, open, moving and threatening. Then noise as a hand, holding something, was raised to rattle the lattice. I was stepping back whilst hearing a hissing sound. I put up an arm in front of my face but a mist, being squirted from the cubicle, was enveloping me, blinding me with an agonising pain.

I knew instinctively that we had found Lee van Troung and confirmation came from Helen's scream, part fear and part rage as the lattice door crashed open. By the grace of God, my upraised arm had caught most of the pepper spray, but my vision was still blurred as I made out the figure of Helen, agile as a cat as she dodged under the scything blade of his weapon and went racing off towards the High Altar, pursued by the lithe figure of Troung as he ran screaming in hot pursuit. As I followed in their wake, still rubbing at my eyes and face, I could see Helen dodge into the narrow stairwell and stumble as she tackled the ascent with all the speed she could muster.

LvT was right behind her and gaining, I believe, as she reached the balcony of the organ loft, but it was there that the matter ended because standing to greet him was the unexpected figure of Sinbad who must have been inspecting the organ as the drama began. I stopped running and brought up short to gaze up at the denouement. Sinbad was the older man by far but also the taller and the stronger. As Troung advanced on him, swinging his lethal blade, the Afghan stood his ground, ducked under a flailing cut and caught the arm which was wielding the weapon. At that point, the fight was ended. Sinbad plucked the sword free and hurled it over the rail of the balcony to fall with a clatter almost at my feet. The blade glinted wickedly in the light of Helen's candle. Seconds later, it was followed by Lee van Troung as Sinbad swung him up in the air and tipped him over the balcony. It was a symbolic moment, another execution in the same manner as for Chico the pirate all those years back but the aisle of our Cathedral, fashioned from stone quarried centuries ago, was less forgiving than the waters of the Indian Ocean. There was a horrid, bloody splat and the body lay still.

To our credit, I believe, all three of us recovered quite quickly from this dramatic shock. Helen limped down the spiral stairs and emerged with an ashen face. Sinbad followed her with composure and placed a comforting arm around her shoulders. I scooped up the sword, the kukri, whatever it was that Troung had been wielding and roughly hid it beneath the Pulpit. Then I allowed myself a brief minute to catch my breath and rub my eyes before I engaged my brain, grabbed my phone from my pocket and rang Mo Odinga. I was lucky there because he answered me from the restaurant only just off Cathedral Square where he was finishing a long, family lunch. He joined us a few minutes later, moving very slowly still and helped by a stick because he was still convalescing from his injuries caused by the bomb in RB. But his appreciation of the situation was immediate, and his actions were sharp. He told me to get out, taking Helen and Sinbad with me. His tone of voice brooked no argument, so we went to find Jerome still standing by the car and I asked him to take us straight to my apartment. I sat beside him as we drove and, relying on his discretion, told him what had happened. On arrival, I sent Helen off to have a shower and change while I spoke to Sinbad. I told him that his departure must now be delayed while I sorted out some details but that I would rearrange his journey as quickly as possible. I believe he understood all that was in my mind. Then I put him back in the Grenadier with Jerome who drove him back to the Vacation Inn to rest up until I made further contact with him. Before he left, I gave him my most sincere and grateful thanks. His decisive action had saved the life of the person most dear to me. I was in his debt.

I remember very little of the rest of that Saturday evening. It wasn't late but I was still shaking in shock and stumbling aimlessly around the apartment. Helen was in better shape, helped perhaps by her lengthy shower but more likely by life experience. Neither of us felt like eating. I had a couple of stiff whisky's and she accounted for most of a bottle of Sancerre and numerous cigarettes. Eventually, we fell into bed and slept. Sunday morning dawned beautifully but for once, I didn't go out walking on the beach. Helen slept in until nearly nine and I was anxious to be around for Mo Odinga who I felt instinctively would call in person rather than ring. I was right about that.

Helen was in the bathroom when he knocked at the door. I was touched that Mo was in full uniform, complete with swagger stick under his arm but still using a cane for support. His demeanour was grave but confident. He didn't waste words, refusing a cup of coffee and a chair.

'We've cleaned up in the Cathedral, Olty. There's no sign left of a struggle, no bloodstains remaining. The weapon has gone to landfill. The body is in the morgue and will be cremated tomorrow first thing. We found his passport and UN Identity Card along with a bit of cash in US dollars. I'll have all that, along with the ashes, couriered to Geneva on Tuesday's flight. So, ... drama over and evidence gone.'

Dumbly, I nodded my thanks as he went on, 'but Olty, I don't have to tell you that I'm breaking all the rules here. There should be a proper enquiry, but I don't see benefit in that for anyone. It means, though, that you must get your man out of Century urgently - today if possible.'

'I'll get on it, Mo. I know you're right.' Then I hesitated before adding, 'I just wonder how Troung could have known. Known that we were going to be there ... and then.'

'I can't answer all of that, Olty, but I do know that he had been lying up somewhere round here for days. There's a camera in the fountain, you see, and we ran through the footage last night. He first shows up at the beginning of last week. I reckon he sneaked into Century from RB sometime after the bomb there and he'd been waiting for you ever since then. I believe you were his target.'

Mo didn't linger and as soon as he was gone, I realised that I mustn't either. I rang Jerome and while he was coming round with my car, I chased up Helen who was groggy from exhausted sleep but recovering fast. Within half an hour of Odinga's brief visit, we were in the back of the Grenadier, moving swiftly along Sunday morning roads towards the city. I called Beatrice from the car, and she arrived at the Secretariat shortly after us.

Bea - to the best of my belief - remains one of the very few who know the detail of LvT's demise and she had, of course, already met Sinbad. She went to work immediately on her contacts and store of information. Before midday, she had found a direct flight from Century to Nairobi and from there, a small, regional service which would get him into Mogadishu late the following evening, Monday. The travel cost was more than Michaela had paid but I was happy to fund it and Sinbad was happier still when I gave him the news. The three of us sat together having coffee in the lounge of the Vacation Inn. We didn't say much: there was little more to say but Sinbad did have a question for Helen.

'I'll be glad to get home to Michaela. But can I tell her that you'll be over yourself to see her before too long?'

'You can, Sinbad. I promise. And it will be just as soon as I can get my life in Geneva tidied up. I'll send you a message first, of course, let you know when I'm arriving.'

He sighed in contentment. 'That's very good to hear,' he said, 'she'll be so pleased.' After a pause, he went on, 'You two go on back to the beach now. I can manage well enough on my own from here and best if we're not seen together. I'll catch a cab to the airport in the morning.'

I didn't argue as I knew he was right. We all stood. He and Helen hugged tightly: I shook his hand, and his grip was fierce. Then Sinbad sauntered off towards the lifts without a further word. He was a staunch friend at a time of great need, and I wish he could have been with us for longer. I'm sad to say that I've never seen him again since that day.

But I was, myself, at Heaven International Airport soon enough, although on a very different mission. On the Tuesday, 9th December, Helen took the direct flight to Geneva, the same plane as carried the courier package of Lee van Troung documents. I drove her to the airport myself and felt heartache as I watched her pass the final check and into the Departure Lounge. We shared a last wave and I returned to my car, feeling lonely and bereft.

Then started a very busy time. My days at the Secretariat were taken up with detail and then there was some travel around the country. Most of this was at the behest of Kane

Merrick who had been voted in by a unanimous Panel decision to assume the Presidency for the remaining four years of what would have been Laetitia Valbuena's time in Office. Quite properly, Kane was anxious to understand every aspect of all that was expected of him and as part of this learning process, he wanted to visit all the provinces ... and the Secretariat Office in each of them. I managed to persuade him to defer the country tour for ten days, during which time I took him through all the procedural stuff which was Century based and also agreed a date for Hector Valbuena and his daughters to move out of Government House so that Kane and Elspeth Merrick could move in.

There was another, unspoken reason for not immediately leaving the secure and reliable communications guaranteed by the Secretariat building in Century City and that, of course, was Helen. I had many phone conversations with her while she was in Geneva and every one of them seemed to finish too soon. But I was reassured. She sounded bright, bubbly and brimming with news. She had found another American girl to take over the lease on her apartment, she had seen plenty of friends and colleagues with whom she had worked at UNHCR Headquarters, and she had spent a couple of days with Juanita who had driven over from her home outside Pau in France.

Then there had been an interview with Prosper Aguilas, accompanied by his wife Aggie. They had been welcoming and solicitous. Prosper had tried to persuade her to stay on, saying that he was very impressed with her work and especially her initiative in establishing the university in

Rheina Blanca. He wanted her to step up and assume the role vacated by Lee van Troung's death. But Helen had held to the line that it was time for her to move on and she managed to avoid the detail of LvT's demise, saying that he had eventually been found, dossing down in a small house somewhere amongst the warren of alleys in the Old Quarter of Century City. He had died of a heroin overdose. She had told the same story to Juanita and I approved the subterfuge. There was nothing now to be gained by spelling out the drama which had taken place.

Then Helen left Geneva. As I was climbing into the back of my Grenadier, with Jerome at the wheel and President Merrick by my side, she was boarding a plane for London where she changed onto a direct flight to Colorado. There, her adopted mother, Melanie Priest met her, and they spent a night at a Denver Airport hotel before starting the long drive north to Hulett, Wyoming. Mel was then in her early eighties but still spry and energetic, driving herself and relishing the late autumn of life.

Helen was still in Wyoming when I got back to Century from the country tour with President Merrick. It was then just before the Christmas break, and we started on a few particularly happy days. She had treated herself to a new phone, complete with the very latest technology camera which gave such resolution, audio excellence and handheld control such that she could make her own home movie. So, I could put them on the big screen in my sitting room and welcome them into the apartment. I found Mel to be marvellously good company, shrewd in judgment with an excellent sense of humour and a healthy disregard for the formalities of life.

They took me with them one afternoon and although the camera was a bit wobbly, I could join them in seeing the highlights of Hulett, Wyoming: the Church, the Library, the School which had educated Helen and the Town Hall. Mel drove us, her beady head on its sparse, short frame, hardly showing above the steering wheel of her lengthy American station wagon. But the greater treat was returning to her house and sitting in the sun on her veranda - the white railed porch as she called it - gazing out over the miles of cattle grazing grassland.

Later that evening, Mel had a private word with me. 'I like you, Oliver and I approve of you, but understand this: Helen is a precious asset so mind you look after her. Or I'll be after you from either side of the grave!'

Helen left Hulett the following day. Before leaving, she spoke to me to say that she would miss my birthday but would still get back to Millennium in the early New Year. She travelled via New York and a direct flight to Nairobi where she changed to a feeder service into Mogadishu. I got word from Sinbad that she had arrived safely and was planning to stay for a week before making her way back to me.

I started to get excited and to make plans for her welcome home to Century and my apartment on Rainbow Beach.

After a week, I was anxious. After two, I was unsure. After three weeks, I was certain. She wasn't coming back.

It was nearly five weeks before this was confirmed with an explanation. An old-fashioned letter arrived through a courier service. It had been typed out and despatched by Sinbad. I still have it today, rather creased from much study and I will quote only some of it, the part which says, "I am distressed to make you suffer and I wish I was with you now, walking on the sand and sitting on the balcony, watching the sun come down over the ocean. You are the only love of my life and I yearn, body, soul and spirit to be with you now and for a lifetime. But it cannot be. I am the baby of Bangladesh but the child of Somalia. There is so much that I can do for people here - especially women and girls - and I know that is my life's mission from now on. I'll be here for Sala, of course, as well as for myself. I'm lucky that I can make a base here with Michaela until I sort myself out, even though I would so much rather be with you. That's why, Oliver, I must ask you not to tempt me. Please don't come over here. Don't ring or write or message in any way. Try to find some other companionship and remember me kindly for the love we have shared."

Chapter Thirty-One

That was fifteen years ago, and I have obeyed her instruction. I have had no further contact with Helen in all that time, but I still miss her fiercely. In the beginning, I thought she would relent and come back to me. Then I went through a phase which lasted a year or more of plotting and planning, scheming to engineer a reunion which would seem to be by chance. But during these months I maintained frequent contact with Mel in Wyoming who gave me detail of how matters were progressing for Helen in Mogadishu: where she was living, where she was working, how her circle of contacts was expanding and her influence enlarging. In parallel, I received painstaking reports from Michaela of the highs and lows of life in that city which, although much improved from the days of Helen's childhood, was still a testing environment which threatened danger at every turn. I was touched and flattered by one message, passed by E Mail from Sinbad's PC, which quoted Helen as 'struggling to create a Millennium of the East Coast'.

Little by painful little, I came to accept the status quo, to turn my attention to other things and people. But the memories have never left me or diminished and there have been so many evenings over these past years when I have sat out on the balcony with our sort of music playing and my favourite photograph of Helen lighting up the big screen in my living area - a study of her standing slim and straight, looking over Banana Beach close to the spot where her brother left us, her head turned back towards me, a strand of hair blowing across her face but not hiding her shy and playful smile.

Tomorrow, the first of January 2052, will be my 60th Birthday, also the first day of my retirement. I handed over to Pascal Brana as we started the Christmas break and I'll leave him in peace to put his own stamp on the Secretariat. My swansong, really, was a couple of years back when we were flat out with arrangements for marking the fiftieth anniversary of Millennium, the day when this country was established by my grandfather's invasion. The highlight of our celebrations was a State Visit by King William and Queen Kate, accompanied by a platoon of British Diplomats and Civil Servants, including Humphrey Corton who had spent so much time at the Diving Club in Rheina Blanca. He is married to Giselle, Ethiopian born and they took their son Edward to see the Club which Humphrey continues to support. I hope he's not troubled by memories of the bomb attack which he survived, thanks to the self-sacrifice of Royce Harrison. Whilst in RB, the Monarch opened the latest extension to the Technology Park which surrounds the University. I'm touched that the impressive Library there is still known to locals as "Helen House". It was both planned and fitting that the Royal visit coincided with the conclusion of Distance Okuyu's Term of Office, he being our first President of full African descent.

Of course, the Old Guard, the Millennium originals, are all long gone now. Hugh and Alexa Dundas died within a month of each other, back in '38. Both were well into their nineties, and neither was sick, just weary of life. Tina

Fullerton passed on during the following year and, to my sad surprise, Fergus Carradine, whom I had thought indestructible, was lost to kidney failure and sepsis in the winter of 2040. Maurice (Mo) Odinga faded away at much the same time and then we said farewell to Troy who walked off to the south towards his birthplace and was never seen again. By then, Absalom had departed but not before siring a line of descendants of which the latest, Josiah, is now lying at my feet.

And back in the UK, my Dad Oscar died at his desk, serving his local community to the end whilst still grieving for Mum and not having enough fun out of life. Almost simultaneously, real tragedy struck our family with the death from ovarian cancer of my sister Christina, but my brother Edward is going strong and against the odds, my fun but wicked uncle Pete still flourishes and comes out here from time to time.

All is not doom and gloom. Arthur Baine replaced Mo Odinga as Police Commissioner, meaning a move from RB to Century and now I see a good deal of him and Selina. Her sister, Bea, my marvellous PA, left it late to meet her husband but he is a fine fellow. Jim Hunter hails from the Somerset Levels in England and Bea has managed to produce four lively children whilst they developed a considerable land holding in the arid country around Tamalourene in the East. And Jack Kirchoff continues to be very productive: he has recently published the second volume of his history, this entitled *"The Maturing of Millennium"*.

I will keep myself busy. I play tennis and golf every week, plus some snooker at weekends. I have quite a social time and an occasional dalliance. I enjoy this country and city very much, but I love especially expeditions to see the game and the birdlife which is concentrated in Leopard Province.

I won't write more. This is *my* finale, and I will leave the concluding words to AE Housman, the English poet who died exactly a hundred years before I met Helen, and he caught her memory for me in his lines from A Shropshire Lad.

That is the land of lost regret

I see it shining plain

Those happy highways where I went

And cannot come again

Thursday, 26th October 2023

90180ww

For MDA, for Flicka

And for the love of Africa

This is the final novel in a trilogy which includes:

Wings of the Morning

Millennium

Finale

Printed in Great Britain
by Amazon